All Roads Lead to Calvary

All Roads Lead to Calvary

Jerome K. Jerome

MINT EDITIONS

All Roads Lead to Calvary was first published in 1919.

This edition published by Mint Editions 2021.

ISBN 9781513278582 | E-ISBN 9781513279046

Published by Mint Editions®

 MINT
EDITIONS

minteditionbooks.com

Publishing Director: Jennifer Newens
Design & Production: Rachel Lopez Metzger
Project Manager: Micaela Clark
Typesetting: Westchester Publishing Services

Contents

I

She had not meant to stay for the service. The door had stood invitingly open, and a glimpse of the interior had suggested to her the idea that it would make good copy. "Old London Churches: Their Social and Historical Associations." It would be easy to collect anecdotes of the famous people who had attended them. She might fix up a series for one of the religious papers. It promised quite exceptional material, this particular specimen, rich in tombs and monuments. There was character about it, a scent of bygone days. She pictured the vanished congregations in their powdered wigs and stiff brocades. How picturesque must have been the marriages that had taken place there, say in the reign of Queen Anne or of the early Georges. The church would have been ancient even then. With its air of faded grandeur, its sculptured recesses and dark niches, the tattered banners hanging from its roof, it must have made an admirable background. Perhaps an historical novel in the Thackeray vein? She could see her heroine walking up the aisle on the arm of her proud old soldier father. Later on, when her journalistic position was more established, she might think of it. It was still quite early. There would be nearly half an hour before the first worshippers would be likely to arrive: just time enough to jot down a few notes. If she did ever take to literature it would be the realistic school, she felt, that would appeal to her. The rest, too, would be pleasant after her long walk from Westminster. She would find a secluded seat in one of the high, stiff pews, and let the atmosphere of the place sink into her.

And then the pew-opener had stolen up unobserved, and had taken it so for granted that she would like to be shown round, and had seemed so pleased and eager, that she had not the heart to repel her. A curious little old party with a smooth, peach-like complexion and white soft hair that the fading twilight, stealing through the yellow glass, turned to gold. So that at first sight Joan took her for a child. The voice, too, was so absurdly childish—appealing, and yet confident. Not until they were crossing the aisle, where the clearer light streamed in through the open doors, did Joan see that she was very old and feeble, with about her figure that curious patient droop that comes to the work-worn. She proved to be most interesting and full of helpful information. Mary Stopperton was her name. She had lived in the neighbourhood all her life; had as a girl worked for the Leigh Hunts and had "assisted" Mrs. Carlyle. She had been very frightened of the great man himself, and had always hidden herself behind doors or squeezed herself into corners and stopped breathing whenever there had been any fear of meeting him upon the stairs. Until one day having darted into a cupboard to escape from him and drawn the door to after her, it turned out to be the cupboard in which Carlyle was used to keep his boots. So that there was quite a struggle between them; she holding grimly on to the door inside and Carlyle equally determined to open it and get his boots. It had ended in her exposure, with trembling knees and scarlet face, and Carlyle had addressed her as "woman," and had insisted on knowing what she was doing there. And after that she had lost all terror of him. And he had even allowed her with a grim smile to enter occasionally the sacred study with her broom and pan. It had evidently made a lasting impression upon her, that privilege.

"They didn't get on very well together, Mr. and Mrs. Carlyle?" Joan queried, scenting the opportunity of obtaining first-class evidence.

"There wasn't much difference, so far as I could see, between them and most of us," answered the little old lady. "You're not married, dear," she continued, glancing at Joan's ungloved hand, "but people must have a deal of patience when they have to live with us for twenty-four hours a day. You see, little things we do and say without thinking, and little ways we have that we do not notice ourselves, may all the time be irritating to other people."

"What about the other people irritating us?" suggested Joan.

"Yes, dear, and of course that can happen too," agreed the little old lady.

"Did he, Carlyle, ever come to this church?" asked Joan.

Mary Stopperton was afraid he never had, in spite of its being so near. "And yet he was a dear good Christian—in his way," Mary Stopperton felt sure.

"How do you mean 'in his way'?" demanded Joan. It certainly, if Froude was to be trusted, could not have been the orthodox way.

"Well, you see, dear," explained the little old lady, "he gave up things. He could have ridden in his carriage"—she was quoting, it seemed, the words of the Carlyles' old servant—"if he'd written the sort of lies that people pay for being told, instead of throwing the truth at their head."

"But even that would not make him a Christian," argued Joan.

"It is part of it, dear, isn't it?" insisted Mary Stopperton. "To suffer for one's faith. I think Jesus must have liked him for that."

JEROME K. JEROME

They had commenced with the narrow strip of burial ground lying between the south side of the church and Cheyne Walk. And there the little pew-opener had showed her the grave of Anna, afterwards Mrs. Spragg. "Who long declining wedlock and aspiring above her sex fought under her brother with arms and manly attire in a flagship against the French." As also of Mary Astell, her contemporary, who had written a spirited "Essay in Defence of the Fair Sex." So there had been a Suffrage Movement as far back as in the days of Pope and Swift.

Returning to the interior, Joan had duly admired the Cheyne monument, but had been unable to disguise her amusement before the tomb of Mrs. Colvile, whom the sculptor had represented as a somewhat impatient lady, refusing to await the day of resurrection, but pushing through her coffin and starting for Heaven in her grave-clothes. Pausing in front of the Dacre monument, Joan wondered if the actor of that name, who had committed suicide in Australia, and whose London address she remembered had been Dacre House just round the corner, was descended from the family; thinking that, if so, it would give an up-to-date touch to the article. She had fully decided now to write it. But Mary Stopperton could not inform her. They had ended up in the chapel of Sir Thomas More. He, too, had "given up things," including his head. Though Mary Stopperton, siding with Father Morris, was convinced he had now got it back, and that with the remainder of his bones it rested in the tomb before them.

There, the little pew-opener had left her, having to show the early-comers to their seats; and Joan had found an out-of-the-way pew from where she could command a view of the whole church. They were chiefly poor folk, the congregation; with here and there a sprinkling of faded gentility. They seemed in keeping with the place. The twilight faded and a snuffy old man shuffled round and lit the gas.

It was all so sweet and restful. Religion had never appealed to her before. The business-like service in the bare cold chapel where she had sat swinging her feet and yawning as a child had only repelled her. She could recall her father, aloof and awe-inspiring in his Sunday black, passing round the bag. Her mother, always veiled, sitting beside her, a thin, tall woman with passionate eyes and ever restless hands; the women mostly overdressed, and the sleek, prosperous men trying to look meek. At school and at Girton, chapel, which she had attended no oftener than she was obliged, had had about it the same atmosphere of chill compulsion. But here was poetry. She wondered if, after all, religion might not have its place in the world—in company with the other arts. It would be a pity for it to die out. There seemed nothing to take its place. All these lovely cathedrals, these dear little old churches, that for centuries had been the focus of men's thoughts and aspirations. The harbour lights, illumining the troubled waters of their lives. What could be done with them? They could hardly be maintained out of the public funds as mere mementoes of the past. Besides, there were too many of them. The tax-payer would naturally grumble. As Town Halls, Assembly Rooms? The idea was unthinkable. It would be like a performance of Barnum's Circus in the Coliseum at Rome. Yes, they would disappear. Though not, she was glad to think, in her time. In towns, the space would be required for other buildings. Here and there some gradually decaying specimen would be allowed to survive, taking its place with the feudal castles and walled cities of the Continent: the joy of the American tourist, the text-book of the antiquary. A pity! Yes, but then from the aesthetic point of view it was a pity that the groves of ancient Greece had ever been cut down and replanted with currant bushes, their altars scattered; that the stones of the temples of Isis should have come to be the shelter of the fisher of the Nile; and the corn wave in the wind above the buried shrines of Mexico. All these dead truths that from time to time had encumbered the living world. Each in its turn had had to be cleared away.

And yet was it altogether a dead truth: this passionate belief in a personal God who had ordered all things for the best: who could be appealed to for comfort, for help? Might it not be as good an explanation as any other of the mystery surrounding us? It had been so universal. She was not sure where, but somewhere she had come across an analogy that had strongly impressed her. "The fact that a man feels thirsty—though at the time he may be wandering through the Desert of Sahara—proves that somewhere in the world there is water." Might not the success of Christianity in responding to human needs be evidence in its favour? The Love of God, the Fellowship of the Holy Ghost, the Grace of Our Lord Jesus Christ. Were not all human needs provided for in that one comprehensive promise: the desperate need of man to be convinced that behind all the seeming muddle was a loving hand guiding towards good; the need of the soul in its loneliness for fellowship, for strengthening; the need of man in his weakness for the kindly grace of human sympathy, of human example.

And then, as fate would have it, the first lesson happened to be the story of Jonah and the whale. Half a dozen shocked faces turned suddenly towards her told Joan that at some point in the thrilling history she must unconsciously have laughed. Fortunately she was alone in the pew, and feeling herself scarlet, squeezed herself into its farthest corner and drew down her veil.

No, it would have to go. A religion that solemnly demanded of grown men and women in the twentieth century that they should sit and listen with reverential awe to a prehistoric edition of "Grimm's Fairy Stories," including Noah and his ark, the adventures of Samson and Delilah, the conversations between Balaam and his ass, and culminating in what if it were not so appallingly wicked an idea would be the most comical of them all: the conception of an elaborately organized Hell, into which the God of the Christians plunged his creatures for all eternity! Of what use was such a religion as that going to be to the world of the future?

She must have knelt and stood mechanically, for the service was ended. The pulpit was occupied by an elderly uninteresting-looking man with a troublesome cough. But one sentence he had let fall had gripped her attention. For a moment she could not remember it, and then it came to her: "All Roads lead to Calvary." It struck her as rather good. Perhaps he was going to be worth listening to. "To all of us, sooner or later," he was saying, "comes a choosing of two ways: either the road leading to success, the gratification of desires, the honour and approval of our fellow-men—or the path to Calvary."

And then he had wandered off into a maze of detail. The tradesman, dreaming perhaps of becoming a Whiteley, having to choose whether to go forward or remain for all time in the little shop. The statesman—should he abide by the faith that is in him and suffer loss of popularity, or renounce his God and enter the Cabinet? The artist, the writer, the mere labourer—there were too many of them. A few well-chosen examples would have sufficed. And then that irritating cough!

And yet every now and then he would be arresting. In his prime, Joan felt, he must have been a great preacher. Even now, decrepit and wheezy, he was capable of flashes of magnetism, of eloquence. The passage where he pictured the Garden of Gethsemane. The fair Jerusalem, only hidden from us by the shadows. So easy to return to. Its soft lights shining through the trees, beckoning to us; its mingled voices stealing to us through the silence, whispering to us of its well-remembered ways, its pleasant places, its open doorways, friends and loved ones waiting for us. And above, the rock-strewn Calvary: and crowning its summit, clear against the starlit sky, the cold, dark cross. "Not perhaps to us the bleeding hands and feet, but to all the bitter tears. Our Calvary may be a very little hill compared with the mountains where Prometheus suffered, but to us it is steep and lonely."

There he should have stopped. It would have been a good note on which to finish. But it seemed there was another point he wished to make. Even to the sinner Calvary calls. To Judas—even to him the gates of the life-giving Garden of Gethsemane had not been closed. "With his thirty pieces of silver he could have stolen away. In some distant crowded city of the Roman Empire have lived unknown, forgotten. Life still had its pleasures, its rewards. To him also had been given the choice. The thirty pieces of silver that had meant so much to him! He flings them at the feet of his tempters. They would not take them back. He rushes out and hangs himself. Shame and death. With his own hands he will build his own cross, none to help him. He, too—even Judas, climbs his Calvary. Enters into the fellowship of those who through all ages have trod its stony pathway."

Joan waited till the last of the congregation had disappeared, and then joined the little pew-opener who was waiting to close the doors. Joan asked her what she had thought of the sermon, but Mary Stopperton, being a little deaf, had not heard it.

"It was quite good—the matter of it," Joan told her. "All Roads lead to Calvary. The idea is that there comes a time to all of us when we have to choose. Whether, like your friend Carlyle, we will 'give up things' for our faith's sake. Or go for the carriage and pair."

Mary Stopperton laughed. "He is quite right, dear," she said. "It does seem to come, and it is so hard. You have to pray and pray and pray. And even then we cannot always do it." She touched with her little withered fingers Joan's fine white hand. "But you are so strong and brave," she continued, with another little laugh. "It won't be so difficult for you."

It was not until well on her way home that Joan, recalling the conversation, found herself smiling at Mary Stopperton's literal acceptation of the argument. At the time, she remembered, the shadow of a fear had passed over her.

Mary Stopperton did not know the name of the preacher. It was quite common for chance substitutes to officiate there, especially in the evening. Joan had insisted on her acceptance of a shilling, and had made a note of her address, feeling instinctively that the little old woman would "come in useful" from a journalistic point of view.

Shaking hands with her, she had turned eastward, intending to walk to Sloane Square and there take the bus. At the corner of Oakley Street she overtook him. He was evidently a stranger to the neighbourhood, and was peering up through his glasses to see the name of the street; and Joan caught sight of his face beneath a gas lamp.

And suddenly it came to her that it was a face she knew. In the dim-lit church she had not seen him clearly. He was still peering upward. Joan stole another glance. Yes, she had met him somewhere. He was very changed, quite different, but she was sure of it. It was a long time ago. She must have been quite a child.

II

One of Joan's earliest recollections was the picture of herself standing before the high cheval glass in her mother's dressing-room. Her clothes lay scattered far and wide, falling where she had flung them; not a shred of any kind of covering was left to her. She must have been very small, for she could remember looking up and seeing high above her head the two brass knobs by which the glass was fastened to its frame. Suddenly, out of the upper portion of the glass, there looked a scared red face. It hovered there a moment, and over it in swift succession there passed the expressions, first of petrified amazement, secondly of shocked indignation, and thirdly of righteous wrath. And then it swooped down upon her, and the image in the glass became a confusion of small naked arms and legs mingled with green cotton gloves and purple bonnet strings.

"You young imp of Satan!" demanded Mrs. Munday—her feelings of outraged virtue exaggerating perhaps her real sentiments. "What are you doing?"

"Go away. I'se looking at myself," had explained Joan, struggling furiously to regain the glass.

"But where are your clothes?" was Mrs. Munday's wonder.

"I'se tooked them off," explained Joan. A piece of information that really, all things considered, seemed unnecessary.

"But can't you see yourself, you wicked child, without stripping yourself as naked as you were born?"

"No," maintained Joan stoutly. "I hate clothes." As a matter of fact she didn't, even in those early days. On the contrary, one of her favourite amusements was "dressing up." This sudden overmastering desire to arrive at the truth about herself had been a new conceit.

"I wanted to see myself. Clothes ain't me," was all she would or could vouchsafe; and Mrs. Munday had shook her head, and had freely confessed that there were things beyond her and that Joan was one of them; and had succeeded, partly by force, partly by persuasion, in restoring to Joan once more the semblance of a Christian child.

It was Mrs. Munday, poor soul, who all unconsciously had planted the seeds of disbelief in Joan's mind. Mrs. Munday's God, from Joan's point of view, was a most objectionable personage. He talked a lot—or rather Mrs. Munday talked for Him—about His love for little children.

JEROME K. JEROME

But it seemed He only loved them when they were good. Joan was under no delusions about herself. If those were His terms, well, then, so far as she could see, He wasn't going to be of much use to her. Besides, if He hated naughty children, why did He make them naughty? At a moderate estimate quite half Joan's wickedness, so it seemed to Joan, came to her unbidden. Take for example that self-examination before the cheval glass. The idea had come into her mind. It had never occurred to her that it was wicked. If, as Mrs. Munday explained, it was the Devil that had whispered it to her, then what did God mean by allowing the Devil to go about persuading little girls to do indecent things? God could do everything. Why didn't He smash the Devil? It seemed to Joan a mean trick, look at it how you would. Fancy leaving a little girl to fight the Devil all by herself. And then get angry because the Devil won! Joan came to cordially dislike Mrs. Munday's God.

Looking back it was easy enough to smile, but the agony of many nights when she had lain awake for hours battling with her childish terrors had left a burning sense of anger in Joan's heart. Poor mazed, bewildered Mrs. Munday, preaching the eternal damnation of the wicked—who had loved her, who had only thought to do her duty, the blame was not hers. But that a religion capable of inflicting such suffering upon the innocent should still be preached; maintained by the State! That its educated followers no longer believed in a physical Hell, that its more advanced clergy had entered into a conspiracy of silence on the subject was no answer. The great mass of the people were not educated. Official Christendom in every country still preached the everlasting torture of the majority of the human race as a well thought out part of the Creator's scheme. No leader had been bold enough to come forward and denounce it as an insult to his God. As one grew older, kindly mother Nature, ever seeking to ease the self-inflicted burdens of her foolish brood, gave one forgetfulness, insensibility. The condemned criminal puts the thought of the gallows away from him as long as may be: eats, and sleeps and even jokes. Man's soul grows pachydermoid. But the children! Their sensitive brains exposed to every cruel breath. No philosophic doubt permitted to them. No learned disputation on the relationship between the literal and the allegorical for the easing of their frenzied fears. How many million tiny white-faced figures scattered over Christian Europe and America, stared out each night into a vision of black horror; how many million tiny hands clutched wildly at the bedclothes. The Society for the Prevention of Cruelty to Children, if they had done their duty, would have prosecuted before now the Archbishop of Canterbury.

Of course she would go to Hell. As a special kindness some generous relative had, on Joan's seventh birthday, given her an edition of Dante's "Inferno," with illustrations by Doré. From it she was able to form some notion of what her eternity was likely to be. And God all the while up in His Heaven, surrounded by that glorious band of praise-trumpeting angels, watching her out of the corner of His eye. Her courage saved her from despair. Defiance came to her aid. Let Him send her to Hell! She was not going to pray to Him and make up to Him. He was a wicked God. Yes, He was: a cruel, wicked God. And one night she told Him so to His face.

It had been a pretty crowded day, even for so busy a sinner as little Joan. It was springtime, and they had gone into the country for her mother's health. Maybe it was the season: a stirring of the human sap, conducing to that feeling of being "too big for one's boots," as the saying is. A dangerous period of the year. Indeed, on the principle that prevention is better than cure, Mrs. Munday had made it a custom during April and May to administer to Joan a cooling mixture; but on this occasion had unfortunately come away without it. Joan, dressed for use rather than show, and without either shoes or stockings, had stolen stealthily downstairs: something seemed to be calling to her. Silently— "like a thief in the night," to adopt Mrs. Munday's metaphor—had slipped the heavy bolts; had joined the thousand creatures of the wood—had danced and leapt and shouted; had behaved, in short, more as if she had been a Pagan nymph than a happy English child. She had regained the house unnoticed, as she thought, the Devil, no doubt, assisting her; and had hidden her wet clothes in the bottom of a mighty chest. Deceitfulness in her heart, she had greeted Mrs. Munday in sleepy tones from beneath the sheets; and before breakfast, assailed by suspicious questions, had told a deliberate lie. Later in the morning, during an argument with an active young pig who was willing enough to play at Red Riding Hood so far as eating things out of a basket was concerned, but who would not wear a night-cap, she had used a wicked word. In the afternoon she "might have killed" the farmer's only son and heir. They had had a row. In one of those sad lapses from the higher Christian standards into which Satan was always egging her, she had pushed him; and he had tumbled head over heels into the horse-pond.

The reason, that instead of lying there and drowning he had got up and walked back to the house howling fit to wake the Seven Sleepers, was that God, watching over little children, had arranged for the incident taking place on that side of the pond where it was shallow. Had the scrimmage occurred on the opposite bank, beneath which the water was much deeper, Joan in all probability would have had murder on her soul. It seemed to Joan that if God, all-powerful and all-foreseeing, had been so careful in selecting the site, He might with equal ease have prevented the row from ever taking place. Why couldn't the little beast have been guided back from school through the orchard, much the shorter way, instead of being brought round by the yard, so as to come upon her at a moment when she was feeling a bit short-tempered, to put it mildly? And why had God allowed him to call her "Carrots"? That Joan should have "put it" this way, instead of going down on her knees and thanking the Lord for having saved her from a crime, was proof of her inborn evil disposition. In the evening was reached the culminating point. Just before going to bed she had murdered old George the cowman. For all practical purposes she might just as well have been successful in drowning William Augustus earlier in the day. It seemed to be one of those things that had to be. Mr. Hornflower still lived, it was true, but that was not Joan's fault. Joan, standing in white night-gown beside her bed, everything around her breathing of innocence and virtue: the spotless bedclothes, the chintz curtains, the white hyacinths upon the window-ledge, Joan's Bible, a present from Aunt Susan; her prayer-book, handsomely bound in calf, a present from Grandpapa, upon their little table; Mrs. Munday in evening black and cameo brooch (pale red with tomb and weeping willow in white relief) sacred to the memory of the departed Mr. Munday— Joan standing there erect, with pale, passionate face, defying all these aids to righteousness, had deliberately wished Mr. Hornflower dead. Old George Hornflower it was who, unseen by her, had passed her that morning in the wood. Grumpy old George it was who had overheard the wicked word with which she had cursed the pig; who had met William Augustus on his emergence from the pond. To Mr. George Hornflower, the humble instrument in the hands of Providence, helping her towards possible salvation, she ought to have been grateful. And instead of that she had flung into the agonized face of Mrs. Munday these awful words:

"I wish he was dead!"

"He who in his heart—" there was verse and chapter for it. Joan was a murderess. Just as well, so far as Joan was concerned, might she have taken a carving-knife and stabbed Deacon Hornflower to the heart.

Joan's prayers that night, to the accompaniment of Mrs. Munday's sobs, had a hopeless air of unreality about them. Mrs. Munday's kiss was cold.

How long Joan lay and tossed upon her little bed she could not tell. Somewhere about the middle of the night, or so it seemed to her, the frenzy seized her. Flinging the bedclothes away she rose to her feet. It is difficult to stand upon a spring mattress, but Joan kept her balance. Of course He was there in the room with her. God was everywhere, spying upon her. She could distinctly hear His measured breathing. Face to face with Him, she told Him what she thought of Him. She told Him He was a cruel, wicked God.

There are no Victoria Crosses for sinners, or surely little Joan that night would have earned it. It was not lack of imagination that helped her courage. God and she alone, in the darkness. He with all the forces of the Universe behind Him. He armed with His eternal pains and penalties, and eight-year-old Joan: the creature that He had made in His Own Image that He could torture and destroy. Hell yawned beneath her, but it had to be said. Somebody ought to tell Him.

"You are a wicked God," Joan told Him. "Yes, You are. A cruel, wicked God."

And then that she might not see the walls of the room open before her, hear the wild laughter of the thousand devils that were coming to bear her off, she threw herself down, her face hidden in the pillow, and clenched her hands and waited.

And suddenly there burst a song. It was like nothing Joan had ever heard before. So clear and loud and near that all the night seemed filled with harmony. It sank into a tender yearning cry throbbing with passionate desire, and then it rose again in thrilling ecstasy: a song of hope, of victory.

Joan, trembling, stole from her bed and drew aside the blind. There was nothing to be seen but the stars and the dim shape of the hills. But still that song, filling the air with its wild, triumphant melody.

Years afterwards, listening to the overture to *Tannhauser*, there came back to her the memory of that night. Ever through the mad Satanic discords she could hear, now faint, now conquering, the Pilgrims' onward march. So through the jangled discords of the world one heard the Song of Life. Through the dim aeons of man's savage infancy; through the centuries of bloodshed and of horror; through the dark ages of tyranny and superstition; through wrong, through cruelty, through hate; heedless of doom, heedless of death, still the nightingale's song: "I love you. I love you. I love you. We will build a nest. We will rear our brood. I love you. I love you. Life shall not die."

Joan crept back into bed. A new wonder had come to her. And from that night Joan's belief in Mrs. Munday's God began to fade, circumstances helping.

Firstly there was the great event of going to school. She was glad to get away from home, a massive, stiffly furnished house in a wealthy suburb of Liverpool. Her mother, since she could remember, had been an invalid, rarely leaving her bedroom till the afternoon. Her father, the owner of large engineering works, she only saw, as a rule, at dinner-time, when she would come down to dessert. It had been different when she was very young, before her mother had been taken ill. Then she had been more with them both. She had dim recollections of her father playing with her, pretending to be a bear and growling at her from behind the sofa. And then he would seize and hug her and they would both laugh, while he tossed her into the air and caught her. He had looked so big and handsome. All through her childhood there had been the desire to recreate those days, to spring into the air and catch her arms about his neck. She could have loved him dearly if he had only let her. Once, seeking explanation, she had opened her heart a little to Mrs. Munday. It was disappointment, Mrs. Munday thought, that she had not been a boy; and with that Joan had to content herself. Maybe also her mother's illness had helped to sadden him. Or perhaps it was mere temperament, as she argued to herself later, for which they were both responsible. Those little tricks of coaxing, of tenderness, of wilfulness, by means of which other girls wriggled their way so successfully into a warm nest of cosy affection: she had never been able to employ them. Beneath her self-confidence was a shyness, an immovable reserve that had always prevented her from expressing her emotions. She had inherited it, doubtless enough, from him. Perhaps one day, between them, they would break down the barrier, the strength of which seemed to lie in its very flimsiness, its impalpability.

And then during college vacations, returning home with growing notions and views of her own, she had found herself so often in antagonism with him. His fierce puritanism, so opposed to all her enthusiasms.

Arguing with him, she might almost have been listening to one of his Cromwellian ancestors risen from the dead. There had been disputes between him and his work-people, and Joan had taken the side of the men. He had not been angry with her, but coldly contemptuous. And yet, in spite of it all, if he had only made a sign! She wanted to fling herself crying into his arms and shake him—make him listen to her wisdom, sitting on his knee with her hands clasped round his neck. He was not really intolerant and stupid. That had been proved by his letting her go to a Church of England school. Her mother had expressed no wish. It was he who had selected it.

Of her mother she had always stood somewhat in fear, never knowing when the mood of passionate affection would give place to a chill aversion that seemed almost like hate. Perhaps it had been good for her, so she told herself in after years, her lonely, unguided childhood. It had forced her to think and act for herself. At school she reaped the benefit. Self-reliant, confident, original, leadership was granted to her as a natural prerogative. Nature had helped her. Nowhere does a young girl rule more supremely by reason of her beauty than among her fellows. Joan soon grew accustomed to having her boots put on and taken off for her; all her needs of service anticipated by eager slaves, contending with one another for the privilege. By giving a command, by bestowing a few moments of her conversation, it was within her power to make some small adoring girl absurdly happy for the rest of the day; while her displeasure would result in tears, in fawning pleadings for forgiveness. The homage did not spoil her. Rather it helped to develop her. She accepted it from the beginning as in the order of things. Power had been given to her. It was her duty to see to it that she did not use it capriciously, for her own gratification. No conscientious youthful queen could have been more careful in the distribution of her favours—that they should be for the encouragement of the deserving, the reward of virtue; more sparing of her frowns, reserving them for the rectification of error.

At Girton it was more by force of will, of brain, that she had to make her position. There was more competition. Joan welcomed it, as giving more zest to life. But even there her beauty was by no means a negligible quantity. Clever, brilliant young women, accustomed to sweep aside all opposition with a blaze of rhetoric, found themselves to their irritation sitting in front of her silent, not so much listening to her as looking at her. It puzzled them for a time. Because a girl's features are classical and her colouring attractive, surely that has nothing to do with the value of her political views? Until one of them discovered by chance that it has.

"Well, what does Beauty think about it?" this one had asked, laughing. She had arrived at the end of a discussion just as Joan was leaving the room. And then she gave a long low whistle, feeling that she had stumbled upon the explanation. Beauty, that mysterious force that from the date of creation has ruled the world, what does It think? Dumb, passive, as a rule, exercising its influence unconsciously. But if it should become intelligent, active! A Philosopher has dreamed of the vast influence that could be exercised by a dozen sincere men acting in unity. Suppose a dozen of the most beautiful women in the world could form themselves into a league! Joan found them late in the evening still discussing it.

Her mother died suddenly during her last term, and Joan hurried back to attend the funeral. Her father was out when she reached home. Joan changed her travel-dusty clothes, and then went into the room where her mother lay, and closed the door. She must have been a beautiful woman. Now that the fret and the restlessness had left her it had come back to her. The passionate eyes were closed. Joan kissed the marble lids, and drawing a chair to the bedside, sat down. It grieved her that she had never loved her mother—not as one ought to love one's mother, unquestioningly, unreasoningly, as a natural instinct. For a moment a strange thought came to her, and swiftly, almost guiltily, she stole across, and drawing back a corner of the blind, examined closely her own features in the glass, comparing them with the face of the dead woman, thus called upon to be a silent witness for or against the living. Joan drew a sigh of relief and let fall the blind. There could be no misreading the evidence. Death had smoothed away the lines, given back youth. It was almost uncanny, the likeness between them. It might have been her drowned sister lying there. And they had never known one another. Had this also been temperament again, keeping them apart? Why did it imprison us each one as in a moving cell, so that we never could stretch out our arms to one another, except when at rare intervals Love or Death would unlock for a while the key? Impossible that two beings should have been so alike in feature without being more or less alike in thought and feeling. Whose fault had it been? Surely her own; she was so hideously calculating. Even Mrs. Munday, because the old lady had been fond of her and had shown it, had been of more service to her, more a companion, had been nearer to her than her own mother. In self-excuse she recalled the two or three occasions when she had tried to win her mother. But fate seemed to have decreed that their moods should never correspond. Her mother's sudden fierce outbursts of love, when she would be jealous, exacting, almost cruel, had frightened her when she was a child, and later on had bored her. Other daughters would have shown patience, unselfishness, but she had always been so self-centred. Why had she never fallen in love like other girls? There had been a boy at Brighton when she was at school there— quite a nice boy, who had written her wildly extravagant love-letters. It must have cost him half his pocket-money to get them smuggled in to her. Why had she only been amused at them? They might have been beautiful if only one had read them with sympathy. One day he had caught her alone on the Downs. Evidently he had made it his business to hang about every day waiting for some such chance. He had gone down on his knees and kissed her feet, and had been so abject, so pitiful that she had given him some flowers she was wearing. And he had sworn to dedicate the rest of his life to being worthy of her condescension. Poor lad! She wondered—for the first time since that afternoon—what had become of him. There had been others; a third cousin who still wrote to her from Egypt, sending her presents that perhaps he could ill afford, and whom she answered about once a year. And promising young men she had met at Cambridge, ready, she felt instinctively, to fall down and worship her. And all the use she had had for them was to convert them to her views—a task so easy as to be quite uninteresting—with a vague idea that they might come in handy in the future, when she might need help in shaping that world of the future.

Only once had she ever thought of marriage. And that was in favour of a middle-aged, rheumatic widower with three children, a professor of chemistry, very learned and justly famous. For about a month she had thought herself in love. She pictured herself devoting her life to him, rubbing his poor left shoulder where it seemed he suffered most, and brushing his picturesque hair, inclined to grey. Fortunately his eldest daughter was a young woman of resource, or the poor gentleman, naturally carried off his feet by this adoration of youth and beauty, might have made an ass of himself. But apart from this one episode she had reached the age of twenty-three heart-whole.

She rose and replaced the chair. And suddenly a wave of pity passed over her for the dead woman, who had always seemed so lonely in the great stiffly-furnished house, and the tears came.

She was glad she had been able to cry. She had always hated herself for her lack of tears; it was so unwomanly. Even as a child she had rarely cried.

Her father had always been very tender, very patient towards her mother, but she had not expected to find him so changed. He had aged and his shoulders drooped. She had been afraid that he would want her to stay with him and take charge of the house. It had worried her considerably. It would be so difficult to refuse, and yet she would have to. But when he never broached the subject she was hurt. He had questioned her about her plans the day after the funeral, and had seemed only anxious to assist them. She proposed continuing at Cambridge till the end of the term. She had taken her degree the year before. After that, she would go to London and commence her work.

"Let me know what allowance you would like me to make you, when you have thought it out. Things are not what they were at the works, but there will always be enough to keep you in comfort," he had told her. She had fixed it there and then at two hundred a year. She would not take more, and that only until she was in a position to keep herself.

"I want to prove to myself," she explained, "that I am capable of earning my own living. I am going down into the market-place. If I'm no good, if I can't take care of even one poor woman, I'll come back and ask you to keep me." She was sitting on the arm of his chair, and laughing, she drew his head towards her and pressed it against her. "If I succeed, if I am strong enough to fight the world for myself and win, that will mean I am strong enough and clever enough to help others."

"I am only at the end of a journey when you need me," he had answered, and they had kissed. And next morning she returned to her own life.

III

I t was at Madge Singleton's rooms that the details of Joan's entry into journalistic London were arranged. "The Coming of Beauty," was Flora Lessing's phrase for designating the event. Flora Lessing, known among her associates as "Flossie," was the girl who at Cambridge had accidentally stumbled upon the explanation of Joan's influence. In appearance she was of the Fluffy Ruffles type, with childish innocent eyes, and the "unruly curls" beloved of the *Family Herald* novelist. At the first, these latter had been the result of a habit of late rising and consequent hurried toilet operations; but on the discovery that for the purposes of her profession they possessed a market value they had been sedulously cultivated. Editors of the old order had ridiculed the idea of her being of any use to them, when two years previously she had, by combination of cheek and patience, forced herself into their sanctum; had patted her paternally upon her generally ungloved hand, and told her to go back home and get some honest, worthy young man to love and cherish her.

It was Carleton of the *Daily Dispatch* group who had first divined her possibilities. With a swift glance on his way through, he had picked her out from a line of depressed-looking men and women ranged against the wall of the dark entrance passage; and with a snap of his fingers had beckoned to her to follow him. Striding in front of her up to his room, he had pointed to a chair and had left her sitting there for three-quarters of an hour, while he held discussion with a stream of subordinates, managers and editors of departments, who entered and departed one after another, evidently in pre-arranged order. All of them spoke rapidly, without ever digressing by a single word from the point, giving her the impression of their speeches having been rehearsed beforehand.

Carleton himself never interrupted them. Indeed, one might have thought he was not listening, so engrossed he appeared to be in the pile of letters and telegrams that lay waiting for him on his desk. When they had finished he would ask them questions, still with his attention fixed apparently upon the paper in his hand. Then, looking up for the first time, he would run off curt instructions, much in the tone of a Commander-in-Chief giving orders for an immediate assault; and, finishing abruptly, return to his correspondence. When the last, as it transpired, had closed the door behind him, he swung his chair round and faced her.

"What have you been doing?" he asked her.

"Wasting my time and money hanging about newspaper offices, listening to silly talk from old fossils," she told him.

"And having learned that respectable journalism has no use for brains, you come to me," he answered her. "What do you think you can do?"

"Anything that can be done with a pen and ink," she told him.

"Interviewing?" he suggested.

"I've always been considered good at asking awkward questions," she assured him.

He glanced at the clock. "I'll give you five minutes," he said. "Interview me."

She moved to a chair beside the desk, and, opening her bag, took out a writing-block.

"What are your principles?" she asked him. "Have you got any?"

He looked at her sharply across the corner of the desk.

"I mean," she continued, "to what fundamental rule of conduct do you attribute your success?"

She leant forward, fixing her eyes on him. "Don't tell me," she persisted, "that you had none. That life is all just mere blind chance. Think of the young men who are hanging on your answer. Won't you send them a message?"

"Yes," he answered musingly. "It's your baby face that does the trick. In the ordinary way I should have known you were pulling my leg, and have shown you the door. As it was, I felt half inclined for the moment to reply with some damned silly platitude that would have set all Fleet Street laughing at me. Why do my 'principles' interest you?"

"As a matter of fact they don't," she explained. "But it's what people talk about whenever they discuss you."

"What do they say?" he demanded.

"Your friends, that you never had any. And your enemies, that they are always the latest," she informed him.

"You'll do," he answered with a laugh. "With nine men out of ten that speech would have ended your chances. You sized me up at a glance, and knew it would only interest me. And your instinct is right," he added. "What people are saying: always go straight for that."

He gave her a commission then and there for a heart to heart talk with a gentleman whom the editor of the Home News Department of the *Daily Dispatch* would have referred to as a "Leading Literary Luminary," and who had just invented a new world in two volumes. She had asked him childish questions and had listened with wide-open eyes while he, sitting over against her, and smiling benevolently, had laid bare to her all the seeming intricacies of creation, and had explained to her in simple language the necessary alterations and improvements he was hoping to bring about in human nature. He had the sensation that his hair must be standing on end the next morning after having read in cold print what he had said. Expanding oneself before the admiring gaze of innocent simplicity and addressing the easily amused ear of an unsympathetic public are not the same thing. He ought to have thought of that.

It consoled him, later, that he was not the only victim. The *Daily Dispatch* became famous for its piquant interviews; especially with elderly celebrities of the masculine gender.

"It's dirty work," Flossie confided one day to Madge Singleton. "I trade on my silly face. Don't see that I'm much different to any of these poor devils." They were walking home in the evening from a theatre. "If I hadn't been stony broke I'd never have taken it up. I shall get out of it as soon as I can afford to."

"I should make it a bit sooner than that," suggested the elder woman. "One can't always stop oneself just where one wants to when sliding down a slope. It has a knack of getting steeper and steeper as one goes on."

Madge had asked Joan to come a little earlier so that they could have a chat together before the others arrived.

"I've only asked a few," she explained, as she led Joan into the restful white-panelled sitting-room that looked out upon the gardens. Madge shared a set of chambers in Gray's Inn with her brother who was an actor. "But I have chosen them with care."

Joan murmured her thanks.

"I haven't asked any men," she added, as she fixed Joan in an easy chair before the fire. "I was afraid of its introducing the wrong element."

"Tell me," asked Joan, "am I likely to meet with much of that sort of thing?"

"Oh, about as much as there always is wherever men and women work together," answered Madge. "It's a nuisance, but it has to be faced."

"Nature appears to have only one idea in her head," she continued after a pause, "so far as we men and women are concerned. She's been kinder to the lower animals."

"Man has more interests," Joan argued, "a thousand other allurements to distract him; we must cultivate his finer instincts."

"It doesn't seem to answer," grumbled Madge. "One is always told it is the artist—the brain worker, the very men who have these fine instincts, who are the most sexual."

She made a little impatient movement with her hands that was characteristic of her. "Personally, I like men," she went on. "It is so splendid the way they enjoy life: just like a dog does, whether it's wet or fine. We are always blinking up at the clouds and worrying about our hat. It would be so nice to be able to have friendship with them.

"I don't mean that it's all their fault," she continued. "We do all we can to attract them—the way we dress. Who was it said that to every woman every man is a potential lover. We can't get it out of our minds. It's there even when we don't know it. We will never succeed in civilizing Nature."

"We won't despair of her," laughed Joan. "She's creeping up, poor lady, as Whistler said of her. We have passed the phase when everything she did was right in our childish eyes. Now we dare to criticize her. That shows we are growing up. She will learn from us, later on. She's a dear old thing, at heart."

"She's been kind enough to you," replied Madge, somewhat irrelevantly. There was a note of irritation in her tone. "I suppose you know you are supremely beautiful. You seem so indifferent to it, I wonder sometimes if you do."

"I'm not indifferent to it," answered Joan. "I'm reckoning on it to help me."

"Why not?" she continued, with a flash of defiance, though Madge had not spoken. "It is a weapon like any other—knowledge, intellect, courage. God has given me beauty. I shall use it in His service."

They formed a curious physical contrast, these two women in this moment. Joan, radiant, serene, sat upright in her chair, her head slightly thrown back, her fine hands clasping one another so strongly that the delicate muscles could be traced beneath the smooth white skin. Madge, with puckered brows, leant forward in a crouching attitude, her thin nervous hands stretched out towards the fire.

"How does one know when one is serving God?" she asked after a pause, apparently rather of herself than of Joan. "It seems so difficult."

"One feels it," explained Joan.

"Yes, but didn't they all feel it," Madge suggested. She still seemed to be arguing with herself rather than with Joan. "Nietzsche. I have been reading him. They are forming a Nietzsche Society to give lectures about him—propagate him over here. Eleanor's in it up to the neck. It seems to me awful. Every fibre in my being revolts against him. Yet they're all cocksure that he is the coming prophet. He must have convinced himself that he is serving God. If I were a fighter I should feel I was serving God trying to down Him. How do I know which of us is right? Torquemada—Calvin," she went on, without giving Joan the chance of a reply. "It's easy enough to see they were wrong now. But at the time millions of people believed in them—felt it was God's voice speaking through them. Joan of Arc! Fancy dying to put a thing like that upon a throne. It would be funny if it wasn't so tragic. You can say she drove out the English—saved France. But for what? The Bartholomew massacres. The ruin of the Palatinate by Louis XIV. The horrors of the French Revolution, ending with Napoleon and all the misery and degeneracy that he bequeathed to Europe. History might have worked itself out so much better if the poor child had left it alone and minded her sheep."

"Wouldn't that train of argument lead to nobody ever doing anything?" suggested Joan.

"I suppose it would mean stagnation," admitted Madge. "And yet I don't know. Are there not forces moving towards right that are crying to us to help them, not by violence, which only interrupts—delays them, but by quietly preparing the way for them? You know what I mean. Erasmus always said that Luther had hindered the Reformation by stirring up passion and hate." She broke off suddenly. There were tears in her eyes. "Oh, if God would only say what He wants of us," she almost cried; "call to us in trumpet tones that would ring through the world, compelling us to take sides. Why can't He speak?"

"He does," answered Joan. "I hear His voice. There are things I've got to do. Wrongs that I must fight against. Rights that I must never dare to rest till they are won." Her lips were parted. Her breasts heaving. "He does call to us. He has girded His sword upon me."

Madge looked at her in silence for quite a while. "How confident you are," she said. "How I envy you."

They talked for a time about domestic matters. Joan had established herself in furnished rooms in a quiet street of pleasant Georgian houses just behind the Abbey; a member of Parliament and his wife occupied the lower floors, the landlord, a retired butler, and his wife, an excellent cook, confining themselves to the basement and the attics.

The remaining floor was tenanted by a shy young man—a poet, so the landlady thought, but was not sure. Anyhow he had long hair, lived with a pipe in his mouth, and burned his lamp long into the night. Joan had omitted to ask his name. She made a note to do so.

They discussed ways and means. Joan calculated she could get through on two hundred a year, putting aside fifty for dress. Madge was doubtful if this would be sufficient. Joan urged that she was "stock size" and would be able to pick up "models" at sales; but Madge, measuring her against herself, was sure she was too full.

"You will find yourself expensive to dress," she told her, "cheap things won't go well on you; and it would be madness, even from a business point of view, for you not to make the best of yourself."

"Men stand more in awe of a well dressed woman than they do even of a beautiful woman," Madge was of opinion. "If you go into an office looking dowdy they'll beat you down. Tell them the price they are offering you won't keep you in gloves for a week and they'll be ashamed of themselves. There's nothing *infra dig.* in being mean to the poor; but not to sympathize with the rich stamps you as middle class." She laughed.

Joan was worried. "I told Dad I should only ask him for enough to make up two hundred a year," she explained. "He'll laugh at me for not knowing my own mind."

"I should let him," advised Madge. She grew thoughtful again. "We cranky young women, with our new-fangled, independent ways, I guess we hurt the old folks quite enough as it is."

The bell rang and Madge opened the door herself. It turned out to be Flossie. Joan had not seen her since they had been at Girton together, and was surprised at Flossie's youthful "get up." Flossie explained, and without waiting for any possible attack flew to her own defence.

"The revolution that the world is waiting for," was Flossie's opinion, "is the providing of every man and woman with a hundred and fifty a year. Then we shall all be able to afford to be noble and high-minded. As it is, nine-tenths of the contemptible things we do comes from the necessity of our having to earn our living. A hundred and fifty a year would deliver us from evil."

"Would there not still be the diamond dog-collar and the motor car left to tempt us?" suggested Madge.

"Only the really wicked," contended Flossie. "It would classify us. We should know then which were the sheep and which the goats. At present we're all jumbled together: the ungodly who sin out of mere greed and rapacity, and the just men compelled to sell their birthright of fine instincts for a mess of meat and potatoes."

"Yah, socialist," commented Madge, who was busy with the tea things.

Flossie seemed struck by an idea.

"By Jove," she exclaimed. "Why did I never think of it. With a red flag and my hair down, I'd be in all the illustrated papers. It would put up my price no end. And I'd be able to get out of this silly job of mine. I can't go on much longer. I'm getting too well known. I do believe I'll try it. The shouting's easy enough." She turned to Joan. "Are you going to take up socialism?" she demanded.

"I may," answered Joan. "Just to spank it, and put it down again. I'm rather a believer in temptation—the struggle for existence. I only want to make it a finer existence, more worth the struggle, in which the best man shall rise to the top. Your 'universal security'—that will be the last act of the human drama, the cue for ringing down the curtain."

"But do not all our Isms work towards that end?" suggested Madge.

Joan was about to reply when the maid's announcement of "Mrs. Denton" postponed the discussion.

Mrs. Denton was a short, grey-haired lady. Her large strong features must have made her, when she was young, a hard-looking woman; but time and sorrow had strangely softened them; while about the corners of the thin firm mouth lurked a suggestion of humour that possibly had not always been there. Joan, waiting to be introduced, towered head and shoulders above her; yet when she took the small proffered hand and felt those steely blue eyes surveying her, she had the sensation of being quite insignificant. Mrs. Denton seemed to be reading her, and then still retaining Joan's hand she turned to Madge with a smile.

"So this is our new recruit," she said. "She is come to bring healing to the sad, sick world—to right all the old, old wrongs."

She patted Joan's hand and spoke gravely. "That is right, dear. That is youth's *metier*; to take the banner from our failing hands, bear it still a little onward." Her small gloved hand closed on Joan's with a pressure that made Joan wince.

"And you must not despair," she continued; "because in the end it will seem to you that you have failed. It is the fallen that win the victories."

She released Joan's hand abruptly. "Come and see me to-morrow morning at my office," she said. "We will fix up something that shall be serviceable to us both."

JEROME K. JEROME

Madge flashed Joan a look. She considered Joan's position already secured. Mrs. Denton was the doyen of women journalists. She edited a monthly review and was leader writer of one of the most important dailies, besides being the controlling spirit of various social movements. Anyone she "took up" would be assured of steady work. The pay might not be able to compete with the prices paid for more popular journalism, but it would afford a foundation, and give to Joan that opportunity for influence which was her main ambition.

Joan expressed her thanks. She would like to have had more talk with the stern old lady, but was prevented by the entrance of two new comers. The first was Miss Lavery, a handsome, loud-toned young woman. She ran a nursing paper, but her chief interest was in the woman's suffrage question, just then coming rapidly to the front. She had heard Joan speak at Cambridge and was eager to secure her adherence, being wishful to surround herself with a group of young and good-looking women who should take the movement out of the hands of the "frumps," as she termed them. Her doubt was whether Joan would prove sufficiently tractable. She intended to offer her remunerative work upon the *Nursing News* without saying anything about the real motive behind, trusting to gratitude to make her task the easier.

The second was a clumsy-looking, overdressed woman whom Miss Lavery introduced as "Mrs. Phillips, a very dear friend of mine, who is going to be helpful to us all," adding in a hurried aside to Madge, "I simply had to bring her. Will explain to you another time." An apology certainly seemed to be needed. The woman was absurdly out of her place. She stood there panting and slightly perspiring. She was short and fat, with dyed hair. As a girl she had possibly been pretty in a dimpled, giggling sort of way. Joan judged her, in spite of her complexion, to be about forty.

Joan wondered if she could be the wife of the Member of Parliament who occupied the rooms below her in Cowley Street. His name, so the landlady had told her, was Phillips. She put the suggestion in a whisper to Flossie.

"Quite likely," thought Flossie; "just the type that sort of man does marry. A barmaid, I expect."

Others continued to arrive until altogether there must have been about a dozen women present. One of them turned out to be an old schoolfellow of Joan's and two had been with her at Girton. Madge had selected those who she knew would be sympathetic, and all promised help: those who could not give it direct undertaking to provide introductions and recommendations, though some of them were frankly doubtful of journalism affording Joan anything more than the means—not always too honest—of earning a living.

"I started out to preach the gospel: all that sort of thing," drawled a Miss Simmonds from beneath a hat that, if she had paid for it, would have cost her five guineas. "Now my chief purpose in life is to tickle silly women into spending twice as much upon their clothes as their husbands can afford, bamboozling them into buying any old thing that our Advertising Manager instructs me to boom."

"They talk about the editor's opinions," struck in a fiery little woman who was busy flinging crumbs out of the window to a crowd of noisy sparrows. "It's the Advertiser edits half the papers. Write anything that three of them object to, and your proprietor tells you to change your convictions or go. Most of us change." She jerked down the window with a slam.

"It's the syndicates that have done it," was a Mrs. Elliot's opinion. She wrote "Society Notes" for a Labour weekly. "When one man owned a paper he wanted it to express his views. A company is only out for profit. Your modern newspaper is just a shop. It's only purpose is to attract customers. Look at the *Methodist Herald*, owned by the same syndicate of Jews that runs the *Racing News*. They work it as far as possible with the same staff."

"We're a pack of hirelings," asserted the fiery little woman. "Our pens are for sale to the highest bidder. I had a letter from Jocelyn only two days ago. He was one of the original staff of the *Socialist*. He writes me that he has gone as leader writer to a Conservative paper at twice his former salary. Expected me to congratulate him."

"One of these days somebody will start a Society for the Reformation of the Press," thought Flossie. "I wonder how the papers will take it?"

"Much as Rome took Savonarola," thought Madge.

Mrs. Denton had risen.

"They are right to a great extent," she said to Joan. "But not all the temple has been given over to the hucksters. You shall place your preaching stool in some quiet corner, where the passing feet shall pause awhile to listen."

Her going was the signal for the breaking up of the party. In a short time Joan and Madge found themselves left with only Flossie.

"What on earth induced Helen to bring that poor old Dutch doll along with her?" demanded Flossie. "The woman never opened her mouth all the time. Did she tell you?"

"No," answered Madge, "but I think I can guess. She hopes—or perhaps 'fears' would be more correct—that her husband is going to join the Cabinet, and is trying to fit herself by suddenly studying political and social questions. For a month she's been clinging like a leech to Helen Lavery, who takes her to meetings and gatherings. I suppose they've struck up some sort of a bargain. It's rather pathetic."

"Good Heavens! What a tragedy for the man," commented Flossie.

"What is he like?" asked Joan.

"Not much to look at, if that's what you mean," answered Madge. "Began life as a miner, I believe. Looks like ending as Prime Minister."

"I heard him at the Albert Hall last week," said Flossie. "He's quite wonderful."

"In what way?" questioned Joan.

"Oh, you know," explained Flossie. "Like a volcano compressed into a steam engine."

They discussed Joan's plans. It looked as if things were going to be easy for her.

IV

Yet in the end it was Carleton who opened the door for her.

Mrs. Denton was helpful, and would have been more so, if Joan had only understood. Mrs. Denton lived alone in an old house in Gower Street, with a high stone hall that was always echoing to sounds that no one but itself could ever hear. Her son had settled, it was supposed, in one of the Colonies. No one knew what had become of him, and Mrs. Denton herself never spoke of him; while her daughter, on whom she had centred all her remaining hopes, had died years ago. To those who remembered the girl, with her weak eyes and wispy ginger coloured hair, it would have seemed comical, the idea that Joan resembled her. But Mrs. Denton's memory had lost itself in dreams; and to her the likeness had appeared quite wonderful. The gods had given her child back to her, grown strong and brave and clever. Life would have a new meaning for her. Her work would not die with her.

She thought she could harness Joan's enthusiasm to her own wisdom. She would warn her of the errors and pitfalls into which she herself had fallen: for she, too, had started as a rebel. Youth should begin where age left off. Had the old lady remembered a faded dogs-eared volume labelled "Oddments" that for many years had rested undisturbed upon its shelf in her great library, and opening it had turned to the letter E, she would have read recorded there, in her own precise thin penmanship, this very wise reflection:

"Experience is a book that all men write, but no man reads."

To which she would have found added, by way of complement, "Experience is untranslatable. We write it in the cipher of our sufferings, and the key is hidden in our memories."

And turning to the letter Y, she might have read:

"Youth comes to teach. Age remains to listen," and underneath the following:

"The ability to learn is the last lesson we acquire."

Mrs. Denton had long ago given up the practice of jotting down her thoughts, experience having taught her that so often, when one comes to use them, one finds that one has changed them. But in the case of Joan the recollection of these twin "oddments" might have saved her disappointment. Joan knew of a new road that avoided Mrs. Denton's pitfalls. She grew impatient of being perpetually pulled back.

JEROME K. JEROME

For the *Nursing Times* she wrote a series of condensed biographies, entitled "Ladies of the Lamp," commencing with Elizabeth Fry. They formed a record of good women who had battled for the weak and suffering, winning justice for even the uninteresting. Miss Lavery was delighted with them. But when Joan proposed exposing the neglect and even cruelty too often inflicted upon the helpless patients of private Nursing Homes, Miss Lavery shook her head.

"I know," she said. "One does hear complaints about them. Unfortunately it is one of the few businesses managed entirely by women; and just now, in particular, if we were to say anything, it would be made use of by our enemies to injure the Cause."

There was a summer years ago—it came back to Joan's mind—when she had shared lodgings with a girl chum at a crowded sea-side watering-place. The rooms were shockingly dirty; and tired of dropping hints she determined one morning to clean them herself. She climbed a chair and started on a row of shelves where lay the dust of ages. It was a jerry-built house, and the result was that she brought the whole lot down about her head, together with a quarter of a hundred-weight of plaster.

"Yes, I thought you'd do some mischief," had commented the landlady, wearily.

It seemed typical. A jerry-built world, apparently. With the best intentions it seemed impossible to move in it without doing more harm than good to it, bringing things down about one that one had not intended.

She wanted to abolish steel rabbit-traps. She had heard the little beggars cry. It had struck her as such a harmless reform. But they told her there were worthy people in the neighbourhood of Wolverhampton—quite a number of them—who made their living by the manufacture of steel rabbit-traps. If, thinking only of the rabbits, you prohibited steel rabbit-traps, then you condemned all these worthy people to slow starvation. The local Mayor himself wrote in answer to her article. He drew a moving picture of the sad results that might follow such an ill-considered agitation: hundreds of grey-haired men, too old to learn new jobs, begging from door to door; shoals of little children, white-faced and pinched; sobbing women. Her editor was sorry for the rabbits. Had often spent a pleasant day with them himself. But, after all, the Human Race claimed our first sympathies.

She wanted to abolish sweating. She had climbed the rotting stairways, seen the famished creatures in their holes. But it seemed that if you interfered with the complicated system based on sweating then you dislocated the entire structure of the British export clothing trade. Not only would these poor creatures lose their admittedly wretched living—but still a living—but thousands of other innocent victims would also be involved in the common ruin. All very sad, but half a loaf—or even let us frankly say a thin slice—is better than no bread at all.

She wanted board school children's heads examined. She had examined one or two herself. It seemed to her wrong that healthy children should be compelled to sit for hours within jumping distance of the diseased. She thought it better that the dirty should be made fit company for the clean than the clean should be brought down to the level of the dirty. It seemed that in doing this you were destroying the independence of the poor. Opposition reformers, in letters scintillating with paradox, bristling with classical allusion, denounced her attempt to impose middle-class ideals upon a too long suffering proletariat. Better far a few lively little heads than a broken-spirited people robbed of their parental rights.

Through Miss Lavery she obtained an introduction to the great Sir William. He owned a group of popular provincial newspapers, and was most encouraging. Sir William had often said to himself:

"What can I do for God who has done so much for me?" It seemed only fair.

He asked her down to his "little place in Hampshire," to talk plans over. The "little place," it turned out, ran to forty bedrooms, and was surrounded by three hundred acres of park. God had evidently done his bit quite handsomely.

It was in a secluded corner of the park that Sir William had gone down upon one knee and gallantly kissed her hand. His idea was that if she could regard herself as his "Dear Lady," and allow him the honour and privilege of being her "True Knight," that, between them, they might accomplish something really useful. There had been some difficulty about his getting up again, Sir William being an elderly gentleman subject to rheumatism, and Joan had had to expend no small amount of muscular effort in assisting him; so that the episode which should have been symbolical ended by leaving them both red and breathless.

He referred to the matter again the same evening in the library while Lady William slept peacefully in the blue drawing-room; but as it appeared necessary that the compact should be sealed by a knightly kiss Joan had failed to ratify it.

JEROME K. JEROME

She blamed herself on her way home. The poor old gentleman could easily have been kept in his place. The suffering of an occasional harmless caress would have purchased for her power and opportunity. Had it not been somewhat selfish of her? Should she write to him—see him again?

She knew that she never would. It was something apart from her reason. It would not even listen to her. It bade or forbade as if one were a child without any right to a will of one's own. It was decidedly exasperating.

There were others. There were the editors who frankly told her that the business of a newspaper was to write what its customers wanted to read; and that the public, so far as they could judge, was just about fed up with plans for New Jerusalems at their expense. And the editors who were prepared to take up any number of reforms, insisting only that they should be new and original and promise popularity.

And then she met Greyson.

It was at a lunch given by Mrs. Denton. Greyson was a bachelor and lived with an unmarried sister, a few years older than himself. He was editor and part proprietor of an evening paper. It had ideals and was, in consequence, regarded by the general public with suspicion; but by reason of sincerity and braininess was rapidly becoming a power. He was a shy, reserved man with an aristocratic head set upon stooping shoulders. The face was that of a dreamer, but about the mouth there was suggestion of the fighter. Joan felt at her ease with him in spite of the air of detachment that seemed part of his character. Mrs. Denton had paired them off together; and, during the lunch, one of them—Joan could not remember which—had introduced the subject of reincarnation.

Greyson was unable to accept the theory because of the fact that, in old age, the mind in common with the body is subject to decay.

"Perhaps by the time I am forty—or let us say fifty," he argued, "I shall be a bright, intelligent being. If I die then, well and good. I select a likely baby and go straight on. But suppose I hang about till eighty and die a childish old gentleman with a mind all gone to seed. What am I going to do then? I shall have to begin all over again: perhaps worse off than I was before. That's not going to help us much."

Joan explained it to him: that old age might be likened to an illness. A genius lies upon a bed of sickness and babbles childish nonsense. But with returning life he regains his power, goes on increasing it. The mind, the soul, has not decayed. It is the lines of communication that old age has destroyed.

"But surely you don't believe it?" he demanded.

"Why not?" laughed Joan. "All things are possible. It was the possession of a hand that transformed monkeys into men. We used to take things up, you know, and look at them, and wonder and wonder and wonder, till at last there was born a thought and the world became visible. It is curiosity that will lead us to the next great discovery. We must take things up; and think and think and think till one day there will come knowledge, and we shall see the universe."

Joan always avoided getting excited when she thought of it.

"I love to make you excited," Flossie had once confessed to her in the old student days. "You look so ridiculously young and you are so pleased with yourself, laying down the law."

She did not know she had given way to it. He was leaning back in his chair, looking at her; and the tired look she had noticed in his eyes, when she had been introduced to him in the drawing-room, had gone out of them.

During the coffee, Mrs. Denton beckoned him to come to her; and Miss Greyson crossed over and took his vacant chair. She had been sitting opposite to them.

"I've been hearing so much about you," she said. "I can't help thinking that you ought to suit my brother's paper. He has all your ideas. Have you anything that you could send him?"

Joan considered a moment.

"Nothing very startling," she answered. "I was thinking of a series of articles on the old London Churches—touching upon the people connected with them and the things they stood for. I've just finished the first one."

"It ought to be the very thing," answered Miss Greyson. She was a thin, faded woman with a soft, plaintive voice. "It will enable him to judge your style. He's particular about that. Though I'm confident he'll like it," she hastened to add. "Address it to me, will you. I assist him as much as I can."

Joan added a few finishing touches that evening, and posted it; and a day or two later received a note asking her to call at the office.

"My sister is enthusiastic about your article on Chelsea Church and insists on my taking the whole series," Greyson informed her. "She says you have the Stevensonian touch."

Joan flushed with pleasure.

"And you," she asked, "did you think it had the Stevensonian touch?"

"No," he answered, "it seemed to me to have more of your touch."

"What's that like?" she demanded.

"They couldn't suppress you," he explained. "Sir Thomas More with his head under his arm, bloody old Bluebeard, grim Queen Bess, snarling old Swift, Pope, Addison, Carlyle—the whole grisly crowd of them! I could see you holding your own against them all, explaining things to them, getting excited." He laughed.

His sister joined them, coming in from the next room. She had a proposal to make. It was that Joan should take over the weekly letter from "Clorinda." It was supposed to give the views of a—perhaps unusually—sane and thoughtful woman upon the questions of the day. Miss Greyson had hitherto conducted it herself, but was wishful as she explained to be relieved of it; so that she might have more time for home affairs. It would necessitate Joan's frequent attendance at the office; for there would be letters from the public to be answered, and points to be discussed with her brother. She was standing behind his chair with her hands upon his head. There was something strangely motherly about her whole attitude.

Greyson was surprised, for the Letter had been her own conception, and had grown into a popular feature. But she was evidently in earnest; and Joan accepted willingly. "Clorinda" grew younger, more self-assertive; on the whole more human. But still so eminently "sane" and reasonable.

"We must not forget that she is quite a respectable lady, connected—according to her own account—with the higher political circles," Joan's editor would insist, with a laugh.

Miss Greyson, working in the adjoining room, would raise her head and listen. She loved to hear him laugh.

"It's absurd," Flossie told her one morning, as having met by chance they were walking home together along the Embankment. "You're not 'Clorinda'; you ought to be writing letters to her, not from her, waking her up, telling her to come off her perch, and find out what the earth feels like. I'll tell you what I'll do: I'll trot you round to Carleton. If you're out for stirring up strife and contention, well, that's his game, too. He'll use you for his beastly sordid ends. He'd have roped in John the Baptist if he'd been running the 'Jerusalem Star' at the time, and have given him a daily column for so long as the boom lasted. What's that matter, if he's willing to give you a start?"

Joan jibbed at first. But in the end Flossie's arguments prevailed. One afternoon, a week later, she was shown into Carleton's private room, and the door closed behind her. The light was dim, and for a moment she could see no one; until Carleton, who had been standing near one of the windows, came forward and placed a chair for her. And they both sat down.

"I've glanced through some of your things," he said. "They're all right. They're alive. What's your idea?"

Remembering Flossie's counsel, she went straight to the point. She wanted to talk to the people. She wanted to get at them. If she had been a man, she would have taken a chair and gone to Hyde Park. As it was, she hadn't the nerve for Hyde Park. At least she was afraid she hadn't. It might have to come to that. There was a trembling in her voice that annoyed her. She was so afraid she might cry. She wasn't out for anything crazy. She wanted only those things done that could be done if the people would but lift their eyes, look into one another's faces, see the wrong and the injustice that was all around them, and swear that they would never rest till the pain and the terror had been driven from the land. She wanted soldiers—men and women who would forget their own sweet selves, not counting their own loss, thinking of the greater gain; as in times of war and revolution, when men gave even their lives gladly for a dream, for a hope—

Without warning he switched on the electric lamp that stood upon the desk, causing her to draw back with a start.

"All right," he said. "Go ahead. You shall have your tub, and a weekly audience of a million readers for as long as you can keep them interested. Up with anything you like, and down with everything you don't. Be careful not to land me in a libel suit. Call the whole Bench of Bishops hypocrites, and all the ground landlords thieves, if you will: but don't mention names. And don't get me into trouble with the police. Beyond that, I shan't interfere with you."

She was about to speak.

"One stipulation," he went on, "that every article is headed with your photograph."

He read the sudden dismay in her eyes.

"How else do you think you are going to attract their attention?" he asked her. "By your eloquence! Hundreds of men and women as eloquent as you could ever be are shouting to them every day. Who takes any notice of them? Why should they listen any the more to you—another cranky highbrow: some old maid, most likely, with a bony throat and a beaky nose. If Woman is going to come into the fight she will have to use her own weapons. If she is prepared to do that she'll make things hum with a vengeance. She's the biggest force going, if she only knew it."

He had risen and was pacing the room.

"The advertiser has found that out, and is showing the way." He snatched at an illustrated magazine, fresh from the press, that had been placed upon his desk, and opened it at the first page. "Johnson's Blacking," he read out, "advertised by a dainty little minx, showing her ankles. Who's going to stop for a moment to read about somebody's blacking? If a saucy little minx isn't there to trip him up with her ankles!"

He turned another page. "Do you suffer from gout? Classical lady preparing to take a bath and very nearly ready. The old Johnny in the train stops to look at her. Reads the advertisement because she seems to want him to. Rubber heels. Save your boot leather! Lady in evening dress—jolly pretty shoulders—waves them in front of your eyes. Otherwise you'd never think of them."

He fluttered the pages. Then flung the thing across to her.

"Look at it," he said. "Fountain pens—Corn plasters—Charitable appeals—Motor cars—Soaps—Grand pianos. It's the girl in tights and spangles outside the show that brings them trooping in."

"Let them see you," he continued. "You say you want soldiers. Throw off your veil and call for them. Your namesake of France! Do you think if she had contented herself with writing stirring appeals that Orleans would have fallen? She put on a becoming suit of armour and got upon a horse where everyone could see her. Chivalry isn't dead. You modern women are ashamed of yourselves—ashamed of your sex. You don't give it a chance. Revive it. Stir the young men's blood. Their souls will follow."

He reseated himself and leant across towards her.

"I'm not talking business," he said. "This thing's not going to mean much to me one way or the other. I want you to win. Farm labourers bringing up families on twelve and six a week. Shirt hands working half into the night for three farthings an hour. Stinking dens for men to live in. Degraded women. Half fed children. It's damnable. Tell them it's got to stop. That the Eternal Feminine has stepped out of the poster and commands it."

A dapper young man opened the door and put his head into the room.

"Railway smash in Yorkshire," he announced.

Carleton sat up. "Much of a one?" he asked.

The dapper gentleman shrugged his shoulders. "Three killed, eight injured, so far," he answered.

Carleton's interest appeared to collapse.

"Stop press column?" asked the dapper gentleman.

"Yes, I suppose so," replied Carleton. "Unless something better turns up."

The dapper young gentleman disappeared. Joan had risen.

"May I talk it over with a friend?" she asked. "Myself, I'm inclined to accept."

"You will, if you're in earnest," he answered. "I'll give you twenty-four hours. Look in to-morrow afternoon, and see Finch. It will be for the *Sunday Post*—the Inset. We use surfaced paper for that and can do you justice. Finch will arrange about the photograph." He held out his hand. "Shall be seeing you again," he said.

It was but a stone's throw to the office of the *Evening Gazette*. She caught Greyson just as he was leaving and put the thing before him. His sister was with him.

He did not answer at first. He was walking to and fro; and, catching his foot in the waste paper basket, he kicked it savagely out of his way, so that the contents were scattered over the room.

"Yes, he's right," he said. "It was the Virgin above the altar that popularized Christianity. Her face has always been woman's fortune. If she's going to become a fighter, it will have to be her weapon."

He had used almost the same words that Carleton had used.

"I so want them to listen to me," she said. "After all, it's only like having a very loud voice."

He looked at her and smiled. "Yes," he said, "it's a voice men will listen to."

Mary Greyson was standing by the fire. She had not spoken hitherto.

"You won't give up 'Clorinda'?" she asked.

Joan had intended to do so, but something in Mary's voice caused her, against her will, to change her mind.

"Of course not," she answered. "I shall run them both. It will be like writing Jekyll and Hyde."

"What will you sign yourself?" he asked.

"My own name, I think," she said. "Joan Allway."

Miss Greyson suggested her coming home to dinner with them; but Joan found an excuse. She wanted to be alone.

V

The twilight was fading as she left the office. She turned northward, choosing a broad, ill-lighted road. It did not matter which way she took. She wanted to think; or, rather, to dream.

It would all fall out as she had intended. She would commence by becoming a power in journalism. She was reconciled now to the photograph idea—was even keen on it herself. She would be taken full face so that she would be looking straight into the eyes of her readers as she talked to them. It would compel her to be herself; just a hopeful, loving woman: a little better educated than the majority, having had greater opportunity: a little further seeing, maybe, having had more leisure for thought: but otherwise, no whit superior to any other young, eager woman of the people. This absurd journalistic pose of omniscience, of infallibility—this non-existent garment of supreme wisdom that, like the King's clothes in the fairy story, was donned to hide his nakedness by every strutting nonentity of Fleet Street! She would have no use for it. It should be a friend, a comrade, a fellow-servant of the great Master, taking counsel with them, asking their help. Government by the people for the people! It must be made real. These silent, thoughtful-looking workers, hurrying homewards through the darkening streets; these patient, shrewd-planning housewives casting their shadows on the drawn-down blinds: it was they who should be shaping the world, not the journalists to whom all life was but so much "copy." This monstrous conspiracy, once of the Sword, of the Church, now of the Press, that put all Government into the hands of a few stuffy old gentlemen, politicians, leader writers, without sympathy or understanding: it was time that it was swept away. She would raise a new standard. It should be, not "Listen to me, oh ye dumb," but, "Speak to me. Tell me your hidden hopes, your fears, your dreams. Tell me your experience, your thoughts born of knowledge, of suffering."

She would get into correspondence with them, go among them, talk to them. The difficulty, at first, would be in getting them to write to her, to open their minds to her. These voiceless masses that never spoke, but were always being spoken for by self-appointed "leaders," "representatives," who immediately they had climbed into prominence took their place among the rulers, and then from press and platform shouted to them what they were to think and feel. It was as if the Drill-

JEROME K. JEROME

Sergeant were to claim to be the "leader," the "representative" of his squad; or the sheep-dog to pose as the "delegate" of the sheep. Dealt with always as if they were mere herds, mere flocks, they had almost lost the power of individual utterance. One would have to teach them, encourage them.

She remembered a Sunday class she had once conducted; and how for a long time she had tried in vain to get the children to "come in," to take a hand. That she might get in touch with them, understand their small problems, she had urged them to ask questions. And there had fallen such long silences. Until, at last, one cheeky ragamuffin had piped out:

"Please, Miss, have you got red hair all over you? Or only on your head?"

For answer she had rolled up her sleeve, and let them examine her arm. And then, in her turn, had insisted on rolling up his sleeve, revealing the fact that his arms above the wrists had evidently not too recently been washed; and the episode had ended in laughter and a babel of shrill voices. And, at once, they were a party of chums, discussing matters together.

They were but children, these tired men and women, just released from their day's toil, hastening homeward to their play, or to their evening tasks. A little humour, a little understanding, a recognition of the wonderful likeness of us all to one another underneath our outward coverings was all that was needed to break down the barrier, establish comradeship. She stood aside a moment to watch them streaming by. Keen, strong faces were among them, high, thoughtful brows, kind eyes; they must learn to think, to speak for themselves.

She would build again the Forum. The people's business should no longer be settled for them behind lackey-guarded doors. The good of the farm labourer should be determined not exclusively by the squire and his relations. The man with the hoe, the man with the bent back and the patient ox-like eyes: he, too, should be invited to the Council board. Middle-class domestic problems should be solved not solely by fine gentlemen from Oxford; the wife of the little clerk should be allowed her say. War or peace, it should no longer be regarded as a question concerning only the aged rich. The common people—the cannon fodder, the men who would die, and the women who would weep: they should be given something more than the privilege of either cheering platform patriots or being summoned for interrupting public meetings.

From a dismal side street there darted past her a small, shapeless figure in crumpled cap and apron: evidently a member of that lazy, over-indulged class, the domestic servant. Judging from the talk of the drawing-rooms, the correspondence in the papers, a singularly unsatisfactory body. They toiled not, lived in luxury and demanded grand pianos. Someone had proposed doing something for them. They themselves—it seemed that even they had a sort of conscience—were up in arms against it. Too much kindness even they themselves perceived was bad for them. They were holding a meeting that night to explain how contented they were. Six peeresses had consented to attend, and speak for them.

Likely enough that there were good-for-nothing, cockered menials imposing upon incompetent mistresses. There were pampered slaves in Rome. But these others. These poor little helpless sluts. There were thousands such in every city, over-worked and under-fed, living lonely, pleasureless lives. They must be taught to speak in other voices than the dulcet tones of peeresses. By the light of the guttering candles, from their chill attics, they should write to her their ill-spelt visions.

She had reached a quiet, tree-bordered road, surrounding a great park. Lovers, furtively holding hands, passed her by, whispering.

She would write books. She would choose for her heroine a woman of the people. How full of drama, of tragedy must be their stories: their problems the grim realities of life, not only its mere sentimental embroideries. The daily struggle for bare existence, the ever-shadowing menace of unemployment, of illness, leaving them helpless amid the grinding forces crushing them down on every side. The ceaseless need for courage, for cunning. For in the kingdom of the poor the tyrant and the oppressor still sit in the high places, the robber still rides fearless.

In a noisy, flaring street, a thin-clad woman passed her, carrying a netted bag showing two loaves. In a flash, it came to her what it must mean to the poor; this daily bread that in comfortable homes had come to be regarded as a thing like water; not to be considered, to be used without stint, wasted, thrown about. Borne by those feeble, knotted hands, Joan saw it revealed as something holy: hallowed by labour; sanctified by suffering, by sacrifice; worshipped with fear and prayer.

In quiet streets of stately houses, she caught glimpses through uncurtained windows of richly-laid dinner-tables about which servants moved noiselessly, arranging flowers and silver. She wondered idly if she would every marry. A gracious hostess, gathering around her brilliant men and women, statesmen, writers, artists, captains of industry: counselling them, even learning from them: encouraging shy genius. Perhaps, in a perfectly harmless way, allowing it the inspiration derivable from a well-regulated devotion to herself. A salon that should be the nucleus of all those forces that influence influences, over which she would rule with sweet and wise authority. The idea appealed to her.

Into the picture, slightly to the background, she unconsciously placed Greyson. His tall, thin figure with its air of distinction seemed to fit in; Greyson would be very restful. She could see his handsome, ascetic face flush with pleasure as, after the guests were gone, she would lean over the back of his chair and caress for a moment his dark, soft hair tinged here and there with grey. He would always adore her, in that distant, undemonstrative way of his that would never be tiresome or exacting. They would have children. But not too many. That would make the house noisy and distract her from her work. They would be beautiful and clever; unless all the laws of heredity were to be set aside for her especial injury. She would train them, shape them to be the heirs of her labour, bearing her message to the generations that should follow.

At a corner where the trams and buses stopped she lingered for a while, watching the fierce struggle; the weak and aged being pushed back time after time, hardly seeming to even resent it, regarding it as in the natural order of things. It was so absurd, apart from the injustice, the brutality of it! The poor, fighting among themselves! She felt as once when watching a crowd of birds to whom she had thrown a handful of crumbs in winter time. As if they had not enemies enough: cats, weasels, rats, hawks, owls, the hunger and the cold. And added to all, they must needs make the struggle yet harder for one another: pecking at each other's eyes, joining with one another to attack the fallen. These tired men, these weary women, pale-faced lads and girls, why did they not organize among themselves some system that would do away with this daily warfare of each against all. If only they could be got to grasp the fact that they were one family, bound together by suffering. Then, and not till then, would they be able to make their power felt? That would have to come first: the *Esprit de Corps* of the Poor.

In the end she would go into Parliament. It would be bound to come soon, the woman's vote. And after that the opening of all doors would follow. She would wear her college robes. It would be far more fitting than a succession of flimsy frocks that would have no meaning in them. What pity it was that the art of dressing—its relation to life—

was not better understood. What beauty-hating devil had prompted the workers to discard their characteristic costumes that had been both beautiful and serviceable for these hateful slop-shop clothes that made them look like walking scarecrows. Why had the coming of Democracy coincided seemingly with the spread of ugliness: dull towns, mean streets, paper-strewn parks, corrugated iron roofs, Christian chapels that would be an insult to a heathen idol; hideous factories (Why need they be hideous!); chimney-pot hats, baggy trousers, vulgar advertisements, stupid fashions for women that spoilt every line of their figure: dinginess, drabness, monotony everywhere. It was ugliness that was strangling the soul of the people; stealing from them all dignity, all self-respect, all honour for one another; robbing them of hope, of reverence, of joy in life.

Beauty. That was the key to the riddle. All Nature: its golden sunsets and its silvery dawns; the glory of piled-up clouds, the mystery of moonlit glades; its rivers winding through the meadows; the calling of its restless seas; the tender witchery of Spring; the blazonry of autumn woods; its purple moors and the wonder of its silent mountains; its cobwebs glittering with a thousand jewels; the pageantry of starry nights. Form, colour, music! The feathered choristers of bush and brake raising their matin and their evensong, the whispering of the leaves, the singing of the waters, the voices of the winds. Beauty and grace in every living thing, but man. The leaping of the hares, the grouping of cattle, the flight of swallows, the dainty loveliness of insects' wings, the glossy skin of horses rising and falling to the play of mighty muscles. Was it not seeking to make plain to us that God's language was beauty. Man must learn beauty that he may understand God.

She saw the London of the future. Not the vision popular just then: a soaring whirl of machinery in motion, of moving pavements and flying omnibuses; of screaming gramophones and standardized "homes": a city where Electricity was King and man its soulless slave. But a city of peace, of restful spaces, of leisured men and women; a city of fine streets and pleasant houses, where each could live his own life, learning freedom, individuality; a city of noble schools; of workshops that should be worthy of labour, filled with light and air; smoke and filth driven from the land: science, no longer bound to commercialism, having discovered cleaner forces; a city of gay playgrounds where children should learn laughter; of leafy walks where the creatures of the wood and field should be as welcome guests helping to teach sympathy and kindliness: a city of music, of colour, of gladness. Beauty worshipped as religion; ugliness banished as a sin: no ugly slums, no ugly cruelty, no slatternly women and brutalized men, no ugly, sobbing children; no ugly vice flaunting in every highway its insult to humanity: a city clad in beauty as with a living garment where God should walk with man.

She had reached a neighbourhood of narrow, crowded streets. The women were mostly without hats; and swarthy men, rolling cigarettes, lounged against doorways. The place had a quaint foreign flavour. Tiny cafes, filled with smoke and noise, and clean, inviting restaurants abounded. She was feeling hungry, and, choosing one the door of which stood open, revealing white tablecloths and a pleasant air of cheerfulness, she entered. It was late and the tables were crowded. Only at one, in a far corner, could she detect a vacant place, opposite to a slight, pretty-looking girl very quietly dressed. She made her way across and the girl, anticipating her request, welcomed her with a smile. They ate for a while in silence, divided only by the narrow table, their heads, when they leant forward, almost touching. Joan noticed the short, white hands, the fragrance of some delicate scent. There was something odd about her. She seemed to be unnecessarily conscious of being alone. Suddenly she spoke.

"Nice little restaurant, this," she said. "One of the few places where you can depend upon not being annoyed."

Joan did not understand. "In what way?" she asked.

"Oh, you know, men," answered the girl. "They come and sit down opposite to you, and won't leave you alone. At most of the places, you've got to put up with it or go outside. Here, old Gustav never permits it."

Joan was troubled. She was rather looking forward to occasional restaurant dinners, where she would be able to study London's Bohemia.

"You mean," she asked, "that they force themselves upon you, even if you make it plain—"

"Oh, the plainer you make it that you don't want them, the more sport they think it," interrupted the girl with a laugh.

Joan hoped she was exaggerating. "I must try and select a table where there is some good-natured girl to keep me in countenance," she said with a smile.

"Yes, I was glad to see you," answered the girl. "It's hateful, dining by oneself. Are you living alone?"

"Yes," answered Joan. "I'm a journalist."

"I thought you were something," answered the girl. "I'm an artist. Or, rather, was," she added after a pause.

"Why did you give it up?" asked Joan.

"Oh, I haven't given it up, not entirely," the girl answered. "I can always get a couple of sovereigns for a sketch, if I want it, from one or another of the frame-makers. And they can generally sell them for a fiver. I've seen them marked up. Have you been long in London?"

"No," answered Joan. "I'm a Lancashire lass."

"Curious," said the girl, "so am I. My father's a mill manager near Bolton. You weren't educated there?"

"No," Joan admitted. "I went to Rodean at Brighton when I was ten years old, and so escaped it. Nor were you," she added with a smile, "judging from your accent."

"No," answered the other, "I was at Hastings—Miss Gwyn's. Funny how we seem to have always been near to one another. Dad wanted me to be a doctor. But I'd always been mad about art."

Joan had taken a liking to the girl. It was a spiritual, vivacious face with frank eyes and a firm mouth; and the voice was low and strong.

"Tell me," she said, "what interfered with it?" Unconsciously she was leaning forward, her chin supported by her hands. Their faces were very near to one another.

The girl looked up. She did not answer for a moment. There came a hardening of the mouth before she spoke.

"A baby," she said. "Oh, it was my own fault," she continued. "I wanted it. It was all the talk at the time. You don't remember. Our right to children. No woman complete without one. Maternity, woman's kingdom. All that sort of thing. As if the storks brought them. Don't suppose it made any real difference; but it just helped me to pretend that it was something pretty and high-class. 'Overmastering passion' used to be the explanation, before that. I guess it's all much of a muchness: just natural instinct."

The restaurant had been steadily emptying. Monsieur Gustav and his ample-bosomed wife were seated at a distant table, eating their own dinner.

"Why couldn't you have married?" asked Joan.

The girl shrugged her shoulders. "Who was there for me to marry?" she answered. "The men who wanted me: clerks, young tradesmen, down at home—I wasn't taking any of that lot. And the men I might have fancied were all of them too poor. There was one student. He's got on since. Easy enough for him to talk about waiting. Meanwhile. Well, it's like somebody suggesting dinner to you the day after to-morrow. All right enough, if you're not troubled with an appetite."

The waiter came to clear the table. They were almost the last customers left. The man's tone and manner jarred upon Joan. She had not noticed it before. Joan ordered coffee and the girl, exchanging a joke with the waiter, added a liqueur.

"But why should you give up your art?" persisted Joan. It was that was sticking in her mind. "I should have thought that, if only for the sake of the child, you would have gone on with it."

"Oh, I told myself all that," answered the girl. "Was going to devote my life to it. Did for nearly two years. Till I got sick of living like a nun: never getting a bit of excitement. You see, I've got the poison in me. Or, maybe, it had always been there."

"What's become of it?" asked Joan. "The child?"

"Mother's got it," answered the girl. "Seemed best for the poor little beggar. I'm supposed to be dead, and my husband gone abroad." She gave a short, dry laugh. "Mother brings him up to see me once a year. They've got quite fond of him."

"What are you doing now?" asked Joan, in a low tone.

"Oh, you needn't look so scared," laughed the girl, "I haven't come down to that." Her voice had changed. It had a note of shrillness. In some indescribable way she had grown coarse. "I'm a kept woman," she explained. "What else is any woman?"

She reached for her jacket; and the waiter sprang forward and helped her on with it, prolonging the business needlessly. She wished him "Good evening" in a tone of distant hauteur, and led the way to the door. Outside the street was dim and silent. Joan held out her hand.

"No hope of happy endings," she said with a forced laugh. "Couldn't marry him I suppose?"

"He has asked me," answered the girl with a swagger. "Not sure that it would suit me now. They're not so nice to you when they've got you fixed up. So long."

She turned abruptly and walked rapidly away. Joan moved instinctively in the opposite direction, and after a few minutes found herself in a broad well-lighted thoroughfare. A newsboy was shouting his wares.

"'Orrible murder of a woman. Shockin' details. Speshul," repeating it over and over again in a hoarse, expressionless monotone.

He was selling the papers like hot cakes; the purchasers too eager to even wait for their change. She wondered, with a little lump in her throat, how many would have stopped to buy had he been calling instead: "Discovery of new sonnet by Shakespeare. Extra special."

Through swinging doors, she caught glimpses of foul interiors, crowded with men and women released from their toil, taking their evening pleasure. From coloured posters outside the great theatres and music halls, vulgarity and lewdness leered at her, side by side with announcements that the house was full. From every roaring corner, scintillating lights flared forth the merits of this public benefactor's whisky, of this other celebrity's beer: it seemed the only message the people cared to hear. Even among the sirens of the pavement, she noticed that the quiet and merely pretty were hardly heeded. It was everywhere the painted and the overdressed that drew the roving eyes.

She remembered a pet dog that someone had given her when she was a girl, and how one afternoon she had walked with the tears streaming down her face because, in spite of her scoldings and her pleadings, it would keep stopping to lick up filth from the roadway. A kindly passer-by had laughed and told her not to mind.

"Why, that's a sign of breeding, that is, Missie," the man had explained. "It's the classy ones that are always the worst."

It had come to her afterwards craving with its soft brown, troubled eyes for forgiveness. But she had never been able to break it of the habit.

Must man for ever be chained by his appetites to the unclean: ever be driven back, dragged down again into the dirt by his own instincts: ever be rendered useless for all finer purposes by the baseness of his own desires?

The City of her Dreams! The mingled voices of the crowd shaped itself into a mocking laugh.

It seemed to her that it was she that they were laughing at, pointing her out to one another, jeering at her, reviling her, threatening her.

She hurried onward with bent head, trying to escape them. She felt so small, so helpless. Almost she cried out in her despair.

She must have walked mechanically. Looking up she found herself in her own street. And as she reached her doorway the tears came suddenly.

She heard a quick step behind her, and turning, she saw a man with a latch key in his hand. He passed her and opened the door; and then, facing round, stood aside for her to enter. He was a sturdy, thick-set man with a strong, massive face. It would have been ugly but for the deep, flashing eyes. There was tenderness and humour in them.

"We are next floor neighbours," he said. "My name's Phillips."

Joan thanked him. As he held the door open for her their hands accidentally touched. Joan wished him good-night and went up the stairs. There was no light in her room: only the faint reflection of the street lamp outside.

She could still see him: the boyish smile. And his voice that had sent her tears back again as if at the word of command.

She hoped he had not seen them. What a little fool she was.

A little laugh escaped her.

VI

O ne day Joan, lunching at the club, met Madge Singleton.

"I've had such a funny letter from Flossie," said Joan, "begging me almost with tears in her ink to come to her on Sunday evening to meet a 'gentleman friend' of hers, as she calls him, and give her my opinion of him. What on earth is she up to?"

"It's all right," answered Madge. "She doesn't really want our opinion of him—or rather she doesn't want our real opinion of him. She only wants us to confirm hers. She's engaged to him."

"Flossie engaged!" Joan seemed surprised.

"Yes," answered Madge. "It used to be a custom. Young men used to ask young women to marry them. And if they consented it was called 'being engaged.' Still prevails, so I am told, in certain classes."

"Thanks," said Joan. "I have heard of it."

"I thought perhaps you hadn't from your tone," explained Madge.

"But if she's already engaged to him, why risk criticism of him," argued Joan, ignoring Madge's flippancy. "It's too late."

"Oh, she's going to break it off unless we all assure her that we find him brainy," Madge explained with a laugh. "It seems her father wasn't brainy and her mother was. Or else it was the other way about: I'm not quite sure. But whichever it was, it led to ructions. Myself, if he's at all possible and seems to care for her, I intend to find him brilliant."

"And suppose she repeats her mother's experience," suggested Joan.

"There were the Norton-Browns," answered Madge. "Impossible to have found a more evenly matched pair. They both write novels—very good novels, too; and got jealous of one another; and threw press-notices at one another's head all breakfast-time; until they separated. Don't know of any recipe myself for being happy ever after marriage, except not expecting it."

"Or keeping out of it altogether," added Joan.

"Ever spent a day at the Home for Destitute Gentlewomen at East Sheen?" demanded Madge.

"Not yet," admitted Joan. "May have to, later on."

"It ought to be included in every woman's education," Madge continued. "It is reserved for spinsters of over forty-five. Susan Fleming wrote an article upon it for the *Teacher's Friend*; and spent an afternoon and evening there. A month later she married a grocer with five children.

JEROME K. JEROME

The only sound suggestion for avoiding trouble that I ever came across was in a burlesque of the *Blue Bird*. You remember the scene where the spirits of the children are waiting to go down to earth and be made into babies? Someone had stuck up a notice at the entrance to the gangway: 'Don't get born. It only means worry.'"

Flossie had her dwelling-place in a second floor bed-sitting-room of a lodging house in Queen's Square, Bloomsbury; but the drawing-room floor being for the moment vacant, Flossie had persuaded her landlady to let her give her party there; it seemed as if fate approved of the idea. The room was fairly full when Joan arrived. Flossie took her out on the landing, and closed the door behind them.

"You will be honest with me, won't you?" pleaded Flossie, "because it's so important, and I don't seem able to think for myself. As they say, no man can be his own solicitor, can he? Of course I like him, and all that—very much. And I really believe he loves me. We were children together when Mummy was alive; and then he had to go abroad; and has only just come back. Of course, I've got to think of him, too, as he says. But then, on the other hand, I don't want to make a mistake. That would be so terrible, for both of us; and of course I am clever; and there was poor Mummy and Daddy. I'll tell you all about them one day. It was so awfully sad. Get him into a corner and talk to him. You'll be able to judge in a moment, you're so wonderful. He's quiet on the outside, but I think there's depth in him. We must go in now."

She had talked so rapidly Joan felt as if her hat were being blown away. She had difficulty in recognizing Flossie. All the cocksure pertness had departed. She seemed just a kid.

Joan promised faithfully; and Flossie, standing on tiptoe, suddenly kissed her and then bustled her in.

Flossie's young man was standing near the fire talking, or rather listening, to a bird-like little woman in a short white frock and blue ribbons. A sombre lady just behind her, whom Joan from the distance took to be her nurse, turned out to be her secretary, whose duty it was to be always at hand, prepared to take down any happy idea that might occur to the bird-like little woman in the course of conversation. The bird-like little woman was Miss Rose Tolley, a popular novelist. She was explaining to Flossie's young man, whose name was Sam Halliday, the reason for her having written "Running Waters," her latest novel.

"It is daring," she admitted. "I must be prepared for opposition. But it had to be stated."

"I take myself as typical," she continued. "When I was twenty I could have loved you. You were the type of man I did love."

Mr. Halliday, who had been supporting the weight of his body upon his right leg, transferred the burden to his left.

"But now I'm thirty-five; and I couldn't love you if I tried." She shook her curls at him. "It isn't your fault. It is that I have changed. Suppose I'd married you?"

"Bit of bad luck for both of us," suggested Mr. Halliday.

"A tragedy," Miss Tolley corrected him. "There are millions of such tragedies being enacted around us at this moment. Sensitive women compelled to suffer the embraces of men that they have come to loathe. What's to be done?"

Flossie, who had been hovering impatient, broke in.

"Oh, don't you believe her," she advised Mr. Halliday. "She loves you still. She's only teasing you. This is Joan."

She introduced her. Miss Tolley bowed; and allowed herself to be drawn away by a lank-haired young man who had likewise been waiting for an opening. He represented the Uplift Film Association of Chicago, and was wishful to know if Miss Tolley would consent to altering the last chapter and so providing "Running Waters" with a happy ending. He pointed out the hopelessness of it in its present form, for film purposes.

The discussion was brief. "Then I'll send your agent the contract to-morrow," Joan overheard him say a minute later.

Mr. Sam Halliday she liked at once. He was a clean-shaven, square-jawed young man, with quiet eyes and a pleasant voice.

"Try and find me brainy," he whispered to her, as soon as Flossie was out of earshot. "Talk to me about China. I'm quite intelligent on China."

They both laughed, and then shot a guilty glance in Flossie's direction.

"Do the women really crush their feet?" asked Joan.

"Yes," he answered. "All those who have no use for them. About one per cent. of the population. To listen to Miss Tolley you would think that half the women wanted a new husband every ten years. It's always the one per cent. that get themselves talked about. The other ninety-nine are too busy."

"You are young for a philosopher," said Joan.

He laughed. "I told you I'd be all right if you started me on China," he said.

"Why are you marrying. Flossie?" Joan asked him. She thought his point of view would be interesting.

"Not sure I am yet," he answered with a grin. "It depends upon how I get through this evening." He glanced round the room. "Have I got to pass all this crowd, I wonder?" he added.

Joan's eyes followed. It was certainly an odd collection. Flossie, in her hunt for brains, had issued her invitations broadcast; and her fate had been that of the Charity concert. Not all the stars upon whom she had most depended had turned up. On the other hand not a single freak had failed her. At the moment, the centre of the room was occupied by a gentleman and two ladies in classical drapery. They were holding hands in an attitude suggestive of a bas-relief. Joan remembered them, having seen them on one or two occasions wandering in the King's Road, Chelsea; still maintaining, as far as the traffic would allow, the bas-relief suggestion; and generally surrounded by a crowd of children, ever hopeful that at the next corner they would stop and do something really interesting. They belonged to a society whose object was to lure the London public by the force of example towards the adoption of the early Greek fashions and the simpler Greek attitudes. A friend of Flossie's had thrown in her lot with them, but could never be induced to abandon her umbrella. They also, as Joan told herself, were reformers. Near to them was a picturesque gentleman with a beard down to his waist whose "stunt"—as Flossie would have termed it—was hygienic clothing; it seemed to contain an undue proportion of fresh air. There were ladies in coats and stand-up collars, and gentlemen with ringlets. More than one of the guests would have been better, though perhaps not happier, for a bath.

"I fancy that's the idea," said Joan. "What will you do if you fail? Go back to China?"

"Yes," he answered. "And take her with me. Poor little girl."

Joan rather resented his tone.

"We are not all alike," she remarked. "Some of us are quite sane."

He looked straight into her eyes. "You are," he said. "I have been reading your articles. They are splendid. I'm going to help."

"How can you?" she said. "I mean, how will you?"

"Shipping is my business," he said. "I'm going to help sailor men. See that they have somewhere decent to go to, and don't get robbed. And then there are the Lascars, poor devils. Nobody ever takes their part."

"How did you come across them?" she asked. "The articles, I mean. Did Flo give them to you?"

"No," he answered. "Just chance. Caught sight of your photo."

"Tell me," she said. "If it had been the photo of a woman with a bony throat and a beaky nose would you have read them?"

He thought a moment. "Guess not," he answered. "You're just as bad," he continued. "Isn't it the pale-faced young clergyman with the wavy hair and the beautiful voice that you all flock to hear? No getting away from nature. But it wasn't only that." He hesitated.

"I want to know," she said.

"You looked so young," he answered. "I had always had the idea that it was up to the old people to put the world to rights—that all I had to do was to look after myself. It came to me suddenly while you were talking to me—I mean while I was reading you: that if you were worrying yourself about it, I'd got to come in, too—that it would be mean of me not to. It wasn't like being preached to. It was somebody calling for help."

Instinctively she held out her hand and he grasped it.

Flossie came up at the same instant. She wanted to introduce him to Miss Lavery, who had just arrived.

"Hullo!" she said. "Are you two concluding a bargain?"

"Yes," said Joan. "We are founding the League of Youth. You've got to be in it. We are going to establish branches all round the world."

Flossie's young man was whisked away. Joan, who had seated herself in a small chair, was alone for a few minutes.

Miss Tolley had chanced upon a Human Document, with the help of which she was hopeful of starting a "Press Controversy" concerning the morality, or otherwise, of "Running Waters." The secretary stood just behind her, taking notes. They had drifted quite close. Joan could not help overhearing.

"It always seemed to me immoral, the marriage ceremony," the Human Document was explaining. She was a thin, sallow woman, with an untidy head and restless eyes that seemed to be always seeking something to look at and never finding it. "How can we pledge the future? To bind oneself to live with a man when perhaps we have ceased to care for him; it's hideous."

Miss Tolley murmured agreement.

"Our love was beautiful," continued the Human Document, eager, apparently, to relate her experience for the common good; "just because it was a free gift. We were not fettered to one another. At any moment either of us could have walked out of the house. The idea never occurred to us; not for years—five, to be exact."

The secretary, at a sign from Miss Tolley, made a memorandum of it.

"And then did your feelings towards him change suddenly?" questioned Miss Tolley.

"No," explained the Human Document, in the same quick, even tones; "so far as I was concerned, I was not conscious of any alteration in my own attitude. But he felt the need of more solitude—for his development. We parted quite good friends."

"Oh," said Miss Tolley. "And were there any children?"

"Only two," answered the Human Document, "both girls."

"What has become of them?" persisted Miss Tolley.

The Human Document looked offended. "You do not think I would have permitted any power on earth to separate them from me, do you?" she answered. "I said to him, 'They are mine, mine. Where I go, they go. Where I stay, they stay.' He saw the justice of my argument."

"And they are with you now?" concluded Miss Tolley.

"You must come and see them," the Human Document insisted. "Such dear, magnetic creatures. I superintend their entire education myself. We have a cottage in Surrey. It's rather a tight fit. You see, there are seven of us now. But the three girls can easily turn in together for a night, Abner will be delighted."

"Abner is your second?" suggested Miss Tolley.

"My third," the Human Document corrected her. "After Eustace, I married Ivanoff. I say 'married' because I regard it as the holiest form of marriage. He had to return to his own country. There was a political movement on foot. He felt it his duty to go. I want you particularly to meet the boy. He will interest you."

Miss Tolley appeared to be getting muddled. "Whose boy?" she demanded.

"Ivanoff's," explained the Human Document. "He was our only child."

Flossie appeared, towing a white-haired, distinguished-looking man, a Mr. Folk. She introduced him and immediately disappeared. Joan wished she had been left alone a little longer. She would like to have heard more. Especially was she curious concerning Abner, the lady's third. Would the higher moral law compel him, likewise, to leave the poor lady saddled with another couple of children? Or would she, on this occasion, get in—or rather, get off, first? Her own fancy was to back Abner. She did catch just one sentence before Miss Tolley, having obtained more food for reflection than perhaps she wanted, signalled to her secretary that the note-book might be closed.

"Woman's right to follow the dictates of her own heart, uncontrolled by any law," the Human Document was insisting: "That is one of the first things we must fight for."

Mr. Folk was a well-known artist. He lived in Paris. "You are wonderfully like your mother," he told Joan. "In appearance, I mean," he added. "I knew her when she was Miss Caxton. I acted with her in America."

Joan made a swift effort to hide her surprise. She had never heard of her mother having been upon the stage.

"I did not know that you had been an actor," she answered.

"I wasn't really," explained Mr. Folk. "I just walked and talked naturally. It made rather a sensation at the time. Your mother was a genius. You have never thought of going on the stage yourself?"

"No," said Joan. "I don't think I've got what you call the artistic temperament. I have never felt drawn towards anything of that sort."

"I wonder," he said. "You could hardly be your mother's daughter without it."

"Tell me," said Joan. "What was my mother like? I can only remember her as more or less of an invalid."

He did not reply to her question. "Master or Mistress Eminent Artist," he said; "intends to retire from his or her particular stage, whatever it may be. That paragraph ought always to be put among the obituary notices."

"What's your line?" he asked her. "I take it you have one by your being here. Besides, I am sure you have. I am an old fighter. I can tell the young soldier. What's your regiment?"

Joan laughed. "I'm a drummer boy," she answered. "I beat my drum each week in a Sunday newspaper, hoping the lads will follow."

"You feel you must beat that drum," he suggested. "Beat it louder and louder and louder till all the world shall hear it."

"Yes," Joan agreed, "I think that does describe me."

He nodded. "I thought you were an artist," he said. "Don't let them ever take your drum away from you. You'll go to pieces and get into mischief without it."

"I know an old actress," he continued. "She's the mother of four. They are all on the stage and they've all made their mark. The youngest was born in her dressing-room, just after the curtain had fallen. She was playing the Nurse to your mother's Juliet. She is still the best Nurse that I know. 'Jack's always worrying me to chuck it and devote myself to the children,' she confided to me one evening, while she was waiting for her cue. 'But, as I tell him, I'm more helpful to them being with them half the day alive than all the day dead.' That's an anecdote worth remembering, when your time comes. If God gives woman a drum he doesn't mean man to take it away from her. She hasn't got to be playing it for twenty-four hours a day. I'd like you to have seen your mother's Cordelia."

Flossie was tacking her way towards them. Joan acted on impulse. "I wish you'd give me your address," she said "where I could write to you. Or perhaps you would not mind my coming and seeing you one day. I would like you to tell me more about my mother."

He gave her his address in Paris where he was returning almost immediately.

"Do come," he said. "It will take me back thirty-three years. I proposed to your mother on La Grande Terrasse at St. Germain. We will walk there. I'm still a bachelor." He laughed, and, kissing her hand, allowed himself to be hauled away by Flossie, in exchange for Mrs. Phillips, for whom Miss Lavery had insisted on an invitation.

Joan had met Mrs. Phillips several times; and once, on the stairs, had stopped and spoken to her; but had never been introduced to her formally till now.

"We have been meaning to call on you so often," panted Mrs. Phillips. The room was crowded and the exertion of squeezing her way through had winded the poor lady. "We take so much interest in your articles. My husband—" she paused for a second, before venturing upon the word, and the aitch came out somewhat over-aspirated—"reads them most religiously. You must come and dine with us one evening."

Joan answered that she would be very pleased.

"I will find out when Robert is free and run up and let you know," she continued. "Of course, there are so many demands upon him, especially during this period of national crisis, that I spare him all the social duties that I can. But I shall insist on his making an exception in your case."

Joan murmured her sense of favour, but hoped she would not be allowed to interfere with more pressing calls upon Mr. Phillips's time.

"It will do him good," answered Mrs. Phillips; "getting away from them all for an hour or two. I don't see much of him myself."

She glanced round and lowered her voice. "They tell me," she said, "that you're a B.A."

"Yes," answered Joan. "One goes in for it more out of vanity, I'm afraid, than for any real purpose that it serves."

"I took one or two prizes myself," said Mrs. Phillips. "But, of course, one forgets things. I was wondering if you would mind if I ran up occasionally to ask you a question. Of course, as you know, my 'usband 'as 'ad so few advantages"—the lady's mind was concerned with more important matters, and the aspirates, on this occasion, got themselves neglected—"It is wonderful what he 'as done without them. But if, now and then, I could 'elp him—"

There was something about the poor, foolish painted face, as it looked up pleadingly, that gave it a momentary touch of beauty.

"Do," said Joan, speaking earnestly. "I shall be so very pleased if you will."

"Thank you," said the woman. Miss Lavery came up in a hurry to introduce her to Miss Tolley. "I am telling all my friends to read your articles," she added, resuming the gracious patroness, as she bowed her adieus.

Joan was alone again for a while. A handsome girl, with her hair cut short and parted at the side, was discussing diseases of the spine with a curly-headed young man in a velvet suit. The gentleman was describing some of the effects in detail. Joan felt there was danger of her being taken ill if she listened any longer; and seeing Madge's brother near the door, and unoccupied, she made her way across to him.

Niel Singleton, or Keeley, as he called himself upon the stage, was quite unlike his sister. He was short and plump, with a preternaturally solemn face, contradicted by small twinkling eyes. He motioned Joan to a chair and told her to keep quiet and not disturb the meeting.

"Is he brainy?" he whispered after a minute.

"I like him," said Joan.

"I didn't ask you if you liked him," he explained to her. "I asked you if he was brainy. I'm not too sure that you like brainy men."

"Yes, I do," said Joan. "I like you, sometimes."

"Now, none of that," he said severely. "It's no good your thinking of me. I'm wedded to my art. We are talking about Mr. Halliday."

"What does Madge think of him?" asked Joan.

"Madge has fallen in love with him, and her judgment is not to be relied upon," he said. "I suppose you couldn't answer a straight question, if you tried."

"Don't be so harsh with me," pleaded Joan meekly. "I'm trying to think. Yes," she continued, "decidedly he's got brains."

"Enough for the two of them?" demanded Mr. Singleton. "Because he will want them. Now think before you speak."

Joan considered. "Yes," she answered. "I should say he's just the man to manage her."

"Then it's settled," he said. "We must save her."

"Save her from what?" demanded Joan.

"From his saying to himself: 'This is Flossie's idea of a party. This is the sort of thing that, if I marry her, I am letting myself in for.' If he hasn't broken off the engagement already, we may be in time."

He led the way to the piano. "Tell Madge I want her," he whispered. He struck a few notes; and then in a voice that drowned every other sound in the room, struck up a comic song.

The effect was magical.

He followed it up with another. This one with a chorus, consisting chiefly of "Umpty Umpty Umpty Umpty Ay," which was vociferously encored.

By the time it was done with, Madge had discovered a girl who could sing "Three Little Pigs;" and a sad, pale-faced gentleman who told stories. At the end of one of them Madge's brother spoke to Joan in a tone more of sorrow than of anger.

"Hardly the sort of anecdote that a truly noble and high-minded young woman would have received with laughter," he commented.

"Did I laugh?" said Joan.

"Your having done so unconsciously only makes the matter worse," observed Mr. Singleton. "I had hoped it emanated from politeness, not enjoyment."

"Don't tease her," said Madge. "She's having an evening off."

Joan and the Singletons were the last to go. They promised to show Mr. Halliday a short cut to his hotel in Holborn.

"Have you thanked Miss Lessing for a pleasant evening?" asked Mr. Singleton, turning to Mr. Halliday.

He laughed and put his arm round her. "Poor little woman," he said. "You're looking so tired. It was jolly at the end." He kissed her.

He had passed through the swing doors; and they were standing on the pavement waiting for Joan's bus.

"Why did we all like him?" asked Joan. "Even Miss Lavery. There's nothing extraordinary about him."

"Oh yes there is," said Madge. "Love has lent him gilded armour. From his helmet waves her crest," she quoted. "Most men look fine in that costume. Pity they can't always wear it."

The conductor seemed impatient. Joan sprang upon the step and waved her hand.

VII

Joan was making herself a cup of tea when there came a tap at the door. It was Mrs. Phillips.

"I heard you come in," she said. "You're not busy, are you?"

"No," answered Joan. "I hope you're not. I'm generally in about this time; and it's always nice to gossip over a dish of tea."

"Why do you say 'dish' of tea!" asked Mrs. Phillips, as she lowered herself with evident satisfaction into the easy chair Joan placed for her.

"Oh, I don't know," laughed Joan. "Dr. Johnson always talked of a 'dish' of tea. Gives it a literary flavour."

"I've heard of him," said Mrs. Phillips. "He's worth reading, isn't he?"

"Well, he talked more amusingly than he wrote," explained Joan. "Get Boswell's Life of him. Or I'll lend you mine," she added, "if you'll be careful of it. You'll find all the passages marked that are best worth remembering. At least, I think so."

"Thanks," said Mrs. Phillips. "You see, as the wife of a public man, I get so little time for study."

"Is it settled yet?" asked Joan. "Are they going to make room for him in the Cabinet?

"I'm afraid so," answered Mrs. Phillips. "Oh, of course, I want him to," she corrected herself. "And he must, of course, if the King insists upon it. But I wish it hadn't all come with such a whirl. What shall I have to do, do you think?"

Joan was pouring out the tea. "Oh, nothing," she answered, "but just be agreeable to the right people. He'll tell you who they are. And take care of him."

"I wish I'd taken more interest in politics when I was young," said Mrs. Phillips. "Of course, when I was a girl, women weren't supposed to."

"Do you know, I shouldn't worry about them, if I were you," Joan advised her. "Let him forget them when he's with you. A man can have too much of a good thing," she laughed.

"I wonder if you're right," mused Mrs. Phillips. "He does often say that he'd just as soon I didn't talk about them."

Joan shot a glance from over her cup. The poor puzzled face was staring into the fire. Joan could almost hear him saying it.

"I'm sure I am," she said. "Make home-coming a change to him. As you said yourself the other evening. It's good for him to get away from it all, now and then."

"I must try," agreed Mrs. Phillips, looking up. "What sort of things ought I to talk to him about, do you think?"

Joan gave an inward sigh. Hadn't the poor lady any friends of her own. "Oh, almost anything," she answered vaguely: "so long as it's cheerful and non-political. What used you to talk about before he became a great man?"

There came a wistful look into the worried eyes. "Oh, it was all so different then," she said. "'E just liked to—you know. We didn't seem to 'ave to talk. 'E was a rare one to tease. I didn't know 'ow clever 'e was, then."

It seemed a difficult case to advise upon. "How long have you been married?" Joan asked.

"Fifteen years," she answered. "I was a bit older than 'im. But I've never looked my age, they tell me. Lord, what a boy 'e was! Swept you off your feet, like. 'E wasn't the only one. I'd got a way with me, I suppose. Anyhow, the men seemed to think so. There was always a few 'anging about. Like flies round a 'oney-pot, Mother used to say." She giggled. "But 'e wouldn't take No for an answer. And I didn't want to give it 'im, neither. I was gone on 'im, right enough. No use saying I wasn't."

"You must be glad you didn't say No," suggested Joan.

"Yes," she answered, "'E's got on. I always think of that little poem, 'Lord Burleigh,'" she continued; "whenever I get worrying about myself. Ever read it?"

"Yes," answered Joan. "He was a landscape painter, wasn't he?"

"That's the one," said Mrs. Phillips. "I little thought I was letting myself in for being the wife of a big pot when Bob Phillips came along in 'is miner's jacket."

"You'll soon get used to it," Joan told her. "The great thing is not to be afraid of one's fate, whatever it is; but just to do one's best." It was rather like talking to a child.

"You're the right sort to put 'eart into a body. I'm glad I came up," said Mrs. Phillips. "I get a bit down in the mouth sometimes when 'e goes off into one of 'is brown studies, and I don't seem to know what 'e's thinking about. But it don't last long. I was always one of the light-'earted ones."

They discussed life on two thousand a year; the problems it would present; and Mrs. Phillips became more cheerful. Joan laid herself out to be friendly. She hoped to establish an influence over Mrs. Phillips that should be for the poor lady's good; and, as she felt instinctively, for poor Phillips's also. It was not an unpleasing face. Underneath the paint, it was kind and womanly. Joan was sure he would like it better clean. A few months' attention to diet would make a decent figure of her and improve her wind. Joan watched her spreading the butter a quarter of an inch thick upon her toast and restrained with difficulty the impulse to take it away from her. And her clothes! Joan had seen guys carried through the streets on the fifth of November that were less obtrusive.

She remembered, as she was taking her leave, what she had come for: which was to invite Joan to dinner on the following Friday.

"It's just a homely affair," she explained. She had recovered her form and was now quite the lady again. "Two other guests beside yourself: a Mr. Airlie—I am sure you will like him. He's so dilletanty—and Mr. McKean. He's the young man upstairs. Have you met him?"

Joan hadn't: except once on the stairs when, to avoid having to pass her, he had gone down again and out into the street. From the doorstep she had caught sight of his disappearing coat-tails round the corner. Yielding to impishness, she had run after him, and his expression of blank horror when, glancing over his shoulder, he found her walking abstractedly three yards behind him, had gladdened all her evening.

Joan recounted the episode—so far as the doorstep.

"He tried to be shy with me," said Mrs. Phillips, "but I wouldn't let him. I chipped him out of it. If he's going to write plays, as I told him, he will have to get over his fear of a petticoat."

She offered her cheek, and Joan kissed it, somewhat gingerly.

"You won't mind Robert not wearing evening dress," she said. "He never will if he can help it. I shall just slip on a semi-toilette myself."

Joan had difficulty in deciding on her own frock. Her four evening dresses, as she walked round them, spread out upon the bed, all looked too imposing, for what Mrs. Phillips had warned her would be a "homely affair." She had one other, a greyish-fawn, with sleeves to the elbow, that she had had made expressly for public dinners and political At Homes. But that would be going to the opposite extreme, and might seem discourteous—to her hostess. Besides, "mousey" colours didn't really suit her. They gave her a curious sense of being affected. In the end she decided to risk a black crepe-de-chine, square cut, with a girdle of gold embroidery. There couldn't be anything quieter than black, and the gold embroidery was of the simplest. She would wear it without any jewellery whatever: except just a star in her hair. The result, as she viewed the effect in the long glass, quite satisfied her. Perhaps the jewelled star did scintillate rather. It had belonged to her mother. But her hair was so full of shadows: it wanted something to relieve it. Also she approved the curved line of her bare arms. It was certainly very beautiful, a woman's arm. She took her gloves in her hand and went down.

Mr. Phillips was not yet in the room. Mrs. Phillips, in apple-green with an ostrich feather in her hair, greeted her effusively, and introduced her to her fellow guests. Mr. Airlie was a slight, elegant gentleman of uncertain age, with sandy hair and beard cut Vandyke fashion. He asked Joan's permission to continue his cigarette.

"You have chosen the better part," he informed her, on her granting it. "When I'm not smoking, I'm talking."

Mr. McKean shook her hand vigorously without looking at her.

"And this is Hilda," concluded Mrs. Phillips. "She ought to be in bed if she hadn't a naughty Daddy who spoils her."

A lank, black-haired girl, with a pair of burning eyes looking out of a face that, but for the thin line of the lips, would have been absolutely colourless, rose suddenly from behind a bowl of artificial flowers. Joan could not suppress a slight start; she had not noticed her on entering. The girl came slowly forward, and Joan felt as if the uncanny eyes were eating her up. She made an effort and held out her hand with a smile, and the girl's long thin fingers closed on it in a pressure that hurt. She did not speak.

"She only came back yesterday for the half-term," explained Mrs. Phillips. "There's no keeping her away from her books. 'Twas her own wish to be sent to boarding-school. How would you like to go to Girton and be a B.A. like Miss Allway?" she asked, turning to the child.

Phillips's entrance saved the need of a reply. To the evident surprise of his wife he was in evening clothes.

"Hulloa. You've got 'em on," she said.

He laughed. "I shall have to get used to them sooner or later," he said.

Joan felt relieved—she hardly knew why—that he bore the test. It was a well-built, athletic frame, and he had gone to a good tailor. He looked taller in them; and the strong, clean-shaven face less rugged.

Joan sat next to him at the round dinner-table with the child the other side of him. She noticed that he ate as far as possible with his right hand—his hands were large, but smooth and well shaped—his left remaining under the cloth, beneath which the child's right hand, when free, would likewise disappear. For a while the conversation consisted chiefly of anecdotes by Mr. Airlie. There were few public men and women about whom he did not know something to their disadvantage. Joan, listening, found herself repeating the experience of a night or two previous, when, during a performance of *Hamlet*, Niel Singleton, who was playing the grave-digger, had taken her behind the scenes. Hamlet, the King of Denmark and the Ghost were sharing a bottle of champagne in the Ghost's dressing-room: it happened to be the Ghost's birthday. On her return to the front of the house, her interest in the play was gone. It was absurd that it should be so; but the fact remained.

Mr. Airlie had lunched the day before with a leonine old gentleman who every Sunday morning thundered forth Social Democracy to enthusiastic multitudes on Tower Hill. Joan had once listened to him and had almost been converted: he was so tremendously in earnest. She now learnt that he lived in Curzon Street, Mayfair, and filled, in private life, the perfectly legitimate calling of a company promoter in partnership with a Dutch Jew. His latest prospectus dwelt upon the profits to be derived from an amalgamation of the leading tanning industries: by means of which the price of leather could be enormously increased.

It was utterly illogical; but her interest in the principles of Social Democracy was gone.

A very little while ago, Mr. Airlie, in his capacity of second cousin to one of the ladies concerned, a charming girl but impulsive, had been called upon to attend a family council of a painful nature. The gentleman's name took Joan's breath away: it was the name of one of her heroes, an eminent writer: one might almost say prophet. She had hitherto read his books with grateful reverence. They pictured for her the world made perfect; and explained to her just precisely how it was to be accomplished. But, as far as his own particular corner of it was concerned, he seemed to have made a sad mess of it. Human nature of quite an old-fashioned pattern had crept in and spoilt all his own theories.

Of course it was unreasonable. The sign-post may remain embedded in weeds: it notwithstanding points the way to the fair city. She told herself this, but it left her still short-tempered. She didn't care which way it pointed. She didn't believe there was any fair city.

There was a famous preacher. He lived the simple life in a small house in Battersea, and consecrated all his energies to the service of the poor. Almost, by his unselfish zeal, he had persuaded Joan of the usefulness of the church. Mr. Airlie frequently visited him. They interested one another. What struck Mr. Airlie most was the self-sacrificing devotion with which the reverend gentleman's wife and family surrounded him. It was beautiful to see. The calls upon his moderate purse, necessitated by his wide-spread and much paragraphed activities, left but a narrow margin for domestic expenses: with the result that often the only fire in the house blazed brightly in the study where Mr. Airlie and the reverend gentleman sat talking: while mother and children warmed themselves with sense of duty in the cheerless kitchen. And often, as Mr. Airlie, who was of an inquiring turn of mind, had convinced himself, the only evening meal that resources would permit was the satisfying supper for one brought by the youngest daughter to her father where he sat alone in the small dining-room.

Mr. Airlie, picking daintily at his food, continued his stories: of philanthropists who paid starvation wages: of feminists who were a holy terror to their women folk: of socialists who travelled first-class and spent their winters in Egypt or Monaco: of stern critics of public morals who preferred the society of youthful affinities to the continued company of elderly wives: of poets who wrote divinely about babies' feet and whose children hated them.

"Do you think it's all true?" Joan whispered to her host.

He shrugged his shoulders. "No reason why it shouldn't be," he said. "I've generally found him right."

"I've never been able myself," he continued, "to understand the Lord's enthusiasm for David. I suppose it was the Psalms that did it."

Joan was about to offer comment, but was struck dumb with astonishment on hearing McKean's voice: it seemed he could talk. He was telling of an old Scotch peasant farmer. A mean, cantankerous old cuss whose curious pride it was that he had never given anything away. Not a crust, nor a sixpence, nor a rag; and never would. Many had been the attempts to make him break his boast: some for the joke of the thing and some for the need; but none had ever succeeded. It was his one claim to distinction and he guarded it.

One evening it struck him that the milk-pail, standing just inside the window, had been tampered with. Next day he marked with a scratch the inside of the pan and, returning later, found the level of the milk had sunk half an inch. So he hid himself and waited; and at twilight the next day the window was stealthily pushed open, and two small, terror-haunted eyes peered round the room. They satisfied themselves that no one was about and a tiny hand clutching a cracked jug was thrust swiftly in and dipped into the pan; and the window softly closed.

He knew the thief, the grandchild of an old bedridden dame who lived some miles away on the edge of the moor. The old man stood long, watching the small cloaked figure till it was lost in the darkness. It was not till he lay upon his dying bed that he confessed it. But each evening, from that day, he would steal into the room and see to it himself that the window was left ajar.

After the coffee, Mrs. Phillips proposed their adjourning to the "drawing-room" the other side of the folding doors, which had been left open. Phillips asked her to leave Joan and himself where they were. He wanted to talk to her. He promised not to bore her for more than ten minutes.

The others rose and moved away. Hilda came and stood before Joan with her hands behind her.

"I am going to bed now," she said. "I wanted to see you from what Papa told me. May I kiss you?"

It was spoken so gravely that Joan did not ask her, as in lighter mood she might have done, what it was that Phillips had said. She raised her face quietly, and the child bent forward and kissed her, and went out without looking back at either of them, leaving Joan more serious than there seemed any reason for. Phillips filled his pipe and lighted it.

"I wish I had your pen," he said, suddenly breaking the silence. "I'm all right at talking; but I want to get at the others: the men and women who never come, thinking it has nothing to do with them. I'm shy and awkward when I try to write. There seems a barrier in front of me. You break through it. One hears your voice. Tell me," he said, "are you getting your way? Do they answer you?"

"Yes," said Joan. "Not any great number of them, not yet. But enough to show that I really am interesting them. It grows every week."

"Tell them that," he said. "Let them hear each other. It's the same at a meeting. You wait ten minutes sometimes before one man will summon up courage to put a question; but once one or two have ventured they spring up all round you. I was wondering," he added, "if you would help me; let me use you, now and again."

"It is what I should love," she answered. "Tell me what to do." She was not conscious of the low, vibrating tone in which she spoke.

"I want to talk to them," he said, "about their stomachs. I want them to see the need of concentrating upon the food problem: insisting that it shall be solved. The other things can follow."

"There was an old Egyptian chap," he said, "a governor of one of their provinces, thousands of years before the Pharaohs were ever heard of. They dug up his tomb a little while ago. It bore this inscription: 'In my time no man went hungry.' I'd rather have that carved upon my gravestone than the boastings of all the robbers and the butchers of history. Think what it must have meant in that land of drought and famine: only a narrow strip of river bank where a grain of corn would grow; and that only when old Nile was kind. If not, your nearest supplies five hundred miles away across the desert, your only means of transport the slow-moving camel. Your convoy must be guarded against attack, provided with provisions and water for a two months' journey. Yet he never failed his people. Fat year and lean year: 'In my time no man went hungry.' And here, to-day, with our steamships and our railways, with the granaries of the world filled to overflowing, one third of our population lives on the border line of want. In India they die by the roadside. What's the good of it all: your science and your art and your religion! How can you help men's souls if their bodies are starving? A hungry man's a hungry beast.

"I spent a week at Grimsby, some years ago, organizing a fisherman's union. They used to throw the fish back into the sea, tons upon tons of it, that men had risked their lives to catch, that would have fed half London's poor. There was a 'glut' of it, they said. The 'market' didn't want it. Funny, isn't it, a 'glut' of food: and the kiddies can't learn their lessons for want of it. I was talking with a farmer down in Kent. The plums were rotting on his trees. There were too many of them: that was the trouble. The railway carriage alone would cost him more than he could get for them. They were too cheap. So nobody could have them. It's the muddle of the thing that makes me mad—the ghastly muddle-headed way the chief business of the world is managed. There's enough food could be grown in this country to feed all the people and then of the fragments each man might gather his ten basketsful. There's no miracle needed. I went into the matter once with Dalroy of the

Board of Agriculture. He's the best man they've got, if they'd only listen to him. It's never been organized: that's all. It isn't the fault of the individual. It ought not to be left to the individual. The man who makes a corner in wheat in Chicago and condemns millions to privation—likely enough, he's a decent sort of fellow in himself: a kind husband and father—would be upset for the day if he saw a child crying for bread. My dog's a decent enough little chap, as dogs go, but I don't let him run my larder.

"It could be done with a little good will all round," he continued, "and nine men out of every ten would be the better off. But they won't even let you explain. Their newspapers shout you down. It's such a damned fine world for the few: never mind the many. My father was a farm labourer: and all his life he never earned more than thirteen and sixpence a week. I left when I was twelve and went into the mines. There were six of us children; and my mother brought us up healthy and decent. She fed us and clothed us and sent us to school; and when she died we buried her with the money she had put by for the purpose; and never a penny of charity had ever soiled her hands. I can see them now. Talk of your Chancellors of the Exchequer and their problems! She worked herself to death, of course. Well, that's all right. One doesn't mind that where one loves. If they would only let you. She had no opposition to contend with—no thwarting and hampering at every turn—the very people you are working for hounded on against you. The difficulty of a man like myself, who wants to do something, who could do something, is that for the best part of his life he is fighting to be allowed to do it. By the time I've lived down their lies and got my chance, my energy will be gone."

He knocked the ashes from his pipe and relit it.

"I've no quarrel with the rich," he said. "I don't care how many rich men there are, so long as there are no poor. Who does? I was riding on a bus the other day, and there was a man beside me with a bandaged head. He'd been hurt in that railway smash at Morpeth. He hadn't claimed damages from the railway company and wasn't going to. 'Oh, it's only a few scratches,' he said. 'They'll be hit hard enough as it is.' If he'd been a poor devil on eighteen shillings a week it would have been different. He was an engineer earning good wages; so he wasn't feeling sore and bitter against half the world. Suppose you tried to run an army with your men half starved while your officers had more than they could eat. It's been tried and what's been the result? See that your soldiers have their proper rations, and the General can sit down to his six-course dinner, if he will. They are not begrudging it to him.

"A nation works on its stomach. Underfeed your rank and file, and what sort of a fight are you going to put up against your rivals. I want to see England going ahead. I want to see her workers properly fed. I want to see the corn upon her unused acres, the cattle grazing on her wasted pastures. I object to the food being thrown into the sea—left to rot upon the ground while men are hungry—side-tracked in Chicago, while the children grow up stunted. I want the commissariat properly organized."

He had been staring through her rather than at her, so it had seemed to Joan. Suddenly their eyes met, and he broke into a smile.

"I'm so awfully sorry," he said. "I've been talking to you as if you were a public meeting. I'm afraid I'm more used to them than I am to women. Please forgive me."

The whole man had changed. The eyes had a timid pleading in them.

Joan laughed. "I've been feeling as if I were the King of Bavaria," she said.

"How did he feel?" he asked her, leaning forward.

"He had his own private theatre," Joan explained, "where Wagner gave his operas. And the King was the sole audience."

"I should have hated that," he said, "if I had been Wagner."

He looked at her, and a flush passed over his boyish face.

"All right," he said, "if it had been a queen."

Joan found herself tracing patterns with her spoon upon the tablecloth. "But you have won now," she said, still absorbed apparently with her drawing, "you are going to get your chance."

He gave a short laugh. "A trick," he said, "to weaken me. They think to shave my locks; show me to the people bound by their red tape. To put it another way, a rat among the terriers."

Joan laughed. "You don't somehow suggest the rat," she said: "rather another sort of beast."

"What do you advise me?" he asked. "I haven't decided yet."

They were speaking in whispered tones. Through the open doors they could see into the other room. Mrs. Phillips, under Airlie's instructions, was venturing upon a cigarette.

"To accept," she answered. "They won't influence you—the terriers, as you call them. You are too strong. It is you who will sway them. It isn't as if you were a mere agitator. Take this opportunity of showing them that you can build, plan, organize; that you were meant to be a ruler. You can't succeed without them, as things are. You've got to win them over. Prove to them that they can trust you."

He sat for a minute tattooing with his fingers on the table, before speaking.

"It's the frills and flummery part of it that frightens me," he said. "You wouldn't think that sensitiveness was my weak point. But it is. I've stood up to a Birmingham mob that was waiting to lynch me and enjoyed the experience; but I'd run ten miles rather than face a drawing-room of well-dressed people with their masked faces and ironic courtesies. It leaves me for days feeling like a lobster that has lost its shell."

"I wouldn't say it, if I didn't mean it," answered Joan; "but you haven't got to trouble yourself about that. . . You're quite passable." She smiled. It seemed to her that most women would find him more than passable.

He shook his head. "With you," he said. "There's something about you that makes one ashamed of worrying about the little things. But the others: the sneering women and the men who wink over their shoulder while they talk to you, I shall never be able to get away from them, and, of course, wherever I go—"

He stopped abruptly with a sudden tightening of the lips. Joan followed his eyes. Mrs. Phillips had swallowed the smoke and was giggling and spluttering by turns. The yellow ostrich feather had worked itself loose and was rocking to and fro as if in a fit of laughter of its own.

He pushed back his chair and rose. "Shall we join the others?" he said.

He moved so that he was between her and the other room, his back to the open doors. "You think I ought to?" he said.

"Yes," she answered firmly, as if she were giving a command. But he read pity also in her eyes.

"Well, have you two settled the affairs of the kingdom? Is it all decided?" asked Airlie.

"Yes," he answered, laughing. "We are going to say to the people, 'Eat, drink and be wise.'"

He rearranged his wife's feather and smoothed her tumbled hair. She looked up at him and smiled.

Joan set herself to make McKean talk, and after a time succeeded. They had a mutual friend, a raw-boned youth she had met at Cambridge. He was engaged to McKean's sister. His eyes lighted up when he spoke of his sister Jenny. The Little Mother, he called her.

"She's the most beautiful body in all the world," he said. "Though merely seeing her you mightn't know it."

He saw her "home"; and went on up the stairs to his own floor.

Joan stood for a while in front of the glass before undressing; but felt less satisfied with herself. She replaced the star in its case, and took off the regal-looking dress with the golden girdle and laid it carelessly aside. She seemed to be growing smaller.

In her white night dress, with her hair in two long plaits, she looked at herself once more. She seemed to be no one of any importance at all: just a long little girl going to bed. With no one to kiss her good night.

She blew out the candle and climbed into the big bed, feeling very lonesome as she used to when a child. It had not troubled her until to-night. Suddenly she sat up again. She needn't be back in London before Tuesday evening, and to-day was only Friday. She would run down home and burst in upon her father. He would be so pleased to see her.

She would make him put his arms around her.

VIII

S he reached home in the evening. She thought to find her father in his study. But they told her that, now, he usually sat alone in the great drawing-room. She opened the door softly. The room was dark save for a flicker of firelight; she could see nothing. Nor was there any sound.

"Dad," she cried, "are you here?"

He rose slowly from a high-backed chair beside the fire.

"It is you," he said. He seemed a little dazed.

She ran to him and, seizing his listless arms, put them round her.

"Give me a hug, Dad," she commanded. "A real hug."

He held her to him for what seemed a long while. There was strength in his arms, in spite of the bowed shoulders and white hair.

"I was afraid you had forgotten how to do it," she laughed, when at last he released her. "Do you know, you haven't hugged me, Dad, since I was five years old. That's nineteen years ago. You do love me, don't you?"

"Yes," he answered. "I have always loved you."

She would not let him light the gas. "I have dined—in the train," she explained. "Let us talk by the firelight."

She forced him gently back into his chair, and seated herself upon the floor between his knees. "What were you thinking of when I came in?" she asked. "You weren't asleep, were you?"

"No," he answered. "Not that sort of sleep." She could not see his face. But she guessed his meaning.

"Am I very like her?" she asked.

"Yes," he answered. "Marvellously like her as she used to be: except for just one thing. Perhaps that will come to you later. I thought, for the moment, as you stood there by the door. . ." He did not finish the sentence.

"Tell me about her," she said. "I never knew she had been an actress."

He did not ask her how she had learnt it. "She gave it up when we were married," he said. "The people she would have to live among would have looked askance at her if they had known. There seemed no reason why they should."

"How did it all happen?" she persisted. "Was it very beautiful, in the beginning?" She wished she had not added that last. The words had slipped from her before she knew.

"Very beautiful," he answered, "in the beginning."

"It was my fault," he went on, "that it was not beautiful all through. I ought to have let her take up her work again, as she wished to, when she found what giving it up meant to her. The world was narrower then than it is now; and I listened to the world. I thought it another voice."

"It's difficult to tell, isn't it?" she said. "I wonder how one can?"

He did not answer; and they sat for a time in silence.

"Did you ever see her act?" asked Joan.

"Every evening for about six months," he answered. A little flame shot up and showed a smile upon his face.

"I owe to her all the charity and tenderness I know. She taught it to me in those months. I might have learned more if I had let her go on teaching. It was the only way she knew."

Joan watched her as gradually she shaped herself out of the shadows: the poor, thin, fretful lady of the ever restless hands, with her bursts of jealous passion, her long moods of sullen indifference: all her music turned to waste.

"How did she come to fall in love with you?" asked Joan. "I don't mean to be uncomplimentary, Dad." She laughed, taking his hand in hers and stroking it. "You must have been ridiculously handsome, when you were young. And you must always have been strong and brave and clever. I can see such a lot of women falling in love with you. But not the artistic woman."

"It wasn't so incongruous at the time," he answered. "My father had sent me out to America to superintend a contract. It was the first time I had ever been away from home, though I was nearly thirty; and all my pent-up youth rushed out of me at once. It was a harum-scarum fellow, mad with the joy of life, that made love to her; not the man who went out, nor the man who came back. It was at San Francisco that I met her. She was touring the Western States; and I let everything go to the wind and followed her. It seemed to me that Heaven had opened up to me. I fought a duel in Colorado with a man who had insulted her. The law didn't run there in those days; and three of his hired gunmen, as they called them, held us up that night in the train and gave her the alternative of going back with them and kissing him or seeing me dead at her feet. I didn't give her time to answer, nor for them to finish. It seemed a fine death anyhow, that. And I'd have faced Hell itself for the chance of fighting for her. Though she told me afterwards that if I'd died she'd have gone back with them, and killed him."

Joan did not speak for a time. She could see him grave—a little pompous, in his Sunday black, his footsteps creaking down the stone-flagged aisle, the silver-edged collecting bag held stiffly in his hand.

"Couldn't you have saved a bit, Daddy?" she asked, "of all that wealth of youth—just enough to live on?"

"I might," he answered, "if I had known the value of it. I found a cable waiting for me in New York. My father had been dead a month; and I had to return immediately."

"And so you married her and took her drum away from her," said Joan. "Oh, the thing God gives to some of us," she explained, "to make a little noise with, and set the people marching."

The little flame died out. She could feel his body trembling.

"But you still loved her, didn't you, Dad?" she asked. "I was very little at the time, but I can just remember. You seemed so happy together. Till her illness came."

"It was more than love," he answered. "It was idolatry. God punished me for it. He was a hard God, my God."

She raised herself, putting her hands upon his shoulders so that her face was very close to his. "What has become of Him, Dad?" she said. She spoke in a cold voice, as one does of a false friend.

"I do not know," he answered her. "I don't seem to care."

"He must be somewhere," she said: "the living God of love and hope: the God that Christ believed in."

"They were His last words, too," he answered: "'My God, my God, why hast Thou forsaken me?'"

"No, not His last," said Joan: "'Lo, I am with you always, even unto the end of the world.' Love was Christ's God. He will help us to find Him."

Their arms were about one another. Joan felt that a new need had been born in her: the need of loving and of being loved. It was good to lay her head upon his breast and know that he was glad of her coming.

He asked her questions about herself. But she could see that he was tired; so she told him it was too important a matter to start upon so late. She would talk about herself to-morrow. It would be Sunday.

"Do you still go to the chapel?" she asked him a little hesitatingly.

"Yes," he answered. "One lives by habit."

"It is the only Temple I know," he continued after a moment. "Perhaps God, one day, will find me there."

He rose and lit the gas, and a letter on the mantelpiece caught his eye.

"Have you heard from Arthur?" he asked, suddenly turning to her.

"No. Not since about a month," she answered. "Why?"

"He will be pleased to find you here, waiting for him," he said with a smile, handing her the letter. "He will be here some time to-morrow."

Arthur Allway was her cousin, the son of a Nonconformist Minister. Her father had taken him into the works and for the last three years he had been in Egypt, helping in the laying of a tramway line. He was in love with her: at least so they all told her; and his letters were certainly somewhat committal. Joan replied to them—when she did not forget to do so—in a studiously sisterly vein; and always reproved him for unnecessary extravagance whenever he sent her a present. The letter announced his arrival at Southampton. He would stop at Birmingham, where his parents lived, for a couple of days, and be in Liverpool on Sunday evening, so as to be able to get straight to business on Monday morning. Joan handed back the letter. It contained nothing else.

"It only came an hour or two ago," her father explained. "If he wrote to you by the same post, you may have left before it arrived."

"So long as he doesn't think that I came down specially to see him, I don't mind," said Joan.

They both laughed. "He's a good lad," said her father.

They kissed good night, and Joan went up to her own room. She found it just as she had left it. A bunch of roses stood upon the dressing-table. Her father would never let anyone cut his roses but himself.

Young Allway arrived just as Joan and her father had sat down to supper. A place had been laid for him. He flushed with pleasure at seeing her; but was not surprised.

"I called at your diggings," he said. "I had to go through London. They told me you had started. It is good of you."

"No, it isn't," said Joan. "I came down to see Dad. I didn't know you were back." She spoke with some asperity; and his face fell.

"How are you?" she added, holding out her hand. "You've grown quite good-looking. I like your moustache." And he flushed again with pleasure.

He had a sweet, almost girlish face, with delicate skin that the Egyptian sun had deepened into ruddiness; with soft, dreamy eyes and golden hair. He looked lithe and agile rather than strong. He was shy at first, but once set going, talked freely, and was interesting.

His work had taken him into the Desert, far from the beaten tracks. He described the life of the people, very little different from what it must have been in Noah's time. For months he had been the only white man there, and had lived among them. What had struck him was how little he had missed all the paraphernalia of civilization, once he had got over the first shock. He had learnt their sports and games; wrestled and swum and hunted with them. Provided one was a little hungry and tired with toil, a stew of goat's flesh with sweet cakes and fruits, washed down with wine out of a sheep's skin, made a feast; and after, there was music and singing and dancing, or the travelling story-teller would gather round him his rapt audience. Paris had only robbed women of their grace and dignity. He preferred the young girls in their costume of the fourteenth dynasty. Progress, he thought, had tended only to complicate life and render it less enjoyable. All the essentials of happiness—love, courtship, marriage, the home, children, friendship, social intercourse, and play, were independent of it; had always been there for the asking.

Joan thought his mistake lay in regarding man's happiness as more important to him than his self-development. It was not what we got out of civilization but what we put into it that was our gain. Its luxuries and ostentations were, in themselves, perhaps bad for us. But the pursuit of them was good. It called forth thought and effort, sharpened our wits, strengthened our brains. Primitive man, content with his necessities, would never have produced genius. Art, literature, science would have been stillborn.

He hesitated before replying, glancing at her furtively while crumbling his bread. When he did, it was in the tone that one of her younger disciples might have ventured into a discussion with Hypatia. But he stuck to his guns.

How did she account for David and Solomon, Moses and the Prophets? They had sprung from a shepherd race. Yet surely there was genius, literature. Greece owed nothing to progress. She had preceded it. Her thinkers, her poets, her scientists had draws their inspiration from nature, not civilization. Her art had sprung full grown out of the soil. We had never surpassed it.

"But the Greek ideal could not have been the right one, or Greece would not so utterly have disappeared," suggested Mr. Allway. "Unless you reject the law of the survival of the fittest."

He had no qualms about arguing with his uncle.

"So did Archimedes disappear," he answered with a smile. "The nameless Roman soldier remained. That was hardly the survival of the fittest."

He thought it the tragedy of the world that Rome had conquered Greece, imposing her lower ideals upon the race. Rome should have been the servant of Greece: the hands directed by the brain. She would have made roads and harbours, conducted the traffic, reared the market place. She knew of the steam engine, employed it for pumping water in the age of the Antonines. Sooner or later, she would have placed it on rails, and in ships. Rome should have been the policeman, keeping the world in order, making it a fit habitation. Her mistake was in regarding these things as an end in themselves, dreaming of nothing beyond. From her we had inherited the fallacy that man was made for the world, not the world for man. Rome organized only for man's body. Greece would have legislated for his soul.

They went into the drawing-room. Her father asked her to sing and Arthur opened the piano for her and lit the candles. She chose some ballads and a song of Herrick's, playing her own accompaniment while Arthur turned the leaves. She had a good voice, a low contralto. The room was high and dimly lighted. It looked larger than it really was. Her father sat in his usual chair beside the fire and listened with half-closed eyes. Glancing now and then across at him, she was reminded of Orchardson's picture. She was feeling sentimental, a novel sensation to her. She rather enjoyed it.

She finished with one of Burns's lyrics; and then told Arthur that it was now his turn, and that she would play for him. He shook his head, pleading that he was out of practice.

"I wish it," she said, speaking low. And it pleased her that he made no answer but to ask her what he should sing. He had a light tenor voice. It was wobbly at first, but improved as he went on. They ended with a duet.

The next morning she went into town with them. She never seemed to have any time in London, and wanted to do some shopping. They joined her again for lunch and afterwards, at her father's suggestion, she and Arthur went for a walk. They took the tram out of the city and struck into the country. The leaves still lingered brown and red upon the trees. He carried her cloak and opened gates for her and held back brambles while she passed. She had always been indifferent to these small gallantries; but to-day she welcomed them. She wished to feel her power to attract and command. They avoided all subjects on which they could differ, even in words. They talked of people and places they had known together. They remembered their common love of animals and told of the comedies and tragedies that had befallen their pets. Joan's regret was that she had not now even a dog, thinking it cruel to keep them in London. She hated the women she met, dragging the poor little depressed beasts about at the end of a string: savage with them, if they dared to stop for a moment to exchange a passing wag of the tail with some other little lonely sufferer. It was as bad as keeping a lark in a cage. She had tried a cat: but so often she did not get home till late and that was just the time when the cat wanted to be out; so that they seldom met. He suggested a parrot. His experience of them was that they had no regular hours and would willingly sit up all night, if encouraged, and talk all the time. Joan's objection to running a parrot was that it stamped you as an old maid; and she wasn't that, at least, not yet. She wondered if she could make an owl really happy. Minerva had an owl.

He told her how one spring, walking across a common, after a fire, he had found a mother thrush burnt to death upon her nest, her charred wings spread out in a vain endeavour to protect her brood. He had buried her there among the blackened thorn and furze, and placed a little cross of stones above her.

"I hope nobody saw me," he said with a laugh. "But I couldn't bear to leave her there, unhonoured."

"It's one of the things that make me less certain than I want to be of a future existence," said Joan: "the thought that animals can have no part in it; that all their courage and love and faithfulness dies with them and is wasted."

"Are you sure it is?" he answered. "It would be so unreasonable."

They had tea at an old-fashioned inn beside a stream. It was a favourite resort in summer time, but now they had it to themselves. The wind had played pranks with her hair and he found a mirror and knelt before her, holding it.

She stood erect, looking down at him while seeming to be absorbed in the rearrangement of her hair, feeling a little ashamed of herself. She was "encouraging" him. There was no other word for it. She seemed to have developed a sudden penchant for this sort of thing. It would end in his proposing to her; and then she would have to tell him that she cared for him only in a cousinly sort of way—whatever that might mean—and that she could never marry him. She dared not ask herself why. She must manoeuvre to put it off as long as possible; and meanwhile some opening might occur to enlighten him. She would talk to him about her work; and explain to him how she had determined to devote her life to it to the exclusion of all other distractions. If, then, he chose to go on loving her—or if he couldn't help it—that would not be her fault. After all, it did him no harm. She could always be gracious and kind to him. It was not as if she had tricked him. He had always loved her. Kneeling before her, serving her: it was evident it made him supremely happy. It would be cruel of her to end it.

The landlady entered unexpectedly with the tea; but he did not rise till Joan turned away, nor did he seem disconcerted. Neither did the landlady. She was an elderly, quiet-eyed woman, and had served more than one generation of young people with their teas.

They returned home by train. Joan insisted on travelling third class, and selected a compartment containing a stout woman and two children. Arthur had to be at the works. An important contract had got behindhand and they were working overtime. She and her father dined alone. He made her fulfil her promise to talk about herself, and she told him all she thought would interest him. She passed lightly over her acquaintanceship with Phillips. He would regard it as highly undesirable, she told herself, and it would trouble him. He was reading her articles in the *Sunday Post*, as also her Letters from Clorinda: and of the two preferred the latter as being less subversive of law and order. Also he did not like seeing her photograph each week, displayed across two columns with her name beneath in one inch type. He supposed he was old-fashioned. She was getting rather tired of it herself.

"The Editor insisted upon it," she explained. "It was worth it for the opportunity it gives me. I preach every Sunday to a congregation of over a million souls. It's better than being a Bishop. Besides," she added, "the men are just as bad. You see their silly faces everywhere."

"That's like you women," he answered with a smile. "You pretend to be superior; and then you copy us."

She laughed. But the next moment she was serious.

"No, we don't," she said, "not those of us who think. We know we shall never oust man from his place. He will always be the greater. We want to help him; that's all."

"But wasn't that the Lord's idea," he said; "when He gave Eve to Adam to be his helpmeet?"

"Yes, that was all right," she answered. "He fashioned Eve for Adam and saw that Adam got her. The ideal marriage might have been the ideal solution. If the Lord had intended that, he should have kept the match-making in His own hands: not have left it to man. Somewhere in Athens there must have been the helpmeet God had made for Socrates. When they met, it was Xanthippe that she kissed."

A servant brought the coffee and went out again. Her father lighted a cigar and handed her the cigarettes.

"Will it shock you, Dad?" she asked.

"Rather late in the day for you to worry yourself about that, isn't it?" he answered with a smile.

He struck a match and held it for her. Joan sat with her elbows on the table and smoked in silence. She was thinking.

Why had he never "brought her up," never exacted obedience from her, never even tried to influence her? It could not have been mere weakness. She stole a sidelong glance at the tired, lined face with its steel-blue eyes. She had never seen them other than calm, but they must have been able to flash. Why had he always been so just and kind and patient with her? Why had he never scolded her and bullied her and teased her? Why had he let her go away, leaving him lonely in his empty, voiceless house? Why had he never made any claim upon her? The idea came to her as an inspiration. At least, it would ease her conscience. "Why don't you let Arthur live here," she said, "instead of going back to his lodgings? It would be company for you."

He did not answer for some time. She had begun to wonder if he had heard.

"What do you think of him?" he said, without looking at her.

"Oh, he's quite a nice lad," she answered.

It was some while again before he spoke. "He will be the last of the Allways," he said. "I should like to think of the name being continued; and he's a good business man, in spite of his dreaminess. Perhaps he would get on better with the men."

She seized at the chance of changing the subject.

"It was a foolish notion," she said, "that of the Manchester school: that men and women could be treated as mere figures in a sum."

To her surprise, he agreed with her. "The feudal system had a fine idea in it," he said, "if it had been honestly carried out. A master should be the friend, the helper of his men. They should be one family."

She looked at him a little incredulously, remembering the bitter periods of strikes and lock-outs.

"Did you ever try, Dad?" she asked.

"Oh, yes," he answered. "But I tried the wrong way." "The right way might be found," he added, "by the right man, and woman."

She felt that he was watching her through his half-closed eyes. "There are those cottages," he continued, "just before you come to the bridge. They might be repaired and a club house added. The idea is catching on, they tell me. Garden villages, they call them now. It gets the men and women away from the dirty streets; and gives the children a chance."

She knew the place. A sad group of dilapidated little houses forming three sides of a paved quadrangle, with a shattered fountain and withered trees in the centre. Ever since she could remember, they had stood there empty, ghostly, with creaking doors and broken windows, their gardens overgrown with weeds.

"Are they yours?" she asked. She had never connected them with the works, some half a mile away. Though had she been curious, she might have learnt that they were known as "Allway's Folly."

"Your mother's," he answered. "I built them the year I came back from America and gave them to her. I thought it would interest her. Perhaps it would, if I had left her to her own ways."

"Why didn't they want them?" she asked.

"They did, at first," he answered. "The time-servers and the hypocrites among them. I made it a condition that they should be teetotallers, and chapel goers, and everything else that I thought good for them. I thought that I could save their souls by bribing them with cheap rents and share of profits. And then the Union came, and that of course finished it."

So he, too, had thought to build Jerusalem.

"Yes," he said. "I'll sound him about giving up his lodgings."

Joan lay awake for a long while that night. The moon looked in at the window. It seemed to have got itself entangled in the tops of the tall pines. Would it not be her duty to come back—make her father happy, to say nothing of the other. He was a dear, sweet, lovable lad. Together, they might realize her father's dream: repair the blunders, plant gardens where the weeds now grew, drive out the old sad ghosts with living voices. It had been a fine thought, a "King's thought." Others had followed, profiting by his mistakes. But might it not be carried further

JEROME K. JEROME

than even they had gone, shaped into some noble venture that should serve the future.

Was not her America here? Why seek it further? What was this unknown Force, that, against all sense and reason, seemed driving her out into the wilderness to preach. Might it not be mere vanity, mere egoism. Almost she had convinced herself.

And then there flashed remembrance of her mother. She, too, had laid aside herself; had thought that love and duty could teach one to be other than one was. The Ego was the all important thing, entrusted to us as the talents of silver to the faithful servant: to be developed, not for our own purposes, but for the service of the Master.

One did no good by suppressing one's nature. In the end it proved too strong. Marriage with Arthur would be only repeating the mistake. To be worshipped, to be served. It would be very pleasant, when one was in the mood. But it would not satisfy her. There was something strong and fierce and primitive in her nature—something that had come down to her through the generations from some harness-girded ancestress—something impelling her instinctively to choose the fighter; to share with him the joy of battle, healing his wounds, giving him of her courage, exulting with him in the victory.

The moon had risen clear of the entangling pines. It rode serene and free.

Her father came to the station with her in the morning. The train was not in: and they walked up and down and talked. Suddenly she remembered: it had slipped her mind.

"Could I, as a child, have known an old clergyman?" she asked him. "At least he wouldn't have been old then. I dropped into Chelsea Church one evening and heard him preach; and on the way home I passed him again in the street. It seemed to me that I had seen his face before. But not for many years. I meant to write you about it, but forgot."

He had to turn aside for a moment to speak to an acquaintance about business.

"Oh, it's possible," he answered on rejoining her. "What was his name?"

"I do not know," she answered. "He was not the regular Incumbent. But it was someone that I seemed to know quite well—that I must have been familiar with."

"It may have been," he answered carelessly, "though the gulf was wider then than it is now. I'll try and think. Perhaps it is only your fancy."

The train drew in, and he found her a corner seat, and stood talking by the window, about common things.

"What did he preach about?" he asked her unexpectedly.

She was puzzled for the moment. "Oh, the old clergyman," she answered, recollecting. "Oh, Calvary. All roads lead to Calvary, he thought. It was rather interesting."

She looked back at the end of the platform. He had not moved.

IX

A pile of correspondence was awaiting her and, standing by the desk, she began to open and read it. Suddenly she paused, conscious that someone had entered the room and, turning, she saw Hilda. She must have left the door ajar, for she had heard no sound. The child closed the door noiselessly and came across, holding out a letter.

"Papa told me to give you this the moment you came in," she said. Joan had not yet taken off her things. The child must have been keeping a close watch. Save for the signature it contained but one line: "I have accepted."

Joan replaced the letter in its envelope, and laid it down upon the desk. Unconsciously a smile played about her lips.

The child was watching her. "I'm glad you persuaded him," she said.

Joan felt a flush mount to her face. She had forgotten Hilda for the instant.

She forced a laugh. "Oh, I only persuaded him to do what he had made up his mind to do," she explained. "It was all settled."

"No, it wasn't," answered the child. "Most of them were against it. And then there was Mama," she added in a lower tone.

"What do you mean," asked Joan. "Didn't she wish it?"

The child raised her eyes. There was a dull anger in them. "Oh, what's the good of pretending," she said. "He's so great. He could be the Prime Minister of England if he chose. But then he would have to visit kings and nobles, and receive them at his house, and Mama—" She broke off with a passionate gesture of the small thin hands.

Joan was puzzled what to say. She knew exactly what she ought to say: what she would have said to any ordinary child. But to say it to this uncannily knowing little creature did not promise much good.

"Who told you I persuaded him?" she asked.

"Nobody," answered the child. "I knew."

Joan seated herself, and drew the child towards her.

"It isn't as terrible as you think," she said. "Many men who have risen and taken a high place in the world were married to kind, good women unable to share their greatness. There was Shakespeare, you know, who married Anne Hathaway and had a clever daughter. She was just a nice, homely body a few years older than himself. And he seems to have been very fond of her; and was always running down to Stratford to be with her."

"Yes, but he didn't bring her up to London," answered the child. "Mama would have wanted to come; and Papa would have let her, and wouldn't have gone to see Queen Elizabeth unless she had been invited too."

Joan wished she had not mentioned Shakespeare. There had surely been others; men who had climbed up and carried their impossible wives with them. But she couldn't think of one, just then.

"We must help her," she answered somewhat lamely. "She's anxious to learn, I know."

The child shook her head. "She doesn't understand," she said. "And Papa won't tell her. He says it would only hurt her and do no good." The small hands were clenched. "I shall hate her if she spoils his life."

The atmosphere was becoming tragic. Joan felt the need of escaping from it. She sprang up.

"Oh, don't be nonsensical," she said. "Your father isn't the only man married to a woman not as clever as himself. He isn't going to let that stop him. And your mother's going to learn to be the wife of a great man and do the best she can. And if they don't like her they've got to put up with her. I shall talk to the both of them." A wave of motherliness towards the entire Phillips family passed over her. It included Hilda. She caught the child to her and gave her a hug. "You go back to school," she said, "and get on as fast as you can, so that you'll be able to be useful to him."

The child flung her arms about her. "You're so beautiful and wonderful," she said. "You can do anything. I'm so glad you came."

Joan laughed. It was surprising how easily the problem had been solved. She would take Mrs. Phillips in hand at once. At all events she should be wholesome and unobtrusive. It would be a delicate mission, but Joan felt sure of her own tact. She could see his boyish eyes turned upon her with wonder and gratitude.

"I was so afraid you would not be back before I went," said the child. "I ought to have gone this afternoon, but Papa let me stay till the evening."

"You will help?" she added, fixing on Joan her great, grave eyes.

Joan promised, and the child went out. She looked pretty when she smiled. She closed the door behind her noiselessly.

It occurred to Joan that she would like to talk matters over with

Greyson. There was "Clorinda's" attitude to be decided upon; and she was interested to know what view he himself would take. Of course he would be on P——'s side. The *Evening Gazette* had always supported the "gas and water school" of socialism; and to include the people's food was surely only an extension of the principle. She rang him up and Miss Greyson answered, asking her to come round to dinner: they would be alone. And she agreed.

The Greysons lived in a small house squeezed into an angle of the Outer Circle, overlooking Regent's Park. It was charmingly furnished, chiefly with old Chippendale. The drawing-room made quite a picture. It was home-like and restful with its faded colouring, and absence of all show and overcrowding. They sat there after dinner and discussed Joan's news. Miss Greyson was repairing a piece of old embroidery she had brought back with her from Italy; and Greyson sat smoking, with his hands behind his head, and his long legs stretched out towards the fire.

"Carleton will want him to make his food policy include Tariff Reform," he said. "If he prove pliable, and is willing to throw over his free trade principles, all well and good."

"What's Carleton got to do with it?" demanded Joan with a note of indignation.

He turned his head towards her with an amused raising of the eyebrows. "Carleton owns two London dailies," he answered, "and is in treaty for a third: together with a dozen others scattered about the provinces. Most politicians find themselves, sooner or later, convinced by his arguments. Phillips may prove the exception."

"It would be rather interesting, a fight between them," said Joan. "Myself I should back Phillips."

"He might win through," mused Greyson. "He's the man to do it, if anybody could. But the odds will be against him."

"I don't see it," said Joan, with decision.

"I'm afraid you haven't yet grasped the power of the Press," he answered with a smile. "Phillips speaks occasionally to five thousand people. Carleton addresses every day a circle of five million readers."

"Yes, but when Phillips does speak, he speaks to the whole country," retorted Joan.

"Through the medium of Carleton and his like; and just so far as they allow his influence to permeate beyond the platform," answered Greyson.

"But they report his speeches. They are bound to," explained Joan.

"It doesn't read quite the same," he answered. "Phillips goes home under the impression that he has made a great success and has roused the country. He and millions of other readers learn from the next morning's headlines that it was 'A Tame Speech' that he made. What sounded to him 'Loud Cheers' have sunk to mild 'Hear, Hears.' That five minutes' hurricane of applause, during which wildly excited men and women leapt upon the benches and roared themselves hoarse, and which he felt had settled the whole question, he searches for in vain. A few silly interjections, probably pre-arranged by Carleton's young lions, become 'renewed interruptions.' The report is strictly truthful; but the impression produced is that Robert Phillips has failed to carry even his own people with him. And then follow leaders in fourteen widely-circulated Dailies, stretching from the Clyde to the Severn, foretelling how Mr. Robert Phillips could regain his waning popularity by the simple process of adopting Tariff Reform: or whatever the pet panacea of Carleton and Co. may, at the moment, happen to be."

"Don't make us out all alike," pleaded his sister with a laugh. "There are still a few old-fashioned papers that do give their opponents fair play."

"They are not increasing in numbers," he answered, "and the Carleton group is. There is no reason why in another ten years he should not control the entire popular press of the country. He's got the genius and he's got the means."

"The cleverest thing he has done," he continued, turning to Joan, "is your *Sunday Post*. Up till then, the working classes had escaped him. With the *Sunday Post*, he has solved the problem. They open their mouths; and he gives them their politics wrapped up in pictures and gossipy pars."

Miss Greyson rose and put away her embroidery. "But what's his object?" she said. "He must have more money than he can spend; and he works like a horse. I could understand it, if he had any beliefs."

"Oh, we can all persuade ourselves that we are the Heaven-ordained dictator of the human race," he answered. "Love of power is at the bottom of it. Why do our Rockefellers and our Carnegies condemn themselves to the existence of galley slaves, ruining their digestions so that they never can enjoy a square meal. It isn't the money; it's the trouble of their lives how to get rid of that. It is the notoriety, the power that they are out for. In Carleton's case, it is to feel himself the power behind the throne; to know that he can make and unmake statesmen; has the keys of peace and war in his pocket; is able to exclaim: Public opinion? It is I."

"It can be a respectable ambition," suggested Joan.

"It has been responsible for most of man's miseries," he answered. "Every world's conqueror meant to make it happy after he had finished knocking it about. We are all born with it, thanks to the devil." He shifted his position and regarded her with critical eyes. "You've got it badly," he said. "I can see it in the tilt of your chin and the quivering of your nostrils. You beware of it."

Miss Greyson left them. She had to finish an article. They debated "Clorinda's" views; and agreed that, as a practical housekeeper, she would welcome attention being given to the question of the nation's food. The *Evening Gazette* would support Phillips in principle, while reserving to itself the right of criticism when it came to details.

"What's he like in himself?" he asked her. "You've been seeing something of him, haven't you?"

"Oh, a little," she answered. "He's absolutely sincere; and he means business. He won't stop at the bottom of the ladder now he's once got his foot upon it."

"But he's quite common, isn't he?" he asked again. "I've only met him in public."

"No, that's precisely what he isn't," answered Joan. "You feel that he belongs to no class, but his own. The class of the Abraham Lincolns, and the Dantons."

"England's a different proposition," he mused. "Society counts for so much with us. I doubt if we should accept even an Abraham Lincoln: unless in some supreme crisis. His wife rather handicaps him, too, doesn't she?"

"She wasn't born to be the chatelaine of Downing Street," Joan admitted. "But it's not an official position."

"I'm not so sure that it isn't," he laughed. "It's the dinner-table that rules in England. We settle everything round a dinner-table."

She was sitting in front of the fire in a high-backed chair. She never cared to loll, and the shaded light from the electric sconces upon the mantelpiece illumined her.

"If the world were properly stage-managed, that's what you ought to be," he said, "the wife of a Prime Minister. I can see you giving such an excellent performance."

"I must talk to Mary," he added, "see if we can't get you off on some promising young Under Secretary."

"Don't give me ideas above my station," laughed Joan. "I'm a journalist."

"That's the pity of it," he said. "You're wasting the most important thing about you, your personality. You would do more good in a drawing-room, influencing the rulers, than you will ever do hiding behind a pen. It was the drawing-room that made the French Revolution."

The firelight played about her hair. "I suppose every woman dreams of reviving the old French Salon," she answered. "They must have been gloriously interesting." He was leaning forward with clasped hands. "Why shouldn't she?" he said. "The reason that our drawing-rooms have ceased to lead is that our beautiful women are generally frivolous and our clever women unfeminine. What we are waiting for is an English Madame Roland."

Joan laughed. "Perhaps I shall some day," she answered.

He insisted on seeing her as far as the bus. It was a soft, mild night; and they walked round the Circle to Gloucester Gate. He thought there would be more room in the buses at that point.

"I wish you would come oftener," he said. "Mary has taken such a liking to you. If you care to meet people, we can always whip up somebody of interest."

She promised that she would. She always felt curiously at home with the Greysons.

They were passing the long sweep of Chester Terrace. "I like this neighbourhood with its early Victorian atmosphere," she said. "It always makes me feel quiet and good. I don't know why."

"I like the houses, too," he said. "There's a character about them. You don't often find such fine drawing-rooms in London."

"Don't forget your promise," he reminded her, when they parted. "I shall tell Mary she may write to you."

She met Carleton by chance a day or two later, as she was entering the office. "I want to see you," he said; and took her up with him into his room.

"We must stir the people up about this food business," he said, plunging at once into his subject. "Phillips is quite right. It overshadows everything. We must make the country self-supporting. It can be done and must. If a war were to be sprung upon us we could be starved out in a month. Our navy, in face of these new submarines, is no longer able to secure us. France is working day and night upon them. It may be a bogey, or it may not. If it isn't, she would have us at her mercy; and it's too big a risk to run. You live in the same house with him, don't you? Do you often see him?"

"Not often," she answered.

He was reading a letter. "You were dining there on Friday night, weren't you?" he asked her, without looking up.

Joan flushed. What did he mean by cross-examining her in this way? She was not at all used to impertinence from the opposite sex.

"Your information is quite correct," she answered.

Her anger betrayed itself in her tone; and he shot a swift glance at her.

"I didn't mean to offend you," he said. "A mutual friend, a Mr. Airlie, happened to be of the party, and he mentioned you."

He threw aside the letter. "I'll tell you what I want you to do," he said. "It's nothing to object to. Tell him that you've seen me and had a talk. I understand his scheme to be that the country should grow more and more food until it eventually becomes self-supporting; and that the Government should control the distribution. Tell him that with that I'm heart and soul in sympathy; and would like to help him." He pushed aside a pile of papers and, leaning across the desk, spoke with studied deliberation. "If he can see his way to making his policy dependent upon Protection, we can work together."

"And if he can't?" suggested Joan.

He fixed his large, colourless eyes upon her. "That's where you can help him," he answered. "If he and I combine forces, we can pull this through in spite of the furious opposition that it is going to arouse. Without a good Press he is helpless; and where is he going to get his Press backing if he turns me down? From half a dozen Socialist papers whose support will do him more harm than good. If he will bring the working class over to Protection I will undertake that the Tariff Reformers and the Agricultural Interest shall accept his Socialism. It will be a victory for both of us.

"If he gain his end, what do the means matter?" he continued, as Joan did not answer. "Food may be dearer; the Unions can square that by putting up wages; while the poor devil of a farm labourer will at last get fair treatment. We can easily insist upon that. What do you think, yourself?"

"About Protection," she answered. "It's one of the few subjects I haven't made up my mind about."

He laughed. "You will find all your pet reforms depend upon it, when you come to work them out," he said. "You can't have a minimum wage without a minimum price."

They had risen.

"I'll give him your message," said Joan. "But I don't see him exchanging his principles even for your support. I admit it's important."

"Talk it over with him," he said. "And bear this in mind for your own guidance." He took a step forward, which brought his face quite close to hers: "If he fails, and all his life's work goes for nothing, I shall be sorry; but I shan't break my heart. He will."

Joan dropped a note into Phillips's letter-box on her return home, saying briefly that she wished to see him; and he sent up answer asking her if she would come to the gallery that evening, and meet him after his speech, which would be immediately following the dinner hour.

It was the first time he had risen since his appointment, and he was received with general cheers. He stood out curiously youthful against the background of grey-haired and bald-headed men behind him; and there was youth also in his clear, ringing voice that not even the vault-like atmosphere of that shadowless chamber could altogether rob of its vitality. He spoke simply and good-humouredly, without any attempt at rhetoric, relying chiefly upon a crescendo of telling facts that gradually, as he proceeded, roused the House to that tense stillness that comes to it when it begins to think.

"A distinctly dangerous man," Joan overheard a little old lady behind her comment to a friend. "If I didn't hate him, I should like him."

He met her in the corridor, and they walked up and down and talked, too absorbed to be aware of the curious eyes that were turned upon them. Joan gave him Carleton's message.

"It was clever of him to make use of you," he said. "If he'd sent it through anybody else, I'd have published it."

"You don't think it even worth considering?" suggested Joan.

"Protection?" he flashed out scornfully. "Yes, I've heard of that. I've listened, as a boy, while the old men told of it to one another, in thin, piping voices, round the fireside; how the labourers were flung eight-and-sixpence a week to die on, and the men starved in the towns; while the farmers kept their hunters, and got drunk each night on fine old crusted port. Do you know what their toast was in the big hotels on market day, with the windows open to the street: 'To a long war and a bloody one.' It would be their toast to-morrow, if they had their way. Does he think I am going to be a party to the putting of the people's neck again under their pitiless yoke?"

"But the people are more powerful now," argued Joan. "If the farmer demanded higher prices, they could demand higher wages."

"They would never overtake the farmer," he answered, with a laugh. "And the last word would always be with him. I am out to get rid of the landlords," he continued, "not to establish them as the permanent rulers of the country, as they are in Germany. The people are more powerful—just a little, because they are no longer dependent on the land. They can say to the farmer, 'All right, my son, if that's your figure, I'm going to the shop next door—to South America, to Canada, to Russia.' It isn't a satisfactory solution. I want to see England happy and healthy before I bother about the Argentine. It drives our men into the slums when they might be living fine lives in God's fresh air. In the case of war it might be disastrous. There, I agree with him. We must be able to shut our door without fear of having to open it ourselves to ask for bread. How would Protection accomplish that? Did he tell you?"

"Don't eat me," laughed Joan. "I haven't been sent to you as a missionary. I'm only a humble messenger. I suppose the argument is that, good profits assured to him, the farmer would bustle up and produce more."

"Can you see him bustling up?" he answered with a laugh; "organizing himself into a body, and working the thing out from the point of view of the public weal? I'll tell you what nine-tenths of him would do: grow just as much or little as suited his own purposes; and then go to sleep. And Protection would be his security against ever being awakened."

"I'm afraid you don't like him," Joan commented.

"He will be all right in his proper place," he answered: "as the servant of the public: told what to do, and turned out of his job if he doesn't do it. My scheme does depend upon Protection. You can tell him that. But this time, it's going to be Protection for the people."

They were at the far end of the corridor; and the few others still promenading were some distance away. She had not delivered the whole of her message. She crossed to a seat, and he followed her. She spoke with her face turned away from him.

"You have got to consider the cost of refusal," she said. "His offer wasn't help or neutrality: it was help or opposition by every means in his power. He left me in no kind of doubt as to that. He's not used to being challenged and he won't be squeamish. You will have the whole of his Press against you, and every other journalistic and political influence that he possesses. He's getting a hold upon the working classes. The

Sunday Post has an enormous sale in the manufacturing towns; and he's talking of starting another. Are you strong enough to fight him?"

She very much wanted to look at him, but she would not. It seemed to her quite a time before he replied.

"Yes," he answered, "I'm strong enough to fight him. Shall rather enjoy doing it. And it's time that somebody did. Whether I'm strong enough to win has got to be seen."

She turned and looked at him then. She wondered why she had ever thought him ugly.

"You can face it," she said: "the possibility of all your life's work being wasted?"

"It won't be wasted," he answered. "The land is there. I've seen it from afar and it's a good land, a land where no man shall go hungry. If not I, another shall lead the people into it. I shall have prepared the way."

She liked him for that touch of exaggeration. She was so tired of the men who make out all things little, including themselves and their own work. After all, was it exaggeration? Might he not have been chosen to lead the people out of bondage to a land where there should be no more fear.

"You're not angry with me?" he asked. "I haven't been rude, have I?"

"Abominably rude," she answered, "you've defied my warnings, and treated my embassy with contempt." She turned to him and their eyes met. "I should have despised you, if you hadn't," she added.

There was a note of exultation in her voice; and, as if in answer, something leapt into his eyes that seemed to claim her. Perhaps it was well that just then the bell rang for a division; and the moment passed.

He rose and held out his hand. "We will fight him," he said. "And you can tell him this, if he asks, that I'm going straight for him. Parliament may as well close down if a few men between them are to be allowed to own the entire Press of the country, and stifle every voice that does not shout their bidding. We haven't dethroned kings to put up a newspaper Boss. He shall have all the fighting he wants."

They met more often from that day, for Joan was frankly using her two columns in the *Sunday Post* to propagate his aims. Carleton, to her surprise, made no objection. Nor did he seek to learn the result of his ultimatum. It looked, they thought, as if he had assumed acceptance; and was willing for Phillips to choose his own occasion. Meanwhile replies to her articles reached Joan in weekly increasing numbers. There seemed to be a wind arising, blowing towards Protection. Farm labourers, especially, appeared to be enthusiastic for its coming. From their ill-spelt, smeared epistles, one gathered that, after years of doubt and hesitation, they had—however reluctantly—arrived at the conclusion that without it there could be no hope for them. Factory workers, miners, engineers—more fluent, less apologetic—wrote as strong supporters of Phillips's scheme; but saw clearly how upon Protection its success depended. Shopmen, clerks—only occasionally ungrammatical—felt sure that Robert Phillips, the tried friend of the poor, would insist upon the boon of Protection being no longer held back from the people. Wives and mothers claimed it as their children's birthright. Similar views got themselves at the same time, into the correspondence columns of Carleton's other numerous papers. Evidently Democracy had been throbbing with a passion for Protection hitherto unknown, even to itself.

"He means it kindly," laughed Phillips. "He is offering me an excuse to surrender gracefully. We must have a public meeting or two after Christmas, and clear the ground." They had got into the habit of speaking in the plural.

Mrs. Phillips's conversion Joan found more difficult than she had anticipated. She had persuaded Phillips to take a small house and let her furnish it upon the hire system. Joan went with her to the widely advertised "Emporium" in the City Road, meaning to advise her. But, in the end, she gave it up out of sheer pity. Nor would her advice have served much purpose, confronted by the "rich and varied choice" provided for his patrons by Mr. Krebs, the "Furnisher for Connoisseurs."

"We've never had a home exactly," explained Mrs. Phillips, during their journey in the tram. "It's always been lodgings, up to now. Nice enough, some of them; but you know what I mean; everybody else's taste but your own. I've always fancied a little house with one's own things in it. You know, things that you can get fond of."

Oh, the things she was going to get fond of! The things that her poor, round foolish eyes gloated upon the moment that she saw them! Joan tried to enlist the shopman on her side, descending even to flirtation. Unfortunately he was a young man with a high sense of duty, convinced that his employer's interests lay in his support of Mrs. Phillips. The sight of the furniture that, between them, they selected for the dining-room gave Joan a quite distinct internal pain. They ascended to the floor above, devoted to the exhibition of "*Recherche* drawing-room suites." Mrs. Phillips's eye instinctively fastened with passionate desire upon the most atrocious. Joan grew vehement. It was impossible.

"I always was a one for cheerful colours," explained Mrs. Phillips.

Even the shopman wavered. Joan pressed her advantage; directed Mrs. Phillips's attention to something a little less awful. Mrs. Phillips yielded.

"Of course you know best, dear," she admitted. "Perhaps I am a bit too fond of bright things."

The victory was won. Mrs. Phillips had turned away. The shopman was altering the order. Joan moved towards the door, and accidentally caught sight of Mrs. Phillips's face. The flabby mouth was trembling. A tear was running down the painted cheek.

Joan slipped her hand through the other's arm.

"I'm not so sure you're not right after all," she said, fixing a critical eye upon the rival suites. "It is a bit mousey, that other."

The order was once more corrected. Joan had the consolation of witnessing the childish delight that came again into the foolish face; but felt angry with herself at her own weakness.

It was the woman's feebleness that irritated her. If only she had shown a spark of fight, Joan could have been firm. Poor feckless creature, what could have ever been her attraction for Phillips!

She followed, inwardly fuming, while Mrs. Phillips continued to pile monstrosity upon monstrosity. What would Phillips think? And what would Hilda's eyes say when they looked upon that *recherche* drawing-room suite? Hilda, who would have had no sentimental compunctions! The woman would be sure to tell them both that she, Joan, had accompanied her and helped in the choosing. The whole ghastly house would be exhibited to every visitor as the result of their joint taste. She could hear Mr. Airlie's purring voice congratulating her.

She ought to have insisted on their going to a decent shop. The mere advertisement ought to have forewarned her. It was the posters that had captured Mrs. Phillips: those dazzling apartments where bejewelled society reposed upon the "high-class but inexpensive designs" of Mr. Krebs. Artists ought to have more self-respect than to sell their talents for such purposes.

The contract was concluded in Mr. Krebs' private office: a very stout gentleman with a very thin voice, whose dream had always been to one day be of service to the renowned Mr. Robert Phillips. He was clearly under the impression that he had now accomplished it. Even as Mrs. Phillips took up the pen to sign, the wild idea occurred to Joan of snatching the paper away from her, hustling her into a cab, and in some quiet street or square making the woman see for herself that she was a useless fool; that the glowing dreams and fancies she had cherished in her silly head for fifteen years must all be given up; that she must stand aside, knowing herself of no account.

It could be done. She felt it. If only one could summon up the needful brutality. If only one could stifle that still, small voice of Pity.

Mrs. Phillips signed amid splutterings and blots. Joan added her signature as witness.

She did effect an improvement in the poor lady's dress. On Madge's advice she took her to a voluble little woman in the Earl's Court Road who was struck at once by Madame Phillips's remarkable resemblance to the Baroness von Stein. Had not Joan noticed it? Whatever suited the Baroness von Stein—allowed by common consent to be one of the best-dressed women in London—was bound to show up Madame Phillips to equal advantage. By curious coincidence a costume for the Baroness had been put in hand only the day before. It was sent for and pinned upon the delighted Madame Phillips. Perfection! As the Baroness herself would always say: "My frock must be a framework for my personality. It must never obtrude." The supremely well-dressed woman! One never notices what she has on: that is the test. It seemed it was what Mrs. Phillips had always felt herself. Joan could have kissed the voluble, emphatic little woman.

But the dyed hair and the paint put up a fight for themselves.

"I want you to do something very brave," said Joan. She had invited herself to tea with Mrs. Phillips, and they were alone in the small white-panelled room that they were soon to say good-bye to. The new house would be ready at Christmas. "It will be a little hard at first," continued Joan, "but afterwards you will be glad that you have done it. It is a duty you owe to your position as the wife of a great leader of the people."

The firelight showed to Joan a comically frightened face, with round, staring eyes and an open mouth.

"What is it you want me to do?" she faltered

"I want you to be just yourself," said Joan; "a kind, good woman of the people, who will win their respect, and set them an example." She moved across and seating herself on the arm of Mrs. Phillips's chair, touched lightly with her hand the flaxen hair and the rouged cheek. "I want you to get rid of all this," she whispered. "It isn't worthy of you. Leave it to the silly dolls and the bad women."

There was a long silence. Joan felt the tears trickling between her fingers.

"You haven't seen me," came at last in a thin, broken voice.

Joan bent down and kissed her. "Let's try it," she whispered.

A little choking sound was the only answer. But the woman rose and, Joan following, they stole upstairs into the bedroom and Mrs. Phillips turned the key.

It took a long time, and Joan, seated on the bed, remembered a night when she had taken a trapped mouse (if only he had been a quiet mouse!) into the bathroom and had waited while it drowned. It was finished at last, and Mrs. Phillips stood revealed with her hair down, showing streaks of dingy brown.

Joan tried to enthuse; but the words came haltingly. She suggested to Joan a candle that some wind had suddenly blown out. The paint and powder had been obvious, but at least it had given her the mask of youth. She looked old and withered. The life seemed to have gone out of her.

"You see, dear, I began when I was young," she explained; "and he has always seen me the same. I don't think I could live like this."

The painted doll that the child fancied! the paint washed off and the golden hair all turned to drab? Could one be sure of "getting used to it," of "liking it better?" And the poor bewildered doll itself! How could one expect to make of it a statue: "The Woman of the People." One could only bruise it.

It ended in Joan's promising to introduce her to discreet theatrical friends who would tell her of cosmetics less injurious to the skin, and advise her generally in the ancient and proper art of "making up."

It was not the end she had looked for. Joan sighed as she closed her door behind her. What was the meaning of it? On the one hand that unimpeachable law, the greatest happiness of the greatest number; the sacred cause of Democracy; the moral Uplift of the people; Sanity, Wisdom, Truth, the higher Justice; all the forces on which she was relying for the regeneration of the world—all arrayed in stern demand that the flabby, useless Mrs. Phillips should be sacrificed for the general good. Only one voice had pleaded for foolish, helpless Mrs. Phillips— and had conquered. The still, small voice of Pity.

JEROME K. JEROME

X

Arthur sprang himself upon her a little before Christmas. He was full of a great project. It was that she and her father should spend Christmas with his people at Birmingham. Her father thought he would like to see his brother; they had not often met of late, and Birmingham would be nearer for her than Liverpool.

Joan had no intention of being lured into the Birmingham parlour. She thought she could see in it a scheme for her gradual entanglement. Besides, she was highly displeased. She had intended asking her father to come to Brighton with her. As a matter of fact, she had forgotten all about Christmas; and the idea only came into her head while explaining to Arthur how his impulsiveness had interfered with it. Arthur, crestfallen, suggested telegrams. It would be quite easy to alter everything; and of course her father would rather be with her, wherever it was. But it seemed it was too late. She ought to have been consulted. A sudden sense of proprietorship in her father came to her assistance and added pathos to her indignation. Of course, now, she would have to spend Christmas alone. She was far too busy to think of Birmingham. She could have managed Brighton. Argument founded on the length of journey to Birmingham as compared with the journey to Brighton she refused to be drawn into. Her feelings had been too deeply wounded to permit of descent into detail.

But the sinner, confessing his fault, is entitled to forgiveness, and, having put him back into his proper place, she let him kiss her hand. She even went further and let him ask her out to dinner. As the result of her failure to reform Mrs. Phillips she was feeling dissatisfied with herself. It was an unpleasant sensation and somewhat new to her experience. An evening spent in Arthur's company might do her good. The experiment proved successful. He really was quite a dear boy. Eyeing him thoughtfully through the smoke of her cigarette, it occurred to her how like he was to Guido's painting of St. Sebastian; those soft, dreamy eyes and that beautiful, almost feminine, face! There always had been a suspicion of the saint about him even as a boy: nothing one could lay hold of: just that odd suggestion of a shadow intervening between him and the world.

It seemed a favourable opportunity to inform him of that fixed determination of hers: never—in all probability—to marry: but to devote her life to her work. She was feeling very kindly towards him; and was able to soften her decision with touches of gentle regret. He did not appear in the least upset. But 'thought' that her duty might demand, later on, that she should change her mind: that was if fate should offer her some noble marriage, giving her wider opportunity.

She was a little piqued at his unexpected attitude of aloofness. What did he mean by a "noble marriage"—to a Duke, or something of that sort?

He did not think the candidature need be confined to Dukes, though he had no objection to a worthy Duke. He meant any really great man who would help her and whom she could help.

She promised, somewhat shortly, to consider the matter, whenever the Duke, or other class of nobleman, should propose to her. At present no sign of him had appeared above the horizon. Her own idea was that, if she lived long enough, she would become a spinster. Unless someone took pity on her when she was old and decrepit and past her work.

There was a little humorous smile about his mouth. But his eyes were serious and pleading.

"When shall I know that you are old and decrepit?" he asked.

She was not quite sure. She thought it would be when her hair was grey—or rather white. She had been informed by experts that her peculiar shade of hair went white, not grey.

"I shall ask you to marry me when your hair is white," he said. "May I?"

It did not suggest any overwhelming impatience. "Yes," she answered. "In case you haven't married yourself, and forgotten all about me."

"I shall keep you to your promise," he said quite gravely.

She felt the time had come to speak seriously. "I want you to marry," she said, "and be happy. I shall be troubled if you don't."

He was looking at her with those shy, worshipping eyes of his that always made her marvel at her own wonderfulness.

"It need not do that," he answered. "It would be beautiful to be with you always so that I might serve you. But I am quite happy, loving you. Let me see you now and then: touch you and hear your voice."

Behind her drawn-down lids, she offered up a little prayer that she might always be worthy of his homage. She didn't know it would make no difference to him.

She walked with him to Euston and saw him into the train. He had given up his lodgings and was living with her father at The Pines. They were busy on a plan for securing the co-operation of the workmen, and

JEROME K. JEROME

she promised to run down and hear all about it. She would not change her mind about Birmingham, but sent everyone her love.

She wished she had gone when it came to Christmas Day. This feeling of loneliness was growing upon her. The Phillips had gone up north; and the Greysons to some relations of theirs: swell country people in Hampshire. Flossie was on a sea voyage with Sam and his mother, and even Madge had been struck homesick. It happened to be a Sunday, too, of all days in the week, and London in a drizzling rain was just about the limit. She worked till late in the afternoon, but, sitting down to her solitary cup of tea, she felt she wanted to howl. From the basement came faint sounds of laughter. Her landlord and lady were entertaining guests. If they had not been, she would have found some excuse for running down and talking to them, if only for a few minutes.

Suddenly the vision of old Chelsea Church rose up before her with its little motherly old pew-opener. She had so often been meaning to go and see her again, but something had always interfered. She hunted through her drawers and found a comparatively sober-coloured shawl, and tucked it under her cloak. The service was just commencing when she reached the church. Mary Stopperton showed her into a seat and evidently remembered her. "I want to see you afterwards," she whispered; and Mary Stopperton had smiled and nodded. The service, with its need for being continually upon the move, bored her; she was not in the mood for it. And the sermon, preached by a young curate who had not yet got over his Oxford drawl, was uninteresting. She had half hoped that the wheezy old clergyman, who had preached about Calvary on the evening she had first visited the church, would be there again. She wondered what had become of him, and if it were really a fact that she had known him when she was a child, or only her fancy. It was strange how vividly her memory of him seemed to pervade the little church. She had the feeling he was watching her from the shadows. She waited for Mary in the vestibule, and gave her the shawl, making her swear on the big key of the church door that she would wear it herself and not give it away. The little old pew-opener's pink and white face flushed with delight as she took it, and the thin, work-worn hands fingered it admiringly. "But I may lend it?" she pleaded.

They turned up Church Street. Joan confided to Mary what a rotten Christmas she had had, all by herself, without a soul to speak to except her landlady, who had brought her meals and had been in such haste to get away.

"I don't know what made me think of you," she said. "I'm so glad I did." She gave the little old lady a hug. Mary laughed. "Where are you going now, dearie?" she asked.

"Oh, I don't mind so much now," answered Joan. "Now that I've seen a friendly face, I shall go home and go to bed early."

They walked a little way in silence. Mary slipped her hand into Joan's. "You wouldn't care to come home and have a bit of supper with me, would you, dearie?" she asked.

"Oh, may I?" answered Joan.

Mary's hand gave Joan's a little squeeze. "You won't mind if anybody drops in?" she said. "They do sometimes of a Sunday evening."

"You don't mean a party?" asked Joan.

"No, dear," answered Mary. "It's only one or two who have nowhere else to go."

Joan laughed. She thought she would be a fit candidate.

"You see, it makes company for me," explained Mary.

Mary lived in a tiny house behind a strip of garden. It stood in a narrow side street between two public-houses, and was covered with ivy. It had two windows above and a window and a door below. The upstairs rooms belonged to the churchwardens and were used as a storehouse for old parish registers, deemed of little value. Mary Stopperton and her bedridden husband lived in the two rooms below. Mary unlocked the door, and Joan passed in and waited. Mary lit a candle that was standing on a bracket and turned to lead the way.

"Shall I shut the door?" suggested Joan.

Mary blushed like a child that has been found out just as it was hoping that it had not been noticed.

"It doesn't matter, dearie," she explained. "They know, if they find it open, that I'm in."

The little room looked very cosy when Mary had made up the fire and lighted the lamp. She seated Joan in the worn horsehair easy-chair; out of which one had to be careful one did not slip on to the floor; and spread her handsome shawl over the back of the dilapidated sofa.

"You won't mind my running away for a minute," she said. "I shall only be in the next room."

Through the thin partition, Joan heard a constant shrill, complaining voice. At times, it rose into an angry growl. Mary looked in at the door.

"I'm just running round to the doctor's," she whispered. "His medicine hasn't come. I shan't be long."

Joan offered to go in and sit with the invalid. But Mary feared the exertion of talking might be too much for him. "He gets so excited," she explained. She slipped out noiselessly.

It seemed, in spite of its open door, a very silent little house behind its strip of garden. Joan had the feeling that it was listening.

Suddenly she heard a light step in the passage, and the room door opened. A girl entered. She was wearing a large black hat and a black boa round her neck. Between them her face shone unnaturally white. She carried a small cloth bag. She started, on seeing Joan, and seemed about to retreat.

"Oh, please don't go," cried Joan. "Mrs. Stopperton has just gone round to the doctor's. She won't be long. I'm a friend of hers."

The girl took stock of her and, apparently reassured, closed the door behind her.

"What's he like to-night?" she asked, with a jerk of her head in the direction of the next room. She placed her bag carefully upon the sofa, and examined the new shawl as she did so.

"Well, I gather he's a little fretful," answered Joan with a smile.

"That's a bad sign," said the girl. "Means he's feeling better." She seated herself on the sofa and fingered the shawl. "Did you give it her?" she asked.

"Yes," admitted Joan. "I rather fancied her in it."

"She'll only pawn it," said the girl, "to buy him grapes and port wine."

"I felt a bit afraid of her," laughed Joan, "so I made her promise not to part with it. Is he really very ill, her husband?"

"Oh, yes, there's no make-believe this time," answered the girl. "A bad thing for her if he wasn't."

"Oh, it's only what's known all over the neighbourhood," continued the girl. "She's had a pretty rough time with him. Twice I've found her getting ready to go to sleep for the night by sitting on the bare floor with her back against the wall. Had sold every stick in the place and gone off. But she'd always some excuse for him. It was sure to be half her fault and the other half he couldn't help. Now she's got her 'reward' according to her own account. Heard he was dying in a doss-house, and must fetch him home and nurse him back to life. Seems he's getting fonder of her every day. Now that he can't do anything else."

"It doesn't seem to depress her spirits," mused Joan.

"Oh, she! She's all right," agreed the girl. "Having the time of her life: someone to look after for twenty-four hours a day that can't help themselves."

She examined Joan awhile in silence. "Are you on the stage?" she asked.

"No," answered Joan. "But my mother was. Are you?"

"Thought you looked a bit like it," said the girl. "I'm in the chorus. It's better than being in service or in a shop: that's all you can say for it."

"But you'll get out of that," suggested Joan. "You've got the actress face."

The girl flushed with pleasure. It was a striking face, with intelligent eyes and a mobile, sensitive mouth. "Oh, yes," she said, "I could act all right. I feel it. But you don't get out of the chorus. Except at a price."

Joan looked at her. "I thought that sort of thing was dying out," she said.

The girl shrugged her shoulders. "Not in my shop," she answered. "Anyhow, it was the only chance I ever had. Wish sometimes I'd taken it. It was quite a good part."

"They must have felt sure you could act," said Joan. "Next time it will be a clean offer."

The girl shook her head. "There's no next time," she said; "once you're put down as one of the stand-offs. Plenty of others to take your place."

"Oh, I don't blame them," she added. "It isn't a thing to be dismissed with a toss of your head. I thought it all out. Don't know now what decided me. Something inside me, I suppose."

Joan found herself poking the fire. "Have you known Mary Stopperton long?" she asked.

"Oh, yes," answered the girl. "Ever since I've been on my own."

"Did you talk it over with her?" asked Joan.

"No," answered the girl. "I may have just told her. She isn't the sort that gives advice."

"I'm glad you didn't do it," said Joan: "that you put up a fight for all women."

The girl gave a short laugh. "Afraid I wasn't thinking much about that," she said.

"No," said Joan. "But perhaps that's the way the best fights are fought—without thinking."

Mary peeped round the door. She had been lucky enough to find the doctor in. She disappeared again, and they talked about themselves.

JEROME K. JEROME

The girl was a Miss Ensor. She lived by herself in a room in Lawrence Street.

"I'm not good at getting on with people," she explained.

Mary joined them, and went straight to Miss Ensor's bag and opened it. She shook her head at the contents, which consisted of a small, flabby-looking meat pie in a tin dish, and two pale, flat mince tarts.

"It doesn't nourish you, dearie," complained Mary. "You could have bought yourself a nice bit of meat with the same money."

"And you would have had all the trouble of cooking it," answered the girl. "That only wants warming up."

"But I like cooking, you know, dearie," grumbled Mary. "There's no interest in warming things up."

The girl laughed. "You don't have to go far for your fun," she said. "I'll bring a sole next time; and you shall do it *au gratin*."

Mary put the indigestible-looking pasties into the oven, and almost banged the door. Miss Ensor proceeded to lay the table. "How many, do you think?" she asked. Mary was doubtful. She hoped that, it being Christmas Day, they would have somewhere better to go.

"I passed old 'Bubble and Squeak,' just now, spouting away to three men and a dog outside the World's End. I expect he'll turn up," thought Miss Ensor. She laid for four, leaving space for more if need be. "I call it the 'Cadger's Arms,'" she explained, turning to Joan. "We bring our own victuals, and Mary cooks them for us and waits on us; and the more of us the merrier. You look forward to your Sunday evening parties, don't you?" she asked of Mary.

Mary laughed. She was busy in a corner with basins and a saucepan. "Of course I do, dearie," she answered. "I've always been fond of company."

There came another opening of the door. A little hairy man entered. He wore spectacles and was dressed in black. He carried a paper parcel which he laid upon the table. He looked a little doubtful at Joan. Mary introduced them. His name was Julius Simson. He shook hands as if under protest.

"As friends of Mary Stopperton," he said, "we meet on neutral ground. But in all matters of moment I expect we are as far asunder as the poles. I stand for the People."

"We ought to be comrades," answered Joan, with a smile. "I, too, am trying to help the People."

"You and your class," said Mr. Simson, "are friends enough to the People, so long as they remember that they are the People, and keep their proper place—at the bottom. I am for putting the People at the top."

"Then they will be the Upper Classes," suggested Joan. "And I may still have to go on fighting for the rights of the lower orders."

"In this world," explained Mr. Simson, "someone has got to be Master. The only question is who."

Mary had unwrapped the paper parcel. It contained half a sheep's head. "How would you like it done?" she whispered.

Mr. Simson considered. There came a softer look into his eyes. "How did you do it last time?" he asked. "It came up brown, I remember, with thick gravy."

"Braised," suggested Mary.

"That's the word," agreed Mr. Simson. "Braised." He watched while Mary took things needful from the cupboard, and commenced to peel an onion.

"That's the sort that makes me despair of the People," said Mr. Simson. Joan could not be sure whether he was addressing her individually or imaginary thousands. "Likes working for nothing. Thinks she was born to be everybody's servant." He seated himself beside Miss Ensor on the antiquated sofa. It gave a complaining groan but held out.

"Did you have a good house?" the girl asked him. "Saw you from the distance, waving your arms about. Hadn't time to stop."

"Not many," admitted Mr. Simson. "A Christmassy lot. You know. Sort of crowd that interrupts you and tries to be funny. Dead to their own interests. It's slow work."

"Why do you do it?" asked Miss Ensor.

"Damned if I know," answered Mr. Simson, with a burst of candour. "Can't help it, I suppose. Lost me job again."

"The old story?" suggested Miss Ensor.

"The old story," sighed Mr. Simson. "One of the customers happened to be passing last Wednesday when I was speaking on the Embankment. Heard my opinion of the middle classes?"

"Well, you can't expect 'em to like it, can you?" submitted Miss Ensor.

"No," admitted Mr. Simson with generosity. "It's only natural. It's a fight to the finish between me and the Bourgeois. I cover them with ridicule and contempt and they hit back at me in the only way they know."

"Take care they don't get the best of you," Miss Ensor advised him.

"Oh, I'm not afraid," he answered. "I'll get another place all right: give me time. The only thing I'm worried about is my young woman."

"Doesn't agree with you?" inquired Miss Ensor.

"Oh, it isn't that," he answered. "But she's frightened. You know. Says life with me is going to be a bit too uncertain for her. Perhaps she's right."

"Oh, why don't you chuck it," advised Miss Ensor, "give the Bourgeois a rest."

Mr. Simson shook his head. "Somebody's got to tackle them," he said. "Tell them the truth about themselves, to their faces."

"Yes, but it needn't be you," suggested Miss Ensor.

Mary was leaning over the table. Miss Ensor's four-penny veal and ham pie was ready. Mary arranged it in front of her. "Eat it while it's hot, dearie," she counselled. "It won't be so indigestible."

Miss Ensor turned to her. "Oh, you talk to him," she urged. "Here, he's lost his job again, and is losing his girl: all because of his silly politics. Tell him he's got to have sense and stop it."

Mary seemed troubled. Evidently, as Miss Ensor had stated, advice was not her line. "Perhaps he's got to do it, dearie," she suggested.

"What do you mean by got to do it?" exclaimed Miss Ensor. "Who's making him do it, except himself?"

Mary flushed. She seemed to want to get back to her cooking. "It's something inside us, dearie," she thought: "that nobody hears but ourselves."

"That tells him to talk all that twaddle?" demanded Miss Ensor. "Have you heard him?"

"No, dearie," Mary admitted. "But I expect it's got its purpose. Or he wouldn't have to do it."

Miss Ensor gave a gesture of despair and applied herself to her pie. The hirsute face of Mr. Simson had lost the foolish aggressiveness that had irritated Joan. He seemed to be pondering matters.

Mary hoped that Joan was hungry. Joan laughed and admitted that she was. "It's the smell of all the nice things," she explained. Mary promised it should soon be ready, and went back to her corner.

A short, dark, thick-set man entered and stood looking round the room. The frame must once have been powerful, but now it was shrunken and emaciated. The shabby, threadbare clothes hung loosely from the stooping shoulders. Only the head seemed to have retained its vigour. The face, from which the long black hair was brushed straight back, was ghastly white. Out of it, deep set beneath great shaggy, overhanging brows, blazed the fierce, restless eyes of a fanatic. The huge, thin-lipped mouth seemed to have petrified itself into a savage snarl. He gave Joan the idea, as he stood there glaring round him, of a hunted beast at bay.

Miss Ensor, whose bump of reverence was undeveloped, greeted him cheerfully as Boanerges. Mr. Simson, more respectful, rose and offered his small, grimy hand. Mary took his hat and cloak away from him and closed the door behind him. She felt his hands, and put him into a chair close to the fire. And then she introduced him to Joan.

Joan started on hearing his name. It was one well known.

"The Cyril Baptiste?" she asked. She had often wondered what he might be like.

"The Cyril Baptiste," he answered, in a low, even, passionate voice, that he flung at her almost like a blow. "The atheist, the gaol bird, the pariah, the blasphemer, the anti-Christ. I've hoofs instead of feet. Shall I take off my boots and show them to you? I tuck my tail inside my coat. You can't see my horns. I've cut them off close to my head. That's why I wear my hair long: to hide the stumps."

Mary had been searching in the pockets of his cloak. She had found a paper bag. "You mustn't get excited," she said, laying her little work-worn hand upon his shoulder; "or you'll bring on the bleeding."

"Aye," he answered, "I must be careful I don't die on Christmas Day. It would make a fine text, that, for their sermons."

He lapsed into silence: his almost transparent hands stretched out towards the fire.

Mr. Simson fidgeted. The quiet of the room, broken only by Mary's ministering activities, evidently oppressed him.

"Paper going well, sir?" he asked. "I often read it myself."

"It still sells," answered the proprietor, and editor and publisher, and entire staff of *The Rationalist*.

"I like the articles you are writing on the History of Superstition. Quite illuminating," remarked Mr. Simson.

"It's many a year, I am afraid, to the final chapter," thought their author.

"They afford much food for reflection," thought Mr. Simson, "though I cannot myself go as far as you do in including Christianity under that heading."

Mary frowned at him; but Mr. Simson, eager for argument or not noticing, blundered on:—

"Whether we accept the miraculous explanation of Christ's birth," continued Mr. Simson, in his best street-corner voice, "or whether, with the great French writer whose name for the moment escapes me, we regard Him merely as a man inspired, we must, I think, admit that His teaching has been of help: especially to the poor."

The fanatic turned upon him so fiercely that Mr. Simson's arm involuntarily assumed the posture of defence.

"To the poor?" the old man almost shrieked. "To the poor that he has robbed of all power of resistance to oppression by his vile, submissive creed! that he has drugged into passive acceptance of every evil done to them by his false promises that their sufferings here shall win for them some wonderful reward when they are dead. What has been his teaching to the poor? Bow your backs to the lash, kiss the rod that scars your flesh. Be ye humble, oh, my people. Be ye poor in spirit. Let Wrong rule triumphant through the world. Raise no hand against it, lest ye suffer my eternal punishments. Learn from me to be meek and lowly. Learn to be good slaves and give no trouble to your taskmasters. Let them turn the world into a hell for you. The grave—the grave shall be your gate to happiness.

"Helpful to the poor? Helpful to their rulers, to their owners. They take good care that Christ shall be well taught. Their fat priests shall bear his message to the poor. The rod may be broken, the prison door be forced. It is Christ that shall bind the people in eternal fetters. Christ, the lackey, the jackal of the rich."

Mr. Simson was visibly shocked. Evidently he was less familiar with the opinions of *The Rationalist* than he had thought.

"I really must protest," exclaimed Mr. Simson. "To whatever wrong uses His words may have been twisted, Christ Himself I regard as divine, and entitled to be spoken of with reverence. His whole life, His sufferings—"

But the old fanatic's vigour had not yet exhausted itself.

"His sufferings!" he interrupted. "Does suffering entitle a man to be regarded as divine? If so, so also am I a God. Look at me!" He stretched out his long, thin arms with their claw-like hands, thrusting forward his great savage head that the bony, wizened throat seemed hardly strong enough to bear. "Wealth, honour, happiness: I had them once. I had wife, children and a home. Now I creep an outcast, keeping to the shadows, and the children in the street throw stones at me. Thirty years I have starved that I might preach. They shut me in their prisons, they hound me into garrets. They jibe at me and mock me, but they cannot silence me. What of my life? Am I divine?"

Miss Ensor, having finished her supper, sat smoking.

"Why must you preach?" she asked. "It doesn't seem to pay you." There was a curious smile about the girl's lips as she caught Joan's eye.

He turned to her with his last flicker of passion.

"Because to this end was I born, and for this cause came I into the world, that I should bear witness unto the truth," he answered.

He sank back a huddled heap upon the chair. There was foam about his mouth, great beads of sweat upon his forehead. Mary wiped them away with a corner of her apron, and felt again his trembling hands. "Oh, please don't talk to him any more," she pleaded, "not till he's had his supper." She fetched her fine shawl, and pinned it round him. His eyes followed her as she hovered about him. For the first time, since he had entered the room, they looked human.

They gathered round the table. Mr. Baptiste was still pinned up in Mary's bright shawl. It lent him a curious dignity. He might have been some ancient prophet stepped from the pages of the Talmud. Miss Ensor completed her supper with a cup of tea and some little cakes: "just to keep us all company," as Mary had insisted.

The old fanatic's eyes passed from face to face. There was almost the suggestion of a smile about the savage mouth.

"A strange supper-party," he said. "Cyril the Apostate; and Julius who strove against the High Priests and the Pharisees; and Inez a dancer before the people; and Joanna a daughter of the rulers, gathered together in the house of one Mary a servant of the Lord."

"Are you, too, a Christian?" he asked of Joan.

"Not yet," answered Joan. "But I hope to be, one day." She spoke without thinking, not quite knowing what she meant. But it came back to her in after years.

The talk grew lighter under the influence of Mary's cooking. Mr. Baptiste could be interesting when he got away from his fanaticism; and even the apostolic Mr. Simson had sometimes noticed humour when it had chanced his way.

A message came for Mary about ten o'clock, brought by a scared little girl, who whispered it to her at the door. Mary apologized. She had to go out. The party broke up. Mary disappeared into the next room and returned in a shawl and bonnet, carrying a small brown paper parcel. Joan walked with her as far as the King's Road.

"A little child is coming," she confided to Joan. She was quite excited about it.

Joan thought. "It's curious," she said, "one so seldom hears of anybody being born on Christmas Day."

They were passing a lamp. Joan had never seen a face look quite so happy as Mary's looked, just then.

"It always seems to me Christ's birthday," she said, "whenever a child is born."

They had reached the corner. Joan could see her bus in the distance.

She stooped and kissed the little withered face.

"Don't stop," she whispered.

Mary gave her a hug, and almost ran away. Joan watched the little child-like figure growing smaller. It glided in and out among the people.

XI

In the spring, Joan, at Mrs. Denton's request, undertook a mission. It was to go to Paris. Mrs. Denton had meant to go herself, but was laid up with sciatica; and the matter, she considered, would not brook of any delay.

"It's rather a delicate business," she told Joan. She was lying on a couch in her great library, and Joan was seated by her side. "I want someone who can go into private houses and mix with educated people on their own level; and especially I want you to see one or two women: they count in France. You know French pretty well, don't you?"

"Oh, sufficiently," Joan answered. The one thing her mother had done for her had been to talk French with her when she was a child; and at Girton she had chummed on with a French girl, and made herself tolerably perfect.

"You will not go as a journalist," continued Mrs. Denton; "but as a personal friend of mine, whose discretion I shall vouch for. I want you to find out what the people I am sending you among are thinking themselves, and what they consider ought to be done. If we are not very careful on both sides we shall have the newspapers whipping us into war."

The perpetual Egyptian trouble had cropped up again and the Carleton papers, in particular, were already sounding the tocsin. Carleton's argument was that we ought to fall upon France and crush her, before she could develop her supposed submarine menace. His flaming posters were at every corner. Every obscure French newspaper was being ransacked for "Insults and Pinpricks."

"A section of the Paris Press is doing all it can to help him, of course," explained Mrs. Denton. "It doesn't seem to matter to them that Germany is only waiting her opportunity, and that, if Russia comes in, it is bound to bring Austria. Europe will pay dearly one day for the luxury of a free Press."

"But you're surely not suggesting any other kind of Press, at this period of the world's history?" exclaimed Joan.

"Oh, but I am," answered the old lady with a grim tightening of the lips. "Not even Carleton would be allowed to incite to murder or arson. I would have him prosecuted for inciting a nation to war."

"Why is the Press always so eager for war?" mused Joan. "According to their own account, war doesn't pay them."

"I don't suppose it does: not directly," answered Mrs. Denton. "But it helps them to establish their position and get a tighter hold upon the public. War does pay the newspaper in the long run. The daily newspaper lives on commotion, crime, lawlessness in general. If people no longer enjoyed reading about violence and bloodshed half their occupation, and that the most profitable half would be gone. It is the interest of the newspaper to keep alive the savage in human nature; and war affords the readiest means of doing this. You can't do much to increase the number of gruesome murders and loathsome assaults, beyond giving all possible advertisement to them when they do occur. But you can preach war, and cover yourself with glory, as a patriot, at the same time."

"I wonder how many of my ideals will be left to me," sighed Joan. "I always used to regard the Press as the modern pulpit."

"The old pulpit became an evil, the moment it obtained unlimited power," answered Mrs. Denton. "It originated persecution and inflamed men's passions against one another. It, too, preached war for its own ends, taught superstition, and punished thought as a crime. The Press of to-day is stepping into the shoes of the medieval priest. It aims at establishing the worst kind of tyranny: the tyranny over men's minds. They pretend to fight among themselves, but it's rapidly becoming a close corporation. The Institute of Journalists will soon be followed by the Union of Newspaper Proprietors and the few independent journals will be squeezed out. Already we have German shareholders on English papers; and English capital is interested in the St. Petersburg Press. It will one day have its International Pope and its school of cosmopolitan cardinals."

Joan laughed. "I can see Carleton rather fancying himself in a tiara," she said. "I must tell Phillips what you say. He's out for a fight with him. Government by Parliament or Government by Press is going to be his war cry."

"Good man," said Mrs. Denton. "I'm quite serious. You tell him from me that the next revolution has got to be against the Press. And it will be the stiffest fight Democracy has ever had."

The old lady had tired herself. Joan undertook the mission. She thought she would rather enjoy it, and Mrs. Denton promised to let her have full instructions. She would write to her friends in Paris and prepare them for Joan's coming.

Joan remembered Folk, the artist she had met at Flossie's party, who had promised to walk with her on the terrace at St. Germain, and tell her more about her mother. She looked up his address on her return home, and wrote to him, giving him the name of the hotel in the Rue de Grenelle where Mrs. Denton had arranged that she should stay. She found a note from him awaiting her when she arrived there. He thought she would like to be quiet after her journey. He would call round in the morning. He had presumed on the privilege of age to send her some lilies. They had been her mother's favourite flower. "Monsieur Folk, the great artist," had brought them himself, and placed them in her dressing-room, so Madame informed her.

It was one of the half-dozen old hotels still left in Paris, and was built round a garden famous for its mighty mulberry tree. She breakfasted underneath it, and was reading there when Folk appeared before her, smiling and with his hat in his hand. He excused himself for intruding upon her so soon, thinking from what she had written him that her first morning might be his only chance. He evidently considered her remembrance of him a feather in his cap.

"We old fellows feel a little sadly, at times, how unimportant we are," he explained. "We are grateful when Youth throws us a smile."

"You told me my coming would take you back thirty-three years," Joan reminded him. "It makes us about the same age. I shall treat you as just a young man."

He laughed. "Don't be surprised," he said, "if I make a mistake occasionally and call you Lena."

Joan had no appointment till the afternoon. They drove out to St. Germain, and had *dejeuner* at a small restaurant opposite the Chateau; and afterwards they strolled on to the terrace.

"What was my mother doing in Paris?" asked Joan,

"She was studying for the stage," he answered. "Paris was the only school in those days. I was at Julien's studio. We acted together for some charity. I had always been fond of it. An American manager who was present offered us both an engagement, and I thought it would be a change and that I could combine the two arts."

"And it was here that you proposed to her," said Joan.

"Just by that tree that leans forward," he answered, pointing with his cane a little way ahead. "I thought that in America I'd get another chance. I might have if your father hadn't come along. I wonder if he remembers me."

"Did you ever see her again, after her marriage?" asked Joan.

"No," he answered. "We used to write to one another until she gave it

JEROME K. JEROME

up. She had got into the habit of looking upon me as a harmless sort of thing to confide in and ask advice of—which she never took."

"Forgive me," he said. "You must remember that I am still her lover." They had reached the tree that leant a little forward beyond its fellows, and he had halted and turned so that he was facing her. "Did she and your father get on together. Was she happy?"

"I don't think she was happy," answered Joan. "She was at first. As a child, I can remember her singing and laughing about the house, and she liked always to have people about her. Until her illness came. It changed her very much. But my father was gentleness itself, to the end."

They had resumed their stroll. It seemed to her that he looked at her once or twice a little oddly without speaking. "What caused your mother's illness?" he asked, abruptly.

The question troubled her. It struck her with a pang of self-reproach that she had always been indifferent to her mother's illness, regarding it as more or less imaginary. "It was mental rather than physical, I think," she answered. "I never knew what brought it about."

Again he looked at her with that odd, inquisitive expression. "She never got over it?" he asked.

"Oh, there were times," answered Joan, "when she was more like her old self again. But I don't think she ever quite got over it. Unless it was towards the end," she added. "They told me she seemed much better for a little while before she died. I was away at Cambridge at the time."

"Poor dear lady," he said, "all those years! And poor Jack Allway." He seemed to be talking to himself. Suddenly he turned to her. "How is the dear fellow?" he asked.

Again the question troubled her. She had not seen her father since that week-end, nearly six months ago, when she had ran down to see him because she wanted something from him. "He felt my mother's death very deeply," she answered. "But he's well enough in health."

"Remember me to him," he said. "And tell him I thank him for all those years of love and gentleness. I don't think he will be offended."

He drove her back to Paris, and she promised to come and see him in his studio and let him introduce her to his artist friends.

"I shall try to win you over, I warn you," he said. "Politics will never reform the world. They appeal only to men's passions and hatreds. They divide us. It is Art that is going to civilize mankind; broaden his sympathies. Art speaks to him the common language of his loves, his dreams, reveals to him the universal kinship."

Mrs. Denton's friends called upon her, and most of them invited her to their houses. A few were politicians, senators or ministers. Others were bankers, heads of business houses, literary men and women. There were also a few quiet folk with names that were historical. They all thought that war between France and England would be a world disaster, but were not very hopeful of averting it. She learnt that Carleton was in Berlin trying to secure possession of a well-known German daily that happened at the moment to be in low water. He was working for an alliance between Germany and England. In France, the Royalists had come to an understanding with the Clericals, and both were evidently making ready to throw in their lot with the war-mongers, hoping that out of the troubled waters the fish would come their way. Of course everything depended on the people. If the people only knew it! But they didn't. They stood about in puzzled flocks, like sheep, wondering which way the newspaper dog was going to hound them. They took her to the great music halls. Every allusion to war was greeted with rapturous applause. The Marseillaise was demanded and encored till the orchestra rebelled from sheer exhaustion. Joan's patience was sorely tested. She had to listen with impassive face to coarse jests and brutal gibes directed against England and everything English; to sit unmoved while the vast audience rocked with laughter at senseless caricatures of supposed English soldiers whose knees always gave way at the sight of a French uniform. Even in the eyes of her courteous hosts, Joan's quick glance would occasionally detect a curious glint. The fools! Had they never heard of Waterloo and Trafalgar? Even if their memories might be excused for forgetting Crecy and Poictiers and the campaigns of Marlborough. One evening—it had been a particularly trying one for Joan—there stepped upon the stage a wooden-looking man in a kilt with bagpipes under his arm. How he had got himself into the programme Joan could not understand. Managerial watchfulness must have gone to sleep for once. He played Scotch melodies, and the Parisians liked them, and when he had finished they called him back. Joan and her friends occupied a box close to the stage. The wooden-looking Scot glanced up at her, and their eyes met. And as the applause died down there rose the first low warning strains of the Pibroch. Joan sat up in her chair and her lips parted. The savage music quickened. It shrilled and skrealed. The blood came surging through her veins.

And suddenly something lying hidden there leaped to life within her brain. A mad desire surged hold of her to rise and shout defiance at those three thousand pairs of hostile eyes confronting her. She clutched at the arms of her chair and so kept her seat. The pibroch ended with its wild sad notes of wailing, and slowly the mist cleared from her eyes, and the stage was empty. A strange hush had fallen on the house.

She was not aware that her hostess had been watching her. She was a sweet-faced, white-haired lady. She touched Joan lightly on the hand. "That's the trouble," she whispered. "It's in our blood."

Could we ever hope to eradicate it? Was not the survival of this fighting instinct proof that war was still needful to us? In the sculpture-room of an exhibition she came upon a painted statue of Bellona. Its grotesqueness shocked her at first sight, the red streaming hair, the wild eyes filled with fury, the wide open mouth—one could almost hear it screaming—the white uplifted arms with outstretched hands! Appalling! Terrible! And yet, as she gazed at it, gradually the thing grew curiously real to her. She seemed to hear the gathering of the chariots, the neighing of the horses, the hurrying of many feet, the sound of an armouring multitude, the shouting, and the braying of the trumpets.

These cold, thin-lipped calculators, arguing that "War doesn't pay"; those lank-haired cosmopolitans, preaching their "International," as if the only business of mankind were wages! War still was the stern school where men learnt virtue, duty, forgetfulness of self, faithfulness unto death.

This particular war, of course, must be stopped: if it were not already too late. It would be a war for markets; for spheres of commercial influence; a sordid war that would degrade the people. War, the supreme test of a nation's worth, must be reserved for great ideals. Besides, she wanted to down Carleton.

One of the women on her list, and the one to whom Mrs. Denton appeared to attach chief importance, a Madame de Barante, disappointed Joan. She seemed to have so few opinions of her own. She had buried her young husband during the Franco-Prussian war. He had been a soldier. And she had remained unmarried. She was still beautiful.

"I do not think we women have the right to discuss war," she confided to Joan in her gentle, high-bred voice. "I suppose you think that out of date. I should have thought so myself forty years ago. We talk of 'giving' our sons and lovers, as if they were ours to give. It makes me a little angry when I hear pampered women speak like that. It is the men who have to suffer and die. It is for them to decide."

"But perhaps I can arrange a meeting for you with a friend," she added, "who will be better able to help you, if he is in Paris. I will let you know."

She told Joan what she remembered herself of 1870. She had turned her country house into a hospital and had seen a good deal of the fighting.

"It would not do to tell the truth, or we should have our children growing up to hate war," she concluded.

She was as good as her word, and sent Joan round a message the next morning to come and see her in the afternoon. Joan was introduced to a Monsieur de Chaumont. He was a soldierly-looking gentleman, with a grey moustache, and a deep scar across his face.

"Hanged if I can see how we are going to get out of it," he answered Joan cheerfully. "The moment there is any threat of war, it becomes a point of honour with every nation to do nothing to avoid it. I remember my old duelling days. The quarrel may have been about the silliest trifle imaginable. A single word would have explained the whole thing away. But to utter it would have stamped one as a coward. This Egyptian Tra-la-la! It isn't worth the bones of a single grenadier, as our friends across the Rhine would say. But I expect, before it's settled, there will be men's bones sufficient, bleaching on the desert, to build another Pyramid. It's so easily started: that's the devil of it. A mischievous boy can throw a lighted match into a powder magazine, and then it becomes every patriot's business to see that it isn't put out. I hate war. It accomplishes nothing, and leaves everything in a greater muddle than it was before. But if the idea ever catches fire, I shall have to do all I can to fan the conflagration. Unless I am prepared to be branded as a poltroon. Every professional soldier is supposed to welcome war. Most of us do: it's our opportunity. There's some excuse for us. But these men—Carleton and their lot: I regard them as nothing better than the Menades of the Commune. They care nothing if the whole of Europe blazes. They cannot personally get harmed whatever happens. It's fun to them."

"But the people who can get harmed," argued Joan. "The men who will be dragged away from their work, from their business, used as 'cannon fodder.'"

He shrugged his shoulders. "Oh, they are always eager enough for it, at first," he answered. "There is the excitement. The curiosity. You must remember that life is a monotonous affair to the great mass of the people. There's the natural craving to escape from it; to court adventure.

They are not so enthusiastic about it after they have tasted it. Modern warfare, they soon find, is about as dull a business as science ever invented."

There was only one hope that he could see: and that was to switch the people's mind on to some other excitement. His advices from London told him that a parliamentary crisis was pending. Could not Mrs. Denton and her party do something to hasten it? He, on his side, would consult with the Socialist leaders, who might have something to suggest.

He met Joan, radiant, a morning or two later. The English Government had resigned and preparations for a general election were already on foot.

"And God has been good to us, also," he explained.

A well-known artist had been found murdered in his bed and grave suspicion attached to his beautiful young wife.

"She deserves the Croix de Guerre, if it is proved that she did it," he thought. "She will have saved many thousands of lives—for the present."

Folk had fixed up a party at his studio to meet her. She had been there once or twice; but this was a final affair. She had finished her business in Paris and would be leaving the next morning. To her surprise, she found Phillips there. He had come over hurriedly to attend a Socialist conference, and Leblanc, the editor of *Le Nouveau Monde*, had brought him along.

"I took Smedley's place at the last moment," he whispered to her. "I've never been abroad before. You don't mind, do you?"

It didn't strike her as at all odd that a leader of a political party should ask her "if she minded" his being in Paris to attend a political conference. He was wearing a light grey suit and a blue tie. There was nothing about him, at that moment, suggesting that he was a leader of any sort. He might have been just any man, but for his eyes.

"No," she whispered. "Of course not. I don't like your tie." It seemed to depress him, that.

She felt elated at the thought that he would see her for the first time amid surroundings where she would shine. Folk came forward to meet her with that charming air of protective deference that he had adopted towards her. He might have been some favoured minister of state kissing the hand of a youthful Queen. She glanced down the long studio, ending in its fine window overlooking the park. Some of the most distinguished men in Paris were there, and the immediate stir of admiration that her entrance had created was unmistakable. Even the women turned pleased glances at her; as if willing to recognize in her their representative. A sense of power came to her that made her feel kind to all the world. There was no need for her to be clever: to make any effort to attract. Her presence, her sympathy, her approval seemed to be all that was needed of her. She had the consciousness that by the mere exercise of her will she could sway the thoughts and actions of these men: that sovereignty had been given to her. It reflected itself in her slightly heightened colour, in the increased brilliance of her eyes, in the confident case of all her movements. It added a compelling softness to her voice.

She never quite remembered what the talk was about. Men were brought up and presented to her, and hung about her words, and sought to please her. She had spoken her own thoughts, indifferent whether they expressed agreement or not; and the argument had invariably taken another plane. It seemed so important that she should be convinced. Some had succeeded, and had been strengthened. Others had failed, and had departed sorrowful, conscious of the necessity of "thinking it out again."

Guests with other engagements were taking their leave. A piquante little woman, outrageously but effectively dressed—she looked like a drawing by Beardsley—drew her aside. "I've always wished I were a man," she said. "It seemed to me that they had all the power. From this afternoon, I shall be proud of belonging to the governing sex."

She laughed and slipped away.

Phillips was waiting for her in the vestibule. She had forgotten him; but now she felt glad of his humble request to be allowed to see her home. It would have been such a big drop from her crowded hour of triumph to the long lonely cab ride and the solitude of the hotel. She resolved to be gracious, feeling a little sorry for her neglect of him—but reflecting with satisfaction that he had probably been watching her the whole time.

"What's the matter with my tie?" he asked. "Wrong colour?"

She laughed. "Yes," she answered. "It ought to be grey to match your suit. And so ought your socks."

"I didn't know it was going to be such a swell affair, or I shouldn't have come," he said.

She touched his hand lightly.

"I want you to get used to it," she said. "It's part of your work. Put your brain into it, and don't be afraid."

JEROME K. JEROME

"I'll try," he said.

He was sitting on the front seat, facing her. "I'm glad I went," he said with sudden vehemence. "I loved watching you, moving about among all those people. I never knew before how beautiful you are."

Something in his eyes sent a slight thrill of fear through her. It was not an unpleasant sensation—rather exhilarating. She watched the passing street till she felt that his eyes were no longer devouring her.

"You're not offended?" he asked. "At my thinking you beautiful?" he added, in case she hadn't understood.

She laughed. Her confidence had returned to her. "It doesn't generally offend a woman," she answered.

He seemed relieved. "That's what's so wonderful about you," he said. "I've met plenty of clever, brilliant women, but one could forget that they were women. You're everything."

He pleaded, standing below her on the steps of the hotel, that she would dine with him. But she shook her head. She had her packing to do. She could have managed it; but something prudent and absurd had suddenly got hold of her; and he went away with much the same look in his eyes that comes to a dog when he finds that his master cannot be persuaded into an excursion.

She went up to her room. There really was not much to do. She could quite well finish her packing in the morning. She sat down at the desk and set to work to arrange her papers. It was a warm spring evening, and the window was open. A crowd of noisy sparrows seemed to be delighted about something. From somewhere, unseen, a blackbird was singing. She read over her report for Mrs. Denton. The blackbird seemed never to have heard of war. He sang as if the whole world were a garden of languor and love. Joan looked at her watch. The first gong would sound in a few minutes. She pictured the dreary, silent dining-room with its few scattered occupants, and her heart sank at the prospect. To her relief came remembrance of a cheerful but entirely respectable restaurant near to the Louvre to which she had been taken a few nights before. She had noticed quite a number of women dining there alone. She closed her dispatch case with a snap and gave a glance at herself in the great mirror. The blackbird was still singing.

She walked up the Rue des Sts. Peres, enjoying the delicious air. Half way across the bridge she overtook a man, strolling listlessly in front of her. There was something familiar about him. He was wearing a grey suit and had his hands in his pockets. Suddenly the truth flashed upon her. She stopped. If he strolled on, she would be able to slip back. Instead of which he abruptly turned to look down at a passing steamer, and they were face to face.

It made her mad, the look of delight that came into his eyes. She could have boxed his ears. Hadn't he anything else to do but hang about the streets.

He explained that he had been listening to the band in the gardens, returning by the Quai d'Orsay.

"Do let me come with you," he said. "I kept myself free this evening, hoping. And I'm feeling so lonesome."

Poor fellow! She had come to understand that feeling. After all, it wasn't altogether his fault that they had met. And she had been so cross to him!

He was reading every expression on her face.

"It's such a lovely evening," he said. "Couldn't we go somewhere and dine under a tree?"

It would be rather pleasant. There was a little place at Meudon, she remembered. The plane trees would just be in full leaf.

A passing cab had drawn up close to them. The chauffeur was lighting his pipe.

Even Mrs. Grundy herself couldn't object to a journalist dining with a politician!

The stars came out before they had ended dinner. She had made him talk about himself. It was marvellous what he had accomplished with his opportunities. Ten hours a day in the mines had earned for him his living, and the night had given him his leisure. An attic, lighted by a tallow candle, with a shelf of books that left him hardly enough for bread, had been his Alma Mater. History was his chief study. There was hardly an authority Joan could think of with which he was not familiar. *Julius Caesar* was his favourite play. He seemed to know it by heart. At twenty-three he had been elected a delegate, and had entered Parliament at twenty-eight. It had been a life of hardship, of privation, of constant strain; but she found herself unable to pity him. It was a tale of strength, of struggle, of victory, that he told her.

Strength! The shaded lamplight fell upon his fearless kindly face with its flashing eyes and its humorous mouth. He ought to have been drinking out of a horn, not a wine glass that his well-shaped hand could have crushed by a careless pressure. In a winged helmet and a coat of mail he would have looked so much more fitly dressed than in that soft felt hat and ridiculous blue tie.

She led him to talk on about the future. She loved to hear his clear, confident voice with its touch of boyish boastfulness. What was there to stop him? Why should he not climb from power to power till he had reached the end!

And as he talked and dreamed there grew up in her heart a fierce anger. What would her own future be? She would marry probably some man of her own class, settle down to the average woman's "life"; be allowed, like a spoilt child, to still "take an interest" in public affairs: hold "drawing-rooms" attended by cranks and political nonentities: be President, perhaps, of the local Woman's Liberal League. The alternative: to spend her days glued to a desk, penning exhortations to the people that Carleton and his like might or might not allow them to read; while youth and beauty slipped away from her, leaving her one of the ten thousand other lonely, faded women, forcing themselves unwelcome into men's jobs. There came to her a sense of having been robbed of what was hers by primitive eternal law. Greyson had been right. She did love power—power to serve and shape the world. She would have earned it and used it well. She could have helped him, inspired him. They would have worked together: he the force and she the guidance. She would have supplied the things he lacked. It was to her he came for counsel, as it was. But for her he would never have taken the first step. What right had this poor brainless lump of painted flesh to share his wounds, his triumphs? What help could she give him when the time should come that he should need it?

Suddenly he broke off. "What a fool I'm making of myself," he said. "I always was a dreamer."

She forced a laugh. "Why shouldn't it come true?" she asked.

They had the little garden to themselves. The million lights of Paris shone below them.

"Because you won't be there," he answered, "and without you I can't do it. You think I'm always like I am to-night, bragging, confident. So I am when you are with me. You give me back my strength. The plans and hopes and dreams that were slipping from me come crowding round me, laughing and holding out their hands. They are like the children. They need two to care for them. I want to talk about them to someone who understands them and loves them, as I do. I want to feel they are dear to someone else, as well as to myself: that I must work for them for her sake, as well as for my own. I want someone to help me to bring them up."

There were tears in his eyes. He brushed them angrily away. "Oh, I know I ought to be ashamed of myself," he said. "It wasn't her fault. She wasn't to know that a hot-blooded young chap of twenty hasn't all his wits about him, any more than I was. If I had never met you, it wouldn't have mattered. I'd have done my bit of good, and have stopped there, content. With you beside me"—he looked away from her to where the silent city peeped through its veil of night—"I might have left the world better than I found it."

The blood had mounted to her face. She drew back into the shadow, beyond the tiny sphere of light made by the little lamp.

"Men have accomplished great things without a woman's help," she said.

"Some men," he answered. "Artists and poets. They have the woman within them. Men like myself—the mere fighter: we are incomplete in ourselves. Male and female created He them. We are lost without our mate."

He was thinking only of himself. Had he no pity for her. So was she, also, useless without her mate. Neither was she of those, here and there, who can stand alone. Her task was that of the eternal woman: to make a home: to cleanse the world of sin and sorrow, make it a kinder dwelling-place for the children that should come. This man was her true helpmeet. He would have been her weapon, her dear servant; and she could have rewarded him as none other ever could. The lamplight fell upon his ruddy face, his strong white hands resting on the flimsy table. He belonged to an older order than her own. That suggestion about him of something primitive, of something not yet altogether tamed. She felt again that slight thrill of fear that so strangely excited her. A mist seemed to be obscuring all things. He seemed to be coming towards her. Only by keeping her eyes fixed on his moveless hands, still resting on the table, could she convince herself that his arms were not closing about her, that she was not being drawn nearer and nearer to him, powerless to resist.

Suddenly, out of the mist, she heard voices. The waiter was standing beside him with the bill. She reached out her hand and took it. The usual few mistakes had occurred. She explained them, good temperedly, and the waiter, with profuse apologies, went back to have it corrected.

He turned to her as the man went. "Try and forgive me," he said in a low voice. "It all came tumbling out before I thought what I was saying."

JEROME K. JEROME

The blood was flowing back into her veins. "Oh, it wasn't your fault," she answered. "We must make the best we can of it."

He bent forward so that he could see into her eyes.

"Tell me," he said. There was a note of fierce exultation in his voice. "I'll promise never to speak of it again. If I had been a free man, could I have won you?"

She had risen while he was speaking. She moved to him and laid her hands upon his shoulders.

"Will you serve me and fight for me against all my enemies?" she asked.

"So long as I live," he answered.

She glanced round. There was no sign of the returning waiter. She bent over him and kissed him.

"Don't come with me," she said. "There's a cab stand in the Avenue. I shall walk to Sevres and take the train."

She did not look back.

XII

S he reached home in the evening. The Phillips's old rooms had been twice let since Christmas, but were now again empty. The McKean with his silent ways and his everlasting pipe had gone to America to superintend the production of one of his plays. The house gave her the feeling of being haunted. She had her dinner brought up to her and prepared for a long evening's work; but found herself unable to think—except on the one subject that she wanted to put off thinking about. To her relief the last post brought her a letter from Arthur. He had been called to Lisbon to look after a contract, and would be away for a fortnight. Her father was not as well as he had been.

It seemed to just fit in. She would run down and spend a few quiet days at Liverpool. In her old familiar room where the moon peeped in over the tops of the tall pines she would be able to reason things out. Perhaps her father would be able to help her. She had lost her childish conception of him as of someone prim and proper, with cut and dried formulas for all occasions. That glimpse he had shown her of himself had established a fellowship between them. He, too, had wrestled with life's riddles, not sure of his own answers. She found him suffering from his old heart trouble, but more cheerful than she had known him for years. Arthur seemed to be doing wonders with the men. They were coming to trust him.

"The difficulty I have always been up against," explained her father, "has been their suspicion. 'What's the cunning old rascal up to now? What's his little game?' That is always what I have felt they were thinking to themselves whenever I have wanted to do anything for them. It isn't anything he says to them. It seems to be just he, himself."

He sketched out their plans to her. It seemed to be all going in at one ear and out at the other. What was the matter with her? Perhaps she was tired without knowing it. She would get him to tell her all about it to-morrow. Also, to-morrow, she would tell him about Phillips, and ask his advice. It was really quite late. If he talked any more now, it would give her a headache. She felt it coming on.

She made her "good-night" extra affectionate, hoping to disguise her impatience. She wanted to get up to her own room.

But even that did not help her. It seemed in some mysterious way to be no longer her room, but the room of someone she had known and half forgotten: who would never come back. It gave her the same feeling she had experienced on returning to the house in London: that the place was haunted. The high cheval glass from her mother's dressing-room had been brought there for her use. The picture of an absurdly small child—the child to whom this room had once belonged—standing before it naked, rose before her eyes. She had wanted to see herself. She had thought that only her clothes stood in the way. If we could but see ourselves, as in some magic mirror? All the garments usage and education has dressed us up in laid aside. What was she underneath her artificial niceties, her prim moralities, her laboriously acquired restraints, her unconscious pretences and hypocrisies? She changed her clothes for a loose robe, and putting out the light drew back the curtains. The moon peeped in over the top of the tall pines, but it only stared at her, indifferent. It seemed to be looking for somebody else.

Suddenly, and intensely to her own surprise, she fell into a passionate fit of weeping. There was no reason for it, and it was altogether so unlike her. But for quite a while she was unable to control it. Gradually, and of their own accord, her sobs lessened, and she was able to wipe her eyes and take stock of herself in the long glass. She wondered for the moment whether it was really her own reflection that she saw there or that of some ghostly image of her mother. She had so often seen the same look in her mother's eyes. Evidently the likeness between them was more extensive than she had imagined. For the first time she became conscious of an emotional, hysterical side to her nature of which she had been unaware. Perhaps it was just as well that she had discovered it. She would have to keep a stricter watch upon herself. This question of her future relationship with Phillips: it would have to be thought out coldly, dispassionately. Nothing unexpected must be allowed to enter into it.

It was some time before she fell asleep. The high glass faced her as she lay in bed. She could not get away from the idea that it was her mother's face that every now and then she saw reflected there.

She woke late the next morning. Her father had already left for the works. She was rather glad to have no need of talking. She would take a long walk into the country, and face the thing squarely with the help of the cheerful sun and the free west wind that was blowing from the sea. She took the train up north and struck across the hills. Her spirits rose as she walked.

It was only the intellectual part of him she wanted—the spirit, not the man. She would be taking nothing away from the woman, nothing that had ever belonged to her. All the rest of him: his home life, the benefits that would come to her from his improved means, from his social position: all that the woman had ever known or cared for in him would still be hers. He would still remain to her the kind husband and father. What more was the woman capable of understanding? What more had she any right to demand?

It was not of herself she was thinking. It was for his work's sake that she wanted to be near to him always: that she might counsel him, encourage him. For this she was prepared to sacrifice herself, give up her woman's claim on life. They would be friends, comrades—nothing more. That little lurking curiosity of hers, concerning what it would be like to feel his strong arms round her, pressing her closer and closer to him: it was only a foolish fancy. She could easily laugh that out of herself. Only bad women had need to be afraid of themselves. She would keep guard for both of them. Their purity of motive, their high purpose, would save them from the danger of anything vulgar or ridiculous.

Of course they would have to be careful. There must be no breath of gossip, no food for evil tongues. About that she was determined even more for his sake than her own. It would be fatal to his career. She was quite in agreement with the popular demand, supposed to be peculiarly English, that a public man's life should be above reproach. Of what use these prophets without self-control; these social reformers who could not shake the ape out of themselves? Only the brave could give courage to others. Only through the pure could God's light shine upon men.

It was vexing his having moved round the corner, into North Street. Why couldn't the silly woman have been content where she was. Living under one roof, they could have seen one another as often as was needful without attracting attention. Now, she supposed, she would have to be more than ever the bosom friend of Mrs. Phillips—spend hours amid that hideous furniture, surrounded by those bilious wallpapers. Of course he could not come to her. She hoped he would appreciate the sacrifice she would be making for him. Fortunately Mrs. Phillips would give no trouble. She would not even understand.

What about Hilda? No hope of hiding their secret from those sharp eyes. But Hilda would approve. They could trust Hilda. The child might prove helpful.

JEROME K. JEROME

It cast a passing shadow upon her spirits, this necessary descent into details. It brought with it the suggestion of intrigue, of deceit: robbing the thing, to a certain extent, of its fineness. Still, what was to be done? If women were coming into public life these sort of relationships with men would have to be faced and worked out. Sex must no longer be allowed to interfere with the working together of men and women for common ends. It was that had kept the world back. They would be the pioneers of the new order. Casting aside their earthly passions, humbly with pure hearts they would kneel before God's altar. He should bless their union.

A lark was singing. She stood listening. Higher and higher he rose, pouring out his song of worship; till the tiny, fragile body disappeared as if fallen from him, leaving his sweet soul still singing. The happy tears came to her eyes, and she passed on. She did not hear that little last faint sob with which he sank exhausted back to earth beside a hidden nest among the furrows.

She had forgotten the time. It was already late afternoon. Her long walk and the keen air had made her hungry. She had a couple of eggs with her tea at a village inn, and was fortunate enough to catch a train that brought her back in time for dinner. A little ashamed of her unresponsiveness the night before, she laid herself out to be sympathetic to her father's talk. She insisted on hearing again all that he and Arthur were doing, opposing him here and there with criticism just sufficient to stimulate him; careful in the end to let him convince her.

These small hypocrisies were new to her. She hoped she was not damaging her character. But it was good, watching him slyly from under drawn-down lids, to see the flash of triumph that would come into his tired eyes in answer to her half-protesting: "Yes, I see your point, I hadn't thought of that," her half reluctant admission that "perhaps" he was right, there; that "perhaps" she was wrong. It was delightful to see him young again, eager, boyishly pleased with himself. It seemed there was a joy she had not dreamed of in yielding victory as well as in gaining it. A new tenderness was growing up in her. How considerate, how patient, how self-forgetful he had always been. She wanted to mother him. To take him in her arms and croon over him, hushing away remembrance of the old sad days.

Folk's words came back to her: "And poor Jack Allway. Tell him I thank him for all those years of love and gentleness." She gave him the message.

Folk had been right. He was not offended. "Dear old chap," he said. "That was kind of him. He was always generous."

He was silent for a while, with a quiet look on his face.

"Give him our love," he said. "Tell him we came together, at the end."

It was on her tongue to ask him, as so often she had meant to do of late, what had been the cause of her mother's illness—if illness it was: what it was that had happened to change both their lives. But always something had stopped her—something ever present, ever watchful, that seemed to shape itself out of the air, bending towards her with its finger on its lips.

She stayed over the week-end; and on the Saturday, at her suggestion, they took a long excursion into the country. It was the first time she had ever asked him to take her out. He came down to breakfast in a new suit, and was quite excited. In the car his hand had sought hers shyly, and, feeling her responsive pressure, he had continued to hold it; and they had sat for a long time in silence. She decided not to tell him about Phillips, just yet. He knew of him only from the Tory newspapers and would form a wrong idea. She would bring them together and leave Phillips to make his own way. He would like Phillips when he knew him, she felt sure. He, too, was a people's man. The torch passed down to him from his old Ironside ancestors, it still glowed. More than once she had seen it leap to flame. In congenial atmosphere, it would burn clear and steadfast. It occurred to her what a delightful solution of her problem, if later on her father could be persuaded to leave Arthur in charge of the works, and come to live with her in London. There was a fine block of flats near Chelsea Church with long views up and down the river. How happy they could be there; the drawing-room in the Adams style with wine-coloured curtains! He was a father any young woman could be proud to take about. Unconsciously she gave his hand an impulsive squeeze. They lunched at an old inn upon the moors; and the landlady, judging from his shy, attentive ways, had begun by addressing her as Madame.

"You grow wonderfully like your mother," he told her that evening at dinner. "There used to be something missing. But I don't feel that, now."

She wrote to Phillips to meet her, if possible, at Euston. There were things she wanted to talk to him about. There was the question whether she should go on writing for Carleton, or break with him at once. Also one or two points that were worrying her in connection with tariff reform. He was waiting for her on the platform. It appeared he, too,

JEROME K. JEROME

had much to say. He wanted her advice concerning his next speech. He had not dined and suggested supper. They could not walk about the streets. Likely enough, it was only her imagination, but it seemed to her that people in the restaurant had recognized him, and were whispering to one another: he was bound to be well known. Likewise her own appearance, she felt, was against them as regarded their desire to avoid observation. She would have to take to those mousey colours that did not suit her, and wear a veil. She hated the idea of a veil. It came from the East and belonged there. Besides, what would be the use? Unless he wore one too. "Who is the veiled woman that Phillips goes about with?" That is what they would ask. It was going to be very awkward, the whole thing. Viewed from the distance, it had looked quite fine. "Dedicating herself to the service of Humanity" was how it had presented itself to her in the garden at Meudon, the twinkling labyrinth of Paris at her feet, its sordid by-ways hidden beneath its myriad lights. She had not bargained for the dedication involving the loss of her self-respect.

They did not talk as much as they had thought they would. He was not very helpful on the Carleton question. There was so much to be said both for and against. It might be better to wait and see how circumstances shaped themselves. She thought his speech excellent. It was difficult to discover any argument against it.

He seemed to be more interested in looking at her when he thought she was not noticing. That little faint vague fear came back to her and stayed with her, but brought no quickening of her pulse. It was a fear of something ugly. She had the feeling they were both acting, that everything depended upon their not forgetting their parts. In handing things to one another, they were both of them so careful that their hands should not meet and touch.

They walked together back to Westminster and wished each other a short good-night upon what once had been their common doorstep. With her latchkey in her hand, she turned and watched his retreating figure, and suddenly a wave of longing seized her to run after him and call him back—to see his eyes light up and feel the pressure of his hands. It was only by clinging to the railings and counting till she was sure he had entered his own house round the corner and closed the door behind him, that she restrained herself.

It was a frightened face that looked at her out of the glass, as she stood before it taking off her hat.

She decided that their future meetings should be at his own house. Mrs. Phillips's only complaint was that she knocked at the door too seldom.

"I don't know what I should do without you, I really don't," confessed the grateful lady. "If ever I become a Prime Minister's wife, it's you I shall have to thank. You've got so much courage yourself, you can put the heart into him. I never had any pluck to spare myself."

She concluded by giving Joan a hug, accompanied by a sloppy but heartfelt kiss.

She would stand behind Phillips's chair with her fat arms round his neck, nodding her approval and encouragement; while Joan, seated opposite, would strain every nerve to keep her brain fixed upon the argument, never daring to look at poor Phillips's wretched face, with its pleading, apologetic eyes, lest she should burst into hysterical laughter. She hoped she was being helpful and inspiring! Mrs. Phillips would assure her afterwards that she had been wonderful. As for herself, there were periods when she hadn't the faintest idea about what she was talking.

Sometimes Mrs. Phillips, called away by domestic duty, would leave them; returning full of excuses just as they had succeeded in forgetting her. It was evident she was under the impression that her presence was useful to them, making it easier for them to open up their minds to one another.

"Don't you be put off by his seeming a bit unresponsive," Mrs. Phillips would explain. "He's shy with women. What I'm trying to do is to make him feel you are one of the family."

"And don't you take any notice of me," further explained the good woman, "when I seem to be in opposition, like. I chip in now and then on purpose, just to keep the ball rolling. It stirs him up, a bit of contradictoriness. You have to live with a man before you understand him."

One morning Joan received a letter from Phillips, marked immediate. He informed her that his brain was becoming addled. He intended that afternoon to give it a draught of fresh air. He would be at the Robin Hood gate in Richmond Park at three o'clock. Perhaps the gods would be good to him. He would wait there for half an hour to give them a chance, anyway.

She slipped the letter unconsciously into the bosom of her dress, and sat looking out of the window. It promised to be a glorious day, and

JEROME K. JEROME

London was stifling and gritty. Surely no one but an unwholesome-minded prude could jib at a walk across a park. Mrs. Phillips would be delighted to hear that she had gone. For the matter of that, she would tell her—when next they met.

Phillips must have seen her getting off the bus, for he came forward at once from the other side of the gate, his face radiant with boyish delight. A young man and woman, entering the park at the same time, looked at them and smiled sympathetically.

Joan had no idea the park contained such pleasant by-ways. But for an occasional perambulator they might have been in the heart of the country. The fallow deer stole near to them with noiseless feet, regarding them out of their large gentle eyes with looks of comradeship. They paused and listened while a missal thrush from a branch close to them poured out his song of hope and courage. From quite a long way off they could still hear his clear voice singing, telling to the young and brave his gallant message. It seemed too beautiful a day for politics. After all, politics—one has them always with one; but the spring passes.

He saw her on to a bus at Kingston, and himself went back by train. They agreed they would not mention it to Mrs. Phillips. Not that she would have minded. The danger was that she would want to come, too; honestly thinking thereby to complete their happiness. It seemed to be tacitly understood there would be other such excursions.

The summer was propitious. Phillips knew his London well, and how to get away from it. There were winding lanes in Hertfordshire, Surrey hills and commons, deep, cool, bird-haunted woods in Buckingham. Each week there was something to look forward to, something to plan for and manoeuvre. The sense of adventure, a spice of danger, added zest. She still knocked frequently, as before, at the door of the hideously-furnished little house in North Street; but Mrs. Phillips no longer oppressed her as some old man of the sea she could never hope to shake off from her shoulders. The flabby, foolish face, robbed of its terrors, became merely pitiful. She found herself able to be quite gentle and patient with Mrs. Phillips. Even the sloppy kisses she came to bear without a shudder down her spine.

"I know you are only doing it because you sympathize with his aims and want him to win," acknowledged the good lady. "But I can't help feeling grateful to you. I don't feel how useless I am while I've got you to run to."

They still discussed their various plans for the amelioration and improvement of humanity; but there seemed less need for haste than they had thought. The world, Joan discovered, was not so sad a place as she had judged it. There were chubby, rogue-eyed children; whistling lads and smiling maidens; kindly men with ruddy faces; happy mothers crooning over gurgling babies. There was no call to be fretful and vehement. They would work together in patience and in confidence. God's sun was everywhere. It needed only that dark places should be opened up and it would enter.

Sometimes, seated on a lichened log, or on the short grass of some sloping hillside, looking down upon some quiet valley, they would find they had been holding hands while talking. It was but as two happy, thoughtless children might have done. They would look at one another with frank, clear eyes and smile.

Once, when their pathway led through a littered farm-yard, he had taken her up in his arms and carried her and she had felt a glad pride in him that he had borne her lightly as if she had been a child, looking up at her and laughing.

An old bent man paused from his work and watched them. "Lean more over him, missie," he advised her. "That's the way. Many a mile I've carried my lass like that, in flood time; and never felt her weight."

Often on returning home, not knowing why, she would look into the glass. It seemed to her that the girlhood she had somehow missed was awakening in her, taking possession of her, changing her. The lips she had always seen pressed close and firm were growing curved, leaving a little parting, as though they were not quite so satisfied with one another. The level brows were becoming slightly raised. It gave her a questioning look that was new to her. The eyes beneath were less confident. They seemed to be seeking something.

One evening, on her way home from a theatre, she met Flossie. "Can't stop now," said Flossie, who was hurrying. "But I want to see you: most particular. Was going to look you up. Will you be at home to-morrow afternoon at tea-time?"

There was a distinct challenge in Flossie's eye as she asked the question. Joan felt herself flush, and thought a moment.

"Yes," she answered. "Will you be coming alone?"

"That's the idea," answered Flossie; "a heart to heart talk between you and me, and nobody else. Half-past four. Don't forget."

Joan walked on slowly. She had the worried feeling with which, once or twice, when a schoolgirl, she had crawled up the stairs to bed after the head mistress had informed her that she would see her in her private room at eleven o'clock the next morning, leaving her to guess what about. It occurred to her, in Trafalgar Square, that she had promised to take tea with the Greysons the next afternoon, to meet some big pot from America. She would have to get out of that. She felt it wouldn't do to put off Flossie.

She went to bed wakeful. It was marvellously like being at school again. What could Flossie want to see her about that was so important? She tried to pretend to herself that she didn't know. After all, perhaps it wasn't that.

But she knew that it was the instant Flossie put up her hands in order to take off her hat. Flossie always took off her hat when she meant to be unpleasant. It was her way of pulling up her sleeves. They had their tea first. They seemed both agreed that that would be best. And then Flossie pushed back her chair and sat up.

She had just the head mistress expression. Joan wasn't quite sure she oughtn't to stand. But, controlling the instinct, leant back in her chair, and tried to look defiant without feeling it.

"How far are you going?" demanded Flossie.

Joan was not in a comprehending mood.

"If you're going the whole hog, that's something I can understand," continued Flossie. "If not, you'd better pull up."

"What do you mean by the whole hog?" requested Joan, assuming dignity.

"Oh, don't come the kid," advised Flossie. "If you don't mind being talked about yourself, you might think of him. If Carleton gets hold of it, he's done for."

"'A little bird whispers to me that Robert Phillips was seen walking across Richmond Park the other afternoon in company with Miss Joan Allway, formerly one of our contributors.' Is that going to end his political career?" retorted Joan with fine sarcasm.

Flossie fixed a relentless eye upon her. "He'll wait till the bird has got a bit more than that to whisper to him," she suggested.

"There'll be nothing more," explained Joan. "So long as my friendship is of any assistance to Robert Phillips in his work, he's going to have it. What use are we going to be in politics—what's all the fuss about, if men and women mustn't work together for their common aims and help one another?"

"Why can't you help him in his own house, instead of wandering all about the country?" Flossie wanted to know.

"So I do," Joan defended herself. "I'm in and out there till I'm sick of the hideous place. You haven't seen the inside. And his wife knows all about it, and is only too glad."

"Does she know about Richmond Park—and the other places?" asked Flossie.

"She wouldn't mind if she did," explained Joan. "And you know what she's like! How can one think what one's saying with that silly, goggle-eyed face in front of one always."

Flossie, since she had become engaged, had acquired quite a matronly train of thought. She spoke kindly, with a little grave shake of her head. "My dear," she said, "the wife is always in the way. You'd feel just the same whatever her face was like."

Joan grew angry. "If you choose to suspect evil, of course you can," she answered with hauteur. "But you might have known me better. I admire the man and sympathize with him. All the things I dream of are the things he is working for. I can do more good by helping and inspiring him"—she wished she had not let slip that word "inspire." She knew that Flossie would fasten upon it—"than I can ever accomplish by myself. And I mean to do it." She really did feel defiant, now.

"I know, dear," agreed Flossie, "you've both of you made up your minds it shall always remain a beautiful union of twin spirits. Unfortunately you've both got bodies—rather attractive bodies."

"We'll keep it off that plane, if you don't mind," answered Joan with a touch of severity.

"I'm willing enough," answered Flossie. "But what about Old Mother Nature? She's going to be in this, you know."

"Take off your glasses, and look at it straight," she went on, without giving Joan time to reply. "What is it in us that 'inspires' men? If it's only advice and sympathy he's after, what's wrong with dear old Mrs. Denton? She's a good walker, except now and then, when she's got the lumbago. Why doesn't he get her to 'inspire' him?"

"It isn't only that," explained Joan. "I give him courage. I always did have more of that than is any use to a woman. He wants to be worthy of my belief in him. What is the harm if he does admire me—if a smile from me or a touch of the hand can urge him to fresh effort? Suppose he does love me—"

Flossie interrupted. "How about being quite frank?" she suggested. "Suppose we do love one another. How about putting it that way?"

"And suppose we do?" agreed Joan, her courage rising. "Why should we shun one another, as if we were both of us incapable of decency or self-control? Why must love be always assumed to make us weak and contemptible, as if it were some subtle poison? Why shouldn't it strengthen and ennoble us?"

"Why did the apple fall?" answered Flossie. "Why, when it escapes from its bonds, doesn't it soar upward? If it wasn't for the irritating law of gravity, we could skip about on the brink of precipices without danger. Things being what they are, sensible people keep as far away from the edge as possible."

"I'm sorry," she continued; "awfully sorry, old girl. It's a bit of rotten bad luck for both of you. You were just made for one another. And Fate, knowing what was coming, bustles round and gets hold of poor, silly Mrs. Phillips so as to be able to say 'Yah.'"

"Unless it all comes right in the end," she added musingly; "and the poor old soul pegs out. I wouldn't give much for her liver."

"That's not bringing me up well," suggested Joan: "putting those ideas into my head."

"Oh, well, one can't help one's thoughts," explained Flossie. "It would be a blessing all round."

They had risen. Joan folded her hands. "Thank you for your scolding, ma'am," she said. "Shall I write out a hundred lines of Greek? Or do you think it will be sufficient if I promise never to do it again?"

"You mean it?" said Flossie. "Of course you will go on seeing him—visiting them, and all that. But you won't go gadding about, so that people can talk?"

"Only through the bars, in future," she promised. "With the gaoler between us." She put her arms round Flossie and bent her head, so that her face was hidden.

Flossie still seemed troubled. She held on to Joan.

"You are sure of yourself?" she asked. "We're only the female of the species. We get hungry and thirsty, too. You know that, kiddy, don't you?"

Joan laughed without raising her face. "Yes, ma'am, I know that," she answered. "I'll be good."

She sat in the dusk after Flossie had gone; and the laboured breathing of the tired city came to her through the open window. She had rather fancied that martyr's crown. It had not looked so very heavy, the thorns not so very alarming—as seen through the window. She would wear it bravely. It would rather become her.

Facing the mirror of the days to come, she tried it on. It was going to hurt. There was no doubt of that. She saw the fatuous, approving face of the eternal Mrs. Phillips, thrust ever between them, against the background of that hideous furniture, of those bilious wall papers— the loneliness that would ever walk with her, sit down beside her in the crowded restaurant, steal up the staircase with her, creep step by step with her from room to room—the ever unsatisfied yearning for a tender word, a kindly touch. Yes, it was going to hurt.

Poor Robert! It would be hard on him, too. She could not help feeling consolation in the thought that he also would be wearing that invisible crown.

She must write to him. The sooner it was done, the better. Half a dozen contradictory moods passed over her during the composing of that letter; but to her they seemed but the unfolding of a single thought. On one page it might have been his mother writing to him; an experienced, sagacious lady; quite aware, in spite of her affection for him, of his faults and weaknesses; solicitous that he should avoid the dangers of an embarrassing entanglement; his happiness being the only consideration of importance. On others it might have been a queen laying her immutable commands upon some loyal subject, sworn to her service. Part of it might have been written by a laughing philosopher who had learnt the folly of taking life too seriously, knowing that all things pass: that the tears of to-day will be remembered with a smile. And a part of it was the unconsidered language of a loving woman. And those were the pages that he kissed.

His letter in answer was much shorter. Of course he would obey her wishes. He had been selfish, thinking only of himself. As for his political career, he did not see how that was going to suffer by his being occasionally seen in company with one of the most brilliantly intellectual women in London, known to share his views. And he didn't care if it did. But inasmuch as she valued it, all things should be sacrificed to it. It was hers to do what she would with. It was the only thing he had to offer her.

Their meetings became confined, as before, to the little house in North Street. But it really seemed as if the gods, appeased by their submission, had decided to be kind. Hilda was home for the holidays;

and her piercing eyes took in the situation at a flash. She appeared to have returned with a new-born and exacting affection for her mother, that astonished almost as much as it delighted the poor lady. Feeling sudden desire for a walk or a bus ride, or to be taken to an entertainment, no one was of any use to Hilda but her mother. Daddy had his silly politics to think and talk about. He must worry them out alone; or with the assistance of Miss Allway. That was what she was there for. Mrs. Phillips, torn between her sense of duty and fear of losing this new happiness, would yield to the child's coaxing. Often they would be left alone to discuss the nation's needs uninterrupted. Conscientiously they would apply themselves to the task. Always to find that, sooner or later, they were looking at one another, in silence.

One day Phillips burst into a curious laugh. They had been discussing the problem of the smallholder. Joan had put a question to him, and with a slight start he had asked her to repeat it. But it seemed she had forgotten it.

"I had to see our solicitor one morning," he explained, "when I was secretary to a miners' union up north. A point had arisen concerning the legality of certain payments. It was a matter of vast importance to us; but he didn't seem to be taking any interest, and suddenly he jumped up. 'I'm sorry, Phillips,' he said, 'but I've got a big trouble of my own on at home—I guess you know what—and I don't seem to care a damn about yours. You'd better see Delauny, if you're in a hurry.' And I did."

He turned and leant over his desk. "I guess they'll have to find another leader if they're in a hurry," he added. "I don't seem able to think about turnips and cows."

"Don't make me feel I've interfered with your work only to spoil it," said Joan.

"I guess I'm spoiling yours, too," he answered. "I'm not worth it. I might have done something to win you and keep you. I'm not going to do much without you."

"You mean my friendship is going to be of no use to you?" asked Joan.

He raised his eyes and fixed them on her with a pleading, dog-like look.

"For God's sake don't take even that away from me," he said. "Unless you want me to go to pieces altogether. A crust does just keep one alive. One can't help thinking what a fine, strong chap one might be if one wasn't always hungry."

She felt so sorry for him. He looked such a boy, with the angry tears in his clear blue eyes, and that little childish quivering of the kind, strong, sulky mouth.

She rose and took his head between her hands and turned his face towards her. She had meant to scold him, but changed her mind and laid his head against her breast and held it there.

He clung to her, as a troubled child might, with his arms clasped round her, and his head against her breast. And a mist rose up before her, and strange, commanding voices seemed calling to her.

He could not see her face. She watched it herself with dim half consciousness as it changed before her in the tawdry mirror above the mantelpiece, half longing that he might look up and see it, half terrified lest he should.

With an effort that seemed to turn her into stone, she regained command over herself.

"I must go now," she said in a harsh voice, and he released her.

"I'm afraid I'm an awful nuisance to you," he said. "I get these moods at times. You're not angry with me?"

"No," she answered with a smile. "But it will hurt me if you fail. Remember that."

She turned down the Embankment after leaving the house. She always found the river strong and restful. So it was not only bad women that needed to be afraid of themselves—even to the most high-class young woman, with letters after her name, and altruistic interests: even to her, also, the longing for the lover's clasp. Flossie had been right. Mother Nature was not to be flouted of her children—not even of her new daughters; to them, likewise, the family trait.

She would have run away if she could, leaving him to guess at her real reason—if he were smart enough. But that would have meant excuses and explanations all round. She was writing a daily column of notes for Greyson now, in addition to the weekly letter from Clorinda; and Mrs. Denton, having compromised with her first dreams, was delegating to Joan more and more of her work. She wrote to Mrs. Phillips that she was feeling unwell and would be unable to lunch with them on the Sunday, as had been arranged. Mrs. Phillips, much disappointed, suggested Wednesday; but it seemed on Wednesday she was no better. And so it drifted on for about a fortnight, without her finding the courage to come to any decision; and then one morning, turning the corner into Abingdon Street, she felt a slight pull at her sleeve; and

Hilda was beside her. The child had shown an uncanny intuition in not knocking at the door. Joan had been fearing that, and would have sent down word that she was out. But it had to be faced.

"Are you never coming again?" asked the child.

"Of course," answered Joan, "when I'm better. I'm not very well just now. It's the weather, I suppose."

The child turned her head as they walked and looked at her. Joan felt herself smarting under that look, but persisted.

"I'm very much run down," she said. "I may have to go away."

"You promised to help him," said the child.

"I can't if I'm ill," retorted Joan. "Besides, I am helping him. There are other ways of helping people than by wasting their time talking to them."

"He wants you," said the child. "It's your being there that helps him."

Joan stopped and turned. "Did he send you?" she asked.

"No," the child answered. "Mama had a headache this morning, and I slipped out. You're not keeping your promise."

Palace Yard, save for a statuesque policeman, was empty.

"How do you know that my being with him helps him?" asked Joan.

"You know things when you love anybody," explained the child. "You feel them. You will come again, soon?"

Joan did not answer.

"You're frightened," the child continued in a passionate, low voice. "You think that people will talk about you and look down upon you. You oughtn't to think about yourself. You ought to think only about him and his work. Nothing else matters."

"I am thinking about him and his work," Joan answered. Her hand sought Hilda's and held it. "There are things you don't understand. Men and women can't help each other in the way you think. They may try to, and mean no harm in the beginning, but the harm comes, and then not only the woman but the man also suffers, and his work is spoilt and his life ruined."

The small, hot hand clasped Joan's convulsively.

"But he won't be able to do his work if you keep away and never come back to him," she persisted. "Oh, I know it. It all depends upon you. He wants you."

"And I want him, if that's any consolation to you," Joan answered with a short laugh. It wasn't much of a confession. The child was cute enough to have found that out for herself. "Only you see I can't have him. And there's an end of it."

They had reached the Abbey. Joan turned and they retraced their steps slowly.

"I shall be going away soon, for a little while," she said. The talk had helped her to decision. "When I come back I will come and see you all. And you must all come and see me, now and then. I expect I shall have a flat of my own. My father may be coming to live with me. Good-bye. Do all you can to help him."

She stooped and kissed the child, straining her to her almost fiercely. But the child's lips were cold. She did not look back.

Miss Greyson was sympathetic towards her desire for a longish holiday and wonderfully helpful; and Mrs. Denton also approved, and, to Joan's surprise, kissed her; Mrs. Denton was not given to kissing. She wired to her father, and got his reply the same evening. He would be at her rooms on the day she had fixed with his travelling bag, and at her Ladyship's orders. "With love and many thanks," he had added. She waited till the day before starting to run round and say good-bye to the Phillipses. She felt it would be unwise to try and get out of doing that. Both Phillips and Hilda, she was thankful, were out; and she and Mrs. Phillips had tea alone together. The talk was difficult, so far as Joan was concerned. If the woman had been possessed of ordinary intuition, she might have arrived at the truth. Joan almost wished she would. It would make her own future task the easier. But Mrs. Phillips, it was clear, was going to be no help to her.

For her father's sake, she made pretence of eagerness, but as the sea widened between her and the harbour lights it seemed as if a part of herself were being torn away from her.

They travelled leisurely through Holland and the Rhine land, and that helped a little: the new scenes and interests; and in Switzerland they discovered a delightful little village in an upland valley with just one small hotel, and decided to stay there for a while, so as to give themselves time to get their letters. They took long walks and climbs, returning tired and hungry, looking forward to their dinner and the evening talk with the few other guests on the veranda. The days passed restfully in that hidden valley. The great white mountains closed her in. They seemed so strong and clean.

It was on the morning they were leaving that a telegram was put into her hands. Mrs. Phillips was ill at lodgings in Folkestone. She hoped that Joan, on her way back, would come to see her.

JEROME K. JEROME

She showed the telegram to her father. "Do you mind, Dad, if we go straight back?" she asked.

"No, dear," he answered, "if you wish it."

"I would like to go back," she said.

XIII

Mrs. Phillips was sitting up in an easy chair near the heavily-curtained windows when Joan arrived. It was a pleasant little house in the old part of the town, and looked out upon the harbour. She was startlingly thin by comparison with what she had been; but her face was still painted. Phillips would run down by the afternoon train whenever he could get away. She never knew when he was coming, so she explained; and she could not bear the idea of his finding her "old and ugly." She had fought against his wish that she should go into a nursing home; and Joan, who in the course of her work upon the *Nursing Times* had acquired some knowledge of them as a whole, was inclined to agree with her. She was quite comfortable where she was. The landlady, according to her account, was a dear. She had sent the nurse out for a walk on getting Joan's wire, so that they could have a cosy chat. She didn't really want much attendance. It was her heart. It got feeble now and then, and she had to keep very still; that was all. Joan told how her father had suffered for years from much the same complaint. So long as you were careful there was no danger. She must take things easily and not excite herself.

Mrs. Phillips acquiesced. "It's turning me into a lazy-bones," she said with a smile. "I can sit here by the hour, just watching the bustle. I was always one for a bit of life."

The landlady entered with Joan's tea. Joan took an instinctive dislike to her. She was a large, flashy woman, wearing a quantity of cheap jewellery. Her familiarity had about it something almost threatening. Joan waited till she heard the woman's heavy tread descending the stairs, before she expressed her opinion.

"I think she only means to be cheerful," explained Mrs. Phillips. "She's quite a good sort, when you know her." The subject seemed in some way to trouble her, and Joan dropped it.

They watched the loading of a steamer while Joan drank her tea.

"He will come this afternoon, I fancy," said Mrs. Phillips. "I seem to feel it. He will be able to see you home."

Joan started. She had been thinking about Phillips, wondering what she should say to him when they met.

"What does he think," she asked, "about your illness?"

"Oh, it worries him, of course, poor dear," Mrs. Phillips answered. "You see, I've always been such a go-ahead, as a rule. But I think he's getting more hopeful. As I tell him, I'll be all right by the autumn. It was that spell of hot weather that knocked me over."

Joan was still looking out of the window. She didn't quite know what to say. The woman's altered appearance had shocked her. Suddenly she felt a touch upon her hand.

"You'll look after him if anything does happen, won't you?" The woman's eyes were pleading with her. They seemed to have grown larger. "You know what I mean, dear, don't you?" she continued. "It will be such a comfort to me to know that it's all right."

In answer the tears sprang to Joan's eyes. She knelt down and put her arms about the woman.

"Don't be so silly," she cried. "There's nothing going to happen. You're going to get fat and well again; and live to see him Prime Minister."

"I am getting thin, ain't I?" she said. "I always wanted to be thin." They both laughed.

"But I shan't see him that, even if I do live," she went on. "He'll never be that, without you. And I'd be so proud to think that he would. I shouldn't mind going then," she added.

Joan did not answer. There seemed no words that would come.

"You will promise, won't you?" she persisted, in a whisper. "It's only 'in case'—just that I needn't worry myself."

Joan looked up. There was something in the eyes looking down upon her that seemed to be compelling her.

"If you'll promise to try and get better," she answered.

Mrs. Phillips stooped and kissed her. "Of course, dear," she said. "Perhaps I shall, now that my mind is easier."

Phillips came, as Mrs. Phillips had predicted. He was surprised at seeing Joan. He had not thought she could get back so soon. He brought an evening paper with him. It contained a paragraph to the effect that Mrs. Phillips, wife of the Rt. Hon. Robert Phillips, M.P., was progressing favourably and hoped soon to be sufficiently recovered to return to her London residence. It was the first time she had had a paragraph all to herself, headed with her name. She flushed with pleasure; and Joan noticed that, after reading it again, she folded the paper up small and slipped it into her pocket. The nurse came in from her walk a little later and took Joan downstairs with her.

"She ought not to talk to more than one person at a time," the nurse explained, with a shake of the head. She was a quiet, business-like woman. She would not express a definite opinion.

"It's her mental state that is the trouble," was all that she would say. "She ought to be getting better. But she doesn't."

"You're not a Christian Scientist, by any chance?" she asked Joan suddenly.

"No," answered Joan. "Surely you're not one?"

"I don't know," answered the woman. "I believe that would do her more good than anything else. If she would listen to it. She seems to have lost all will-power."

The nurse left her; and the landlady came in to lay the table. She understood that Joan would be dining with Mr. Phillips. There was no train till the eight-forty. She kept looking at Joan as she moved about the room. Joan was afraid she would begin to talk, but she must have felt Joan's antagonism for she remained silent. Once their eyes met, and the woman leered at her.

Phillips came down looking more cheerful. He had detected improvement in Mrs. Phillips. She was more hopeful in herself. They talked in low tones during the meal, as people do whose thoughts are elsewhere. It happened quite suddenly, Phillips explained. They had come down a few days after the rising of Parliament. There had been a spell of hot weather; but nothing remarkable. The first attack had occurred about three weeks ago. It was just after Hilda had gone back to school. He wasn't sure whether he ought to send for Hilda, or not. Her mother didn't want him to—not just yet. Of course, if she got worse, he would have to. What did Joan think?—did she think there was any real danger?

Joan could not say. So much depended upon the general state of health. There was the case of her own father. Of course she would always be subject to attacks. But this one would have warned her to be careful.

Phillips thought that living out of town might be better for her, in the future—somewhere in Surrey, where he could easily get up and down. He could sleep himself at the club on nights when he had to be late.

They talked without looking at one another. They did not speak about themselves.

Mrs. Phillips was in bed when Joan went up to say good-bye. "You'll come again soon?" she asked, and Joan promised. "You've made me so happy," she whispered. The nurse was in the room.

They discussed politics in the train. Phillips had found more support for his crusade against Carleton than he had expected. He was going to open the attack at once, thus forestalling Carleton's opposition to his land scheme.

"It isn't going to be the *Daily This* and the *Daily That* and the *Weekly the Other* all combined to down me. I'm going to tell the people that it's Carleton and only Carleton—Carleton here, Carleton there, Carleton everywhere, against them. I'm going to drag him out into the open and make him put up his own fists."

Joan undertook to sound Greyson. She was sure Greyson would support him, in his balanced, gentlemanly way, that could nevertheless be quite deadly.

They grew less and less afraid of looking at one another as they felt that darkened room further and further behind them.

They parted at Charing Cross. Joan would write. They agreed it would be better to choose separate days for their visits to Folkestone.

She ran against Madge in the morning, and invited herself to tea. Her father had returned to Liverpool, and her own rooms, for some reason, depressed her. Flossie was there with young Halliday. They were both off the next morning to his people's place in Devonshire, from where they were going to get married, and had come to say good-bye. Flossie put Sam in the passage and drew-to the door.

"Have you seen her?" she asked. "How is she?"

"Oh, she's changed a good deal," answered Joan. "But I think she'll get over it all right, if she's careful."

"I shall hope for the best," answered Flossie. "Poor old soul, she's had a good time. Don't send me a present; and then I needn't send you one—when your time comes. It's a silly custom. Besides, I've nowhere to put it. Shall be in a ship for the next six months. Will let you know when we're back."

She gave Joan a hug and a kiss, and was gone. Joan joined Madge in the kitchen, where she was toasting buns.

"I suppose she's satisfied herself that he's brainy," she laughed.

"Oh, brains aren't everything," answered Madge. "Some of the worst rotters the world has ever been cursed with have been brainy enough— men and women. We make too much fuss about brains; just as once upon a time we did about mere brute strength, thinking that was all that was needed to make a man great. Brain is only muscle translated into civilization. That's not going to save us."

"You've been thinking," Joan accused her. "What's put all that into your head?"

Madge laughed. "Mixing with so many brainy people, perhaps," she suggested; "and wondering what's become of their souls."

"Be good, sweet child. And let who can be clever," Joan quoted. "Would that be your text?"

Madge finished buttering her buns. "Kant, wasn't it," she answered, "who marvelled chiefly at two things: the starry firmament above him and the moral law within him. And they're one and the same, if he'd only thought it out. It's rather big to be good."

They carried their tea into the sitting-room.

"Do you really think she'll get over it?" asked Madge. "Or is it one of those things one has to say?"

"I think she could," answered Joan, "if she would pull herself together. It's her lack of will-power that's the trouble."

Madge did not reply immediately. She was watching the rooks settling down for the night in the elm trees just beyond the window. There seemed to be much need of coming and going, of much cawing.

"I met her pretty often during those months that Helen Lavery was running her round," she said at length. "It always seemed to me to have a touch of the heroic, that absurd effort she was making to 'qualify' herself, so that she might be of use to him. I can see her doing something quite big, if she thought it would help him."

The cawing of the rooks grew fainter. One by one they folded their wings.

Neither spoke for a while. Later on, they talked about the coming election. If the Party got back, Phillips would go to the Board of Trade. It would afford him a better platform for the introduction of his land scheme.

"What do you gather is the general opinion?" Joan asked. "That he will succeed?"

"The general opinion seems to be that his star is in the ascendant," Madge answered with a smile; "that all things are working together for his good. It's rather a useful atmosphere to have about one, that. It breeds friendship and support!"

Joan looked at her watch. She had an article to finish. Madge stood on tiptoe and kissed her.

"Don't think me unsympathetic," she said. "No one will rejoice more than I shall if God sees fit to call you to good work. But I can't help letting fall my little tear of fellowship with the weeping."

"And mind your p's and q's," she added. "You're in a difficult position. And not all the eyes watching you are friendly."

Joan bore the germ of worry in her breast as she crossed the Gray's Inn Garden. It was a hard law, that of the world: knowing only winners and losers. Of course, the woman was to be pitied. No one could feel more sorry for her than Joan herself. But what had Madge exactly meant by those words: that she could "see her doing something really big," if she thought it would help him? There was no doubt about her affection for him. It was almost dog-like. And the child, also! There must be something quite exceptional about him to have won the devotion of two such opposite beings. Especially Hilda. It would be hard to imagine any lengths to which Hilda's blind idolatry would not lead her.

She ran down twice to Folkestone during the following week. Her visits made her mind easier. Mrs. Phillips seemed so placid, so contented. There was no suggestion of suffering, either mental or physical.

She dined with the Greysons the Sunday after, and mooted the question of the coming fight with Carleton. Greyson thought Phillips would find plenty of journalistic backing. The concentration of the Press into the hands of a few conscienceless schemers was threatening to reduce the journalist to a mere hireling, and the better-class men were becoming seriously alarmed. He found in his desk the report of a speech made by a well-known leader writer at a recent dinner of the Press Club. The man had risen to respond to the toast of his own health and had taken the opportunity to unpack his heart.

"I am paid a thousand a year," so Greyson read to them, "for keeping my own opinions out of my paper. Some of you, perhaps, earn more, and others less; but you're getting it for writing what you're told. If I were to be so foolish as to express my honest opinion, I'd be on the street, the next morning, looking for another job."

"The business of the journalist," the man had continued, "is to destroy the truth, to lie, to pervert, to vilify, to fawn at the feet of Mammon, to sell his soul for his daily bread. We are the tools and vassals of rich men behind the scenes. We are the jumping-jacks. They pull the strings and we dance. Our talents, our possibilities, our lives are the property of other men."

"We tried to pretend it was only one of Jack's little jokes," explained Greyson as he folded up the cutting; "but it wouldn't work. It was too near the truth."

"I don't see what you are going to do," commented Mary. "So long as men are not afraid to sell their souls, there will always be a Devil's market for them."

Greyson did not so much mind there being a Devil's market, provided he could be assured of an honest market alongside, so that a man could take his choice. What he feared was the Devil's steady encroachment, that could only end by the closing of the independent market altogether. His remedy was the introduction of the American trust law, forbidding any one man being interested in more than a limited number of journals.

"But what's the difference," demanded Joan, "between a man owning one paper with a circulation of, say, six millions; or owning six with a circulation of a million apiece? By concentrating all his energies on one, a man with Carleton's organizing genius might easily establish a single journal that would cover the whole field."

"Just all the difference," answered Greyson, "between Pooh Bah as Chancellor of the Exchequer, or Lord High Admiral, or Chief Executioner, whichever he preferred to be, and Pooh Bah as all the Officers of State rolled into one. Pooh Bah may be a very able statesman, entitled to exert his legitimate influence. But, after all, his opinion is only the opinion of one old gentleman, with possible prejudices and preconceived convictions. The Mikado—or the people, according to locality—would like to hear the views of others of his ministers. He finds that the Lord Chancellor and the Lord Chief Justice and the Groom of the Bedchamber and the Attorney-General—the whole entire Cabinet, in short, are unanimously of the same opinion as Pooh Bah. He doesn't know it's only Pooh Bah speaking from different corners of the stage. The consensus of opinion convinces him. One statesman, however eminent, might err in judgment. But half a score of statesmen, all of one mind! One must accept their verdict."

Mary smiled. "But why shouldn't the good newspaper proprietor hurry up and become a multi-proprietor?" she suggested. "Why don't you persuade Lord Sutcliffe to buy up three or four papers, before they're all gone?"

"Because I don't want the Devil to get hold of him," answered Greyson.

"You've got to face this unalterable law," he continued. "That power derived from worldly sources can only be employed for worldly purposes. The power conferred by popularity, by wealth, by that ability to make use of other men that we term organization—sooner or later the man who wields that power becomes the Devil's servant. So long as Kingship was merely a force struggling against anarchy, it was a holy weapon. As it grew in power so it degenerated into an instrument of tyranny. The Church, so long as it remained a scattered body of meek, lowly men, did the Lord's work. Enthroned at Rome, it thundered its edicts against human thought. The Press is in danger of following precisely the same history. When it wrote in fear of the pillory and of the jail, it fought for Liberty. Now it has become the Fourth Estate, it fawns—as Jack Swinton said of it—at the feet of Mammon. My Proprietor, good fellow, allows me to cultivate my plot amid the wilderness for other purposes than those of quick returns. If he were to become a competitor with the Carletons and the Bloomfields, he would have to look upon it as a business proposition. The Devil would take him up on to the high mountain, and point out to him the kingdom of huge circulations and vast profits, whispering to him: 'All this will I give thee, if thou wilt fall down and worship me.' I don't want the dear good fellow to be tempted."

"Is it impossible, then, to combine duty and success?" questioned Joan.

"The combination sometimes happens, by chance," admitted Greyson. "But it's dangerous to seek it. It is so easy to persuade ourselves that it's our duty to succeed."

"But we must succeed to be of use," urged Mary. "Must God's servants always remain powerless?"

"Powerless to rule. Powerful only to serve," he answered. "Powerful as Christ was powerful; not as Caesar was powerful—powerful as those who have suffered and have failed, leaders of forlorn hopes—powerful as those who have struggled on, despised and vilified; not as those of whom all men speak well—powerful as those who have fought lone battles and have died, not knowing their own victory. It is those that serve, not those that rule, shall conquer."

Joan had never known him quite so serious. Generally there was a touch of irony in his talk, a suggestion of aloofness that had often irritated her.

"I wish you would always be yourself, as you are now," she said, "and never pose."

"Do I pose?" he asked, raising his eyebrows.

"That shows how far it has gone," she told him, "that you don't even know it. You pretend to be a philosopher. But you're really a man."

He laughed. "It isn't always a pose," he explained. "It's some men's way of saying: Thy will be done."

"Ask Phillips to come and see me," he said. "I can be of more help, if I know exactly his views."

He walked with her to the bus. They passed a corner house that he had more than once pointed out to her. It had belonged, years ago, to a well-known artist, who had worked out a wonderful scheme of decoration in the drawing-room. A board was up, announcing that the house was for sale. A gas lamp, exactly opposite, threw a flood of light upon the huge white lettering.

Joan stopped. "Why, it's the house you are always talking about," she said. "Are you thinking of taking it?"

"I did go over it," he answered. "But it would be rather absurd for just Mary and me."

She looked up Phillips at the House, and gave him Greyson's message. He had just returned from Folkestone, and was worried.

"She was so much better last week," he explained. "But it never lasts."

"Poor old girl!" he added. "I believe she'd have been happier if I'd always remained plain Bob Phillips."

Joan had promised to go down on the Friday; but finding, on the Thursday morning, that it would be difficult, decided to run down that afternoon instead. She thought at first of sending a wire. But in Mrs. Phillips's state of health, telegrams were perhaps to be avoided. It could make no difference. The front door of the little house was standing half open. She called down the kitchen stairs to the landlady, but received no answer. The woman had probably run out on some short errand. She went up the stairs softly. The bedroom door, she knew, would be open. Mrs. Phillips had a feeling against being "shut off," as she called it. She meant to tap lightly and walk straight in, as usual. But what she saw through the opening caused her to pause. Mrs. Phillips was sitting up in bed with her box of cosmetics in front of her. She was sensitive of anyone seeing her make-up; and Joan, knowing this, drew back a step. But for some reason, she couldn't help watching. Mrs. Phillips dipped a brush into one of the compartments and then remained with it in her hand, as if hesitating. Suddenly she stuck out her tongue and passed the brush over it. At least, so it seemed to Joan. It was only a side view of Mrs. Phillips's face that she was obtaining, and she may have been mistaken. It might have been the lips. The woman gave a little gasp and sat still for a moment. Then, putting away the brush, she closed the box and slipped it under the pillow.

Joan felt her knees trembling. A cold, creeping fear was taking possession of her. Why, she could not understand. She must have been mistaken. People don't make-up their tongues. It must have been the lips. And even if not—if the woman had licked the brush! It was a silly trick people do. Perhaps she liked the taste. She pulled herself together and tapped at the door.

Mrs. Phillips gave a little start at seeing her; but was glad that she had come. Phillips had not been down for two days and she had been feeling lonesome. She persisted in talking more than Joan felt was good for her. She was feeling so much better, she explained. Joan was relieved when the nurse came back from her walk and insisted on her lying down. She dropped to sleep while Joan and the nurse were having their tea.

Joan went back by the early train. She met some people at the station that she knew and travelled up with them. That picture of Mrs. Phillips's tongue just showing beyond the line of Mrs. Phillips's cheek remained at the back of her mind; but it was not until she was alone in her own rooms that she dared let her thoughts return to it.

The suggestion that was forcing itself into her brain was monstrous—unthinkable. That, never possessed of any surplus vitality, and suffering from the added lassitude of illness, the woman should have become indifferent—willing to let a life that to her was full of fears and difficulties slip peacefully away from her, that was possible. But that she should exercise thought and ingenuity—that she should have reasoned the thing out and deliberately laid her plans, calculating at every point on their success; it was inconceivable.

Besides, what could have put the idea into her head? It was laughable, the presumption that she was a finished actress, capable of deceiving everyone about her. If she had had an inkling of the truth, Joan, with every nerve on the alert, almost hoping for it, would have detected it. She had talked with her alone the day before she had left England, and the woman had been full of hopes and projects for the future.

That picture of Mrs. Phillips, propped up against the pillows, with her make-up box upon her knees was still before her when she went to bed. All night long it haunted her: whether thinking or dreaming of it, she could not tell.

Suddenly, she sat up with a stifled cry. It seemed as if a flash of light had been turned upon her, almost blinding her.

Hilda! Why had she never thought of it? The whole thing was so obvious. "You ought not to think about yourself. You ought to think only of him and of his work. Nothing else matters." If she could say that to Joan, what might she not have said to her mother who, so clearly, she divined to be the incubus—the drag upon her father's career? She could hear the child's dry, passionate tones—could see Mrs. Phillips's flabby cheeks grow white—the frightened, staring eyes. Where her father was concerned the child had neither conscience nor compassion. She had waited her time. It was a few days after Hilda's return to school that Mrs. Phillips had been first taken ill.

She flung herself from the bed and drew the blind. A chill, grey light penetrated the room. It was a little before five. She would go round to Phillips, wake him up. He must be told.

With her hat in her hands, she paused. No. That would not do. Phillips must never know. They must keep the secret to themselves. She would go down and see the woman; reason with her, insist. She went into the other room. It was lighter there. The "A.B.C." was standing in its usual place upon her desk. There was a train to Folkestone at six-fifteen. She had plenty of time. It would be wise to have a cup of tea and something to eat. There would be no sense in arriving there with a headache. She would want her brain clear.

It was half-past five when she sat down with her tea in front of her. It was only ten minutes' walk to Charing Cross—say a quarter of an hour. She might pick up a cab. She grew calmer as she ate and drank. Her reason seemed to be returning to her. There was no such violent hurry. Hadn't she better think things over, in the clear daylight? The woman had been ill now for nearly six weeks: a few hours—a day or two—could make no difference. It might alarm the poor creature, her unexpected appearance at such an unusual hour—cause a relapse. Suppose she had been mistaken? Hadn't she better make a few inquiries first—feel her way? One did harm more often than good, acting on impulse. After all, had she the right to interfere? Oughtn't the thing to be thought over as a whole? Mightn't there be arguments, worth considering, against her interference? Her brain was too much in a whirl. Hadn't she better wait till she could collect and arrange her thoughts?

The silver clock upon her desk struck six. It had been a gift from her father when she was at Girton. It never obtruded. Its voice was a faint musical chime that she need not hear unless she cared to listen. She turned and looked at it. It seemed to be a little face looking back at her out of its two round, blinkless eyes. For the first time during all the years that it had watched beside her, she heard its quick, impatient tick.

She sat motionless, staring at it. The problem, in some way, had simplified itself into a contest between herself, demanding time to think, and the little insistent clock, shouting to her to act upon blind impulse. If she could remain motionless for another five minutes, she would have won.

The ticking of the little clock was filling the room. The thing seemed to have become alive—to be threatening to burst its heart. But the thin, delicate indicator moved on.

Suddenly its ticking ceased. It had become again a piece of lifeless mechanism. The hands pointed to six minutes past. Joan took off her hat and laid it aside.

She must think the whole thing over quietly.

XIV

S he could help him. Without her, he would fail. The woman herself saw that, and wished it. Why should she hesitate? It was not as if she had only herself to consider. The fate—the happiness of millions was at stake. He looked to her for aid—for guidance. It must have been intended. All roads had led to it. Her going to the house. She remembered now, it was the first door at which she had knocked. Her footsteps had surely been directed. Her meeting with Mrs. Phillips in Madge's rooms; and that invitation to dinner, coinciding with that crisis in his life. It was she who had persuaded him to accept. But for her he would have doubted, wavered, let his opportunities slip by. He had confessed it to her.

And she had promised him. He needed her. The words she had spoken to Madge, not dreaming then of their swift application. They came back to her. "God has called me. He girded His sword upon me." What right had she to leave it rusting in its scabbard, turning aside from the pathway pointed out to her because of one weak, useless life, crouching in her way. It was not as if she were being asked to do evil herself that good might come. The decision had been taken out of her hands. All she had to do was to remain quiescent, not interfering, awaiting her orders. Her business was with her own part, not with another's. To be willing to sacrifice oneself: that was at the root of all service. Sometimes it was one's own duty, sometimes that of another. Must one never go forward because another steps out of one's way, voluntarily? Besides, she might have been mistaken. That picture, ever before her, of the woman pausing with the brush above her tongue— that little stilled gasp! It may have been but a phantasm, born of her own fevered imagination. She clung to that, desperately.

It was the task that had been entrusted to her. How could he hope to succeed without her. With her, he would be all powerful—accomplish the end for which he had been sent into the world. Society counts for so much in England. What public man had ever won through without its assistance. As Greyson had said: it is the dinner-table that rules. She could win it over to his side. That mission to Paris that she had undertaken for Mrs. Denton, that had brought her into contact with diplomatists, politicians, the leaders and the rulers, the bearers of names known and honoured in history. They had accepted her as one

JEROME K. JEROME

of themselves. She had influenced them, swayed them. That afternoon at Folk's studio, where all eyes had followed her, where famous men and women had waited to attract her notice, had hung upon her words. Even at school, at college, she had always commanded willing homage. As Greyson had once told her, it was herself—her personality that was her greatest asset. Was it to be utterly wasted? There were hundreds of impersonal, sexless women, equipped for nothing else, with pens as keen if not keener than hers. That was not the talent with which she had been entrusted—for which she would have to account. It was her beauty, her power to charm, to draw after her—to compel by the mere exercise of her will. Hitherto Beauty had been content to barter itself for mere coin of the realm—for ease and luxury and pleasure. She only asked to be allowed to spend it in service. As his wife, she could use it to fine ends. By herself she was helpless. One must take the world as one finds it. It gives the unmated woman no opportunity to employ the special gifts with which God has endowed her—except for evil. As the wife of a rising statesman, she could be a force for progress. She could become another Madame Roland; gather round her all that was best of English social life; give back to it its lost position in the vanguard of thought.

She could strengthen him, give him courage. Without her, he would always remain the mere fighter, doubtful of himself. The confidence, the inspiration, necessary for leadership, she alone could bring to him. Each by themselves was incomplete. Together, they would be the whole. They would build the city of their dreams.

She seemed to have become a wandering spirit rather than a living being. She had no sense of time or place. Once she had started, hearing herself laugh. She was seated at a table, and was talking. And then she had passed back into forgetfulness. Now, from somewhere, she was gazing downward. Roofs, domes and towers lay stretched before her, emerging from a sea of shadows. She held out her arms towards them and the tears came to her eyes. The poor tired people were calling to her to join with him to help them. Should she fail them—turn deaf ears to the myriad because of pity for one useless, feeble life?

She had been fashioned to be his helpmate, as surely as if she had been made of the same bone. Nature was at one with God. Spirit and body both yearned for him. It was not position—power for herself that she craved. The marriage market—if that had been her desire: it had always been open to her. She had the gold that buys these things.

Wealth, ambition: they had been offered to her—spread out temptingly before her eyes. They were always within her means, if ever she chose to purchase them. It was this man alone to whom she had ever felt drawn—this man of the people, with that suggestion about him of something primitive, untamed, causing her always in his presence that faint, compelling thrill of fear, who stirred her blood as none of the polished men of her own class had ever done. His kind, strong, ugly face: it moved beside her: its fearless, tender eyes now pleading, now commanding.

He needed her. She heard his passionate, low voice, as she had heard it in the little garden above Meudon: "Because you won't be there; and without you I can do nothing." What right had this poor, worn-out shadow to stand between them, to the end? Had love and life no claims, but only weakness? She had taken all, had given nothing. It was but reparation she was making. Why stop her?

She was alone in a maze of narrow, silent streets that ended always in a high blank wall. It seemed impossible to get away from this blank wall. Whatever way she turned she was always coming back to it.

What was she to do? Drag the woman back to life against her will—lead her back to him to be a chain about his feet until the end? Then leave him to fight the battle alone?

And herself? All her world had been watching and would know. She had counted her chickens before they were dead. She had set her cap at the man, reckoning him already widowed; and his wife had come to life and snatched it from her head. She could hear the laughter—the half amused, half contemptuous pity for her "rotten bad luck." She would be their standing jest, till she was forgotten.

What would life leave to her? A lonely lodging and a pot of ink that she would come to hate the smell of. She could never marry. It would be but her body that she could give to any other man. Not even for the sake of her dreams could she bring herself to that. It might have been possible before, but not now. She could have won the victory over herself, but for hope, that had kindled the smouldering embers of her passion into flame. What cunning devil had flung open this door, showing her all her heart's desire, merely that she should be called upon to slam it to in her own face?

A fierce anger blazed up in her brain. Why should she listen? Why had reason been given to us if we were not to use it—weigh good and evil in the balance and decide for ourselves where lay the nobler gain?

Were we to be led hither and thither like blind children? What was right—what wrong, but what our own God-given judgment told us? Was it wrong of the woman to perform this act of self-renunciation, yielding up all things to love? No, it was great—heroic of her. It would be her cross of victory, her crown.

If the gift were noble, so also it could not be ignoble to accept it.

To reject it would be to dishonour it.

She would accept it. The wonder of it should cast out her doubts and fears. She would seek to make herself worthy of it. Consecrate it with her steadfastness, her devotion.

She thought it ended. But yet she sat there motionless.

What was plucking at her sleeve—still holding her?

Unknowing, she had entered a small garden. It formed a passage between two streets, and was left open day and night. It was but a narrow strip of rank grass and withered shrubs with an asphalte pathway widening to a circle in the centre, where stood a gas lamp and two seats, facing one another.

And suddenly it came to her that this was her Garden of Gethsemane; and a dull laugh broke from her that she could not help. It was such a ridiculous apology for Gethsemane. There was not a corner in which one could possibly pray. Only these two iron seats, one each side of the gaunt gas lamp that glared down upon them. Even the withered shrubs were fenced off behind a railing. A ragged figure sprawled upon the bench opposite to her. It snored gently, and its breath came laden with the odour of cheap whisky.

But it was her Gethsemane: the best that Fate had been able to do for her. It was here that her choice would be made. She felt that.

And there rose before her the vision of that other Garden of Gethsemane with, below it, the soft lights of the city shining through the trees; and above, clear against the starlit sky, the cold, dark cross.

It was only a little cross, hers, by comparison. She could see that. They seemed to be standing side by side. But then she was only a woman—little more than a girl. And her courage was so small. She thought He ought to know that. For her, it was quite a big cross. She wondered if He had been listening to all her arguments. There was really a good deal of sense in some of them. Perhaps He would understand. Not all His prayer had come down to us. He, too, had put up a fight for life. He, too, was young. For Him, also, life must have seemed but just beginning. Perhaps He, too, had felt that His duty still lay among the people—teaching, guiding, healing them. To Him, too, life must have been sweet with its noble work, its loving comradeship. Even from Him the words had to be wrung: "Thy will, not Mine, be done."

She whispered them at last. Not bravely, at all. Feebly, haltingly, with a little sob: her forehead pressed against the cold iron seat, as if that could help her.

She thought that even then God might reconsider it—see her point of view. Perhaps He would send her a sign.

The ragged figure on the bench opposite opened its eyes, stared at her; then went to sleep again. A prowling cat paused to rub itself against her foot, but meeting no response, passed on. Through an open window, somewhere near, filtered the sound of a child's low whimpering.

It was daylight when she awoke. She was cold and her limbs ached. Slowly her senses came back to her. The seat opposite was vacant. The gas lamp showed but a faint blue point of flame. Her dress was torn, her boots soiled and muddy. Strands of her hair had escaped from underneath her hat.

She looked at her watch. Fortunately it was still early. She would be able to let herself in before anyone was up. It was but a little way. She wondered, while rearranging her hair, what day it was. She would find out, when she got home, from the newspaper.

In the street she paused a moment and looked back through the railings. It seemed even still more sordid in the daylight: the sooty grass and the withered shrubs and the asphalte pathway strewn with dirty paper. And again a laugh she could not help broke from her. Her Garden of Gethsemane!

She sent a brief letter round to Phillips, and a telegram to the nurse, preparing them for what she meant to do. She had just time to pack a small trunk and catch the morning train. At Folkestone, she drove first to a house where she herself had once lodged and fixed things to her satisfaction. The nurse was waiting for her in the downstairs room, and opened the door to her. She was opposed to Joan's interference. But Joan had come prepared for that. "Let me have a talk with her," she said. "I think I've found out what it is that is causing all the trouble."

The nurse shot her a swift glance. "I'm glad of that," she said dryly. She let Joan go upstairs.

Mrs. Phillips was asleep. Joan seated herself beside the bed and waited. She had not yet made herself up for the day and the dyed hair was hidden beneath a white, close-fitting cap. The pale, thin face with its closed eyes looked strangely young. Suddenly the thin hands clasped, and her lips moved, as if she were praying in her sleep. Perhaps she also was dreaming of Gethsemane. It must be quite a crowded garden, if only we could see it.

After a while, her eyes opened. Joan drew her chair nearer and slipped her arm in under her, and their eyes met.

"You're not playing the game," whispered Joan, shaking her head. "I only promised on condition that you would try to get well."

The woman made no attempt to deny. Something told her that Joan had learned her secret. She glanced towards the door. Joan had closed it.

"Don't drag me back," she whispered. "It's all finished." She raised herself up and put her arms about Joan's neck. "It was hard at first, and I hated you. And then it came to me that this was what I had been wanting to do, all my life—something to help him, that nobody else could do. Don't take it from me."

"I know," whispered Joan. "I've been there, too. I knew you were doing it, though I didn't quite know how—till the other day. I wouldn't think. I wanted to pretend that I didn't. I know all you can say. I've been listening to it. It was right of you to want to give it all up to me for his sake. But it would be wrong of me to take it. I don't quite see why. I can't explain it. But I mustn't. So you see it would be no good."

"But I'm so useless," pleaded the woman.

"I said that," answered Joan. "I wanted to do it and I talked and talked, so hard. I said everything I could think of. But that was the only answer: I mustn't do it."

They remained for a while with their arms round one another. It struck Joan as curious, even at the time, that all feeling of superiority had gone out of her. They might have been two puzzled children that had met one another on a path that neither knew. But Joan was the stronger character.

"I want you to give me up that box," she said, "and to come away with me where I can be with you and take care of you until you are well."

Mrs. Phillips made yet another effort. "Have you thought about him?" she asked.

Joan answered with a faint smile. "Oh, yes," she said. "I didn't forget that argument in case it hadn't occurred to the Lord."

"Perhaps," she added, "the helpmate theory was intended to apply only to our bodies. There was nothing said about our souls. Perhaps

God doesn't have to work in pairs. Perhaps we were meant to stand alone."

Mrs. Phillips's thin hands were playing nervously with the bed clothes. There still seemed something that she had to say. As if Joan hadn't thought of everything. Her eyes were fixed upon the narrow strip of light between the window curtains.

"You don't think you could, dear," she whispered, "if I didn't do anything wicked any more. But just let things take their course."

"You see, dear," she went on, her face still turned away, "I thought it all finished. It will be hard for me to go back to him, knowing as I do now that he doesn't want me. I shall always feel that I am in his way. And Hilda," she added after a pause, "she will hate me."

Joan looked at the white patient face and was silent. What would be the use of senseless contradiction. The woman knew. It would only seem an added stab of mockery. She knelt beside the bed, and took the thin hands in hers.

"I think God must want you very badly," she said, "or He wouldn't have laid so heavy a cross upon you. You will come?"

The woman did not answer in words. The big tears were rolling down her cheeks. There was no paint to mingle with and mar them. She drew the little metal box from under the pillow and gave it into Joan's hands.

Joan crept out softly from the room.

The nurse was standing by the window. She turned sharply on Joan's entrance. Joan slipped the box into her hands.

The nurse raised the lid. "What a fool I've been," she said. "I never thought of that."

She held out a large strong hand and gave Joan a longish grip. "You're right," she said, "we must get her out of this house at once. Forgive me."

Phillips had been called up north and wired that he would not be able to get down till the Wednesday evening. Joan met him at the station.

"She won't be expecting you, just yet," she explained. "We might have a little walk."

She waited till they had reached a quiet road leading to the hills.

"You will find her changed," she said. "Mentally, I mean. Though she will try not to show it. She was dying for your sake—to set you free. Hilda seems to have had a talk with her and to have spared her no part of the truth. Her great love for you made the sacrifice possible and even welcome. It was the one gift she had in her hands. She was giving it gladly, proudly. So far as she was concerned, it would have been kinder to let her make an end of it. But during the last few days I have come to the conclusion there is a law within us that we may not argue with. She is coming back to life, knowing you no longer want her, that she is only in the way. Perhaps you may be able to think of something to say or do that will lessen her martyrdom. I can't."

They had paused where a group of trees threw a blot of shadow across the moonlit road.

"You mean she was killing herself?" he asked.

"Quite cleverly. So as to avoid all danger of after discovery: that might have hurt us," she answered.

They walked in silence, and coming to a road that led back into the town, he turned down it. She had the feeling she was following him without his knowing it. A cab was standing outside the gate of a house, having just discharged its fare. He seemed to have suddenly recollected her.

"Do you mind?" he said. "We shall get there so much quicker."

"You go," she said. "I'll stroll on quietly."

"You're sure?" he said.

"I would rather," she answered.

It struck her that he was relieved. He gave the man the address, speaking hurriedly, and jumped in.

She had gone on. She heard the closing of the door behind her, and the next moment the cab passed her.

She did not see him again that night. They met in the morning at breakfast. A curious strangeness to each other seemed to have grown up between them, as if they had known one another long ago, and had half forgotten. When they had finished she rose to leave; but he asked her to stop, and, after the table had been cleared, he walked up and down the room, while she sat sideways on the window seat from where she could watch the little ships moving to and fro across the horizon, like painted figures in a show.

"I had a long talk with Nan last night," he said. "And, trying to explain it to her, I came a little nearer to understanding it myself. My love for you would have been strong enough to ruin both of us. I see that now. It would have dominated every other thought in me. It would have swallowed up my dreams. It would have been blind, unscrupulous. Married to you, I should have aimed only at success. It would not have been your fault. You would not have known. About mere birth I should never have troubled myself. I've met daughters of a hundred earls—more or less: clever, jolly little women I could have chucked under the chin and have been chummy with. Nature creates her own ranks, and puts her ban upon misalliances. Every time I took you in my arms I should have felt that you had stepped down from your proper order to mate yourself with me and that it was up to me to make the sacrifice good to you by giving you power—position. Already within the last few weeks, when it looked as if this thing was going to be possible, I have been thinking against my will of a compromise with Carleton that would give me his support. This coming election was beginning to have terrors for me that I have never before felt. The thought of defeat—having to go back to comparative poverty, to comparative obscurity, with you as my wife, was growing into a nightmare. I should have wanted wealth, fame, victory, for your sake—to see you honoured, courted, envied, finely dressed and finely housed—grateful to me for having won for you these things. It wasn't honest, healthy love—the love that unites, that makes a man willing to take as well as to give, that I felt for you; it was worship that separates a man from a woman, that puts fear between them. It isn't good that man should worship a woman. He can't serve God and woman. Their interests are liable to clash. Nan's my helpmate—just a loving woman that the Lord brought to me and gave me when I was alone—that I still love. I didn't know it till last night. She will never stand in my way. I haven't to put her against my duty. She will leave me free to obey the voice that calls to me. And no man can hear that voice but himself."

He had been speaking in a clear, self-confident tone, as if at last he saw his road before him to the end; and felt that nothing else mattered but that he should go forward hopefully, unfalteringly. Now he paused, and his eyes wandered. But the lines about his strong mouth deepened.

"Perhaps, I am not of the stuff that conquerors are made," he went on. "Perhaps, if I were, I should be thinking differently. It comes to me sometimes that I may be one of those intended only to prepare the way—that for me there may be only the endless struggle. I may have to face unpopularity, abuse, failure. She won't mind."

"Nor would you," he added, turning to her suddenly for the first time, "I know that. But I should be afraid—for you."

She had listened to him without interrupting, and even now she did not speak for a while.

JEROME K. JEROME

It was hard not to. She wanted to tell him that he was all wrong—at least, so far as she was concerned. It. was not the conqueror she loved in him; it was the fighter. Not in the hour of triumph but in the hour of despair she would have yearned to put her arms about him. "Unpopularity, abuse, failure," it was against the fear of such that she would have guarded him. Yes, she had dreamed of leadership, influence, command. But it was the leadership of the valiant few against the hosts of the oppressors that she claimed. Wealth, honours! Would she have given up a life of ease, shut herself off from society, if these had been her standards? "*Mesalliance!*" Had the male animal no instinct, telling it when it was loved with all a woman's being, so that any other union would be her degradation.

It was better for him he should think as he did. She rose and held out her hand.

"I will stay with her for a little while," she said. "Till I feel there is no more need. Then I must get back to work."

He looked into her eyes, holding her hand, and she felt his body trembling. She knew he was about to speak, and held up a warning hand.

"That's all, my lad," she said with a smile. "My love to you, and God speed you."

Mrs. Phillips progressed slowly but steadily. Life was returning to her, but it was not the same. Out of those days there had come to her a gentle dignity, a strengthening and refining. The face, now pale and drawn, had lost its foolishness. Under the thin, white hair, and in spite of its deep lines, it had grown younger. A great patience, a child-like thoughtfulness had come into the quiet eyes.

She was sitting by the window, her hands folded. Joan had been reading to her, and the chapter finished, she had closed the book and her thoughts had been wandering. Mrs. Phillips's voice recalled them.

"Do you remember that day, my dear," she said, "when we went furnishing together. And I would have all the wrong things. And you let me."

"Yes," answered Joan with a laugh. "They were pretty awful, some of them."

"I was just wondering," she went on. "It was a pity, wasn't it? I was silly and began to cry."

"I expect that was it," Joan confessed. "It interferes with our reason at times."

"It was only a little thing, of course, that," she answered. "But I've been thinking it must be that that's at the bottom of it all; and that is why God lets there be weak things—children and little animals and men and women in pain, that we feel sorry for, so that people like you and Robert and so many others are willing to give up all your lives to helping them. And that is what He wants."

"Perhaps God cannot help there being weak things," answered Joan. "Perhaps He, too, is sorry for them."

"It comes to the same thing, doesn't it, dear?" she answered. "They are there, anyhow. And that is how He knows those who are willing to serve Him: by their being pitiful."

They fell into a silence. Joan found herself dreaming.

Yes, it was true. It must have been the beginning of all things. Man, pitiless, deaf, blind, groping in the darkness, knowing not even himself. And to her vision, far off, out of the mist, he shaped himself before her: that dim, first standard-bearer of the Lord, the man who first felt pity. Savage, brutish, dumb—lonely there amid the desolation, staring down at some hurt creature, man or beast it mattered not, his dull eyes troubled with a strange new pain he understood not.

And suddenly, as he stooped, there must have come a great light into his eyes.

Man had heard God's voice across the deep, and had made answer.

XV

The years that followed—till, like some shipwrecked swimmer to whom returning light reveals the land, she felt new life and hopes come back to her—always remained in her memory vague, confused; a jumble of events, thoughts, feelings, without sequence or connection.

She had gone down to Liverpool, intending to persuade her father to leave the control of the works to Arthur, and to come and live with her in London; but had left without broaching the subject. There were nights when she would trapse the streets till she would almost fall exhausted, rather than face the solitude awaiting her in her own rooms. But so also there were moods when, like some stricken animal, her instinct was to shun all living things. At such times his presence, for all his loving patience, would have been as a knife in her wound. Besides, he would always be there, when escape from herself for a while became an absolute necessity. More and more she had come to regard him as her comforter. Not from anything he ever said or did. Rather, it seemed to her, because that with him she felt no need of words.

The works, since Arthur had shared the management, had gradually been regaining their position; and he had urged her to let him increase her allowance.

"It will give you greater freedom," he had suggested with fine assumption of propounding a mere business proposition; "enabling you to choose your work entirely for its own sake. I have always wanted to take a hand in helping things on. It will come to just the same, your doing it for me."

She had suppressed a smile, and had accepted. "Thanks, Dad," she had answered. "It will be nice, having you as my backer."

Her admiration of the independent woman had undergone some modification since she had come in contact with her. Woman was intended to be dependent upon man. It was the part appointed to him in the social scheme. Woman had hers, no less important. Earning her own living did not improve her. It was one of the drawbacks of civilization that so many had to do it of necessity. It developed her on the wrong lines—against her nature. This cry of the unsexed: that woman must always be the paid servant instead of the helper of man— paid for being mother, paid for being wife! Why not carry it to its logical conclusion, and insist that she should be paid for her embraces?

That she should share in man's labour, in his hopes, that was the true comradeship. What mattered it, who held the purse-strings!

Her room was always kept ready for her. Often she would lie there, watching the moonlight creep across the floor; and a curious feeling would come to her of being something wandering, incomplete. She would see as through a mist the passionate, restless child with the rebellious eyes to whom the room had once belonged; and later the strangely self-possessed girl with that impalpable veil of mystery around her who would stand with folded hands, there by the window, seeming always to be listening. And she, too, had passed away. The tears would come into her eyes, and she would stretch out yearning arms towards their shadowy forms. But they would only turn upon her eyes that saw not, and would fade away.

In the day-time, when Arthur and her father were at the works, she would move through the high, square, stiffly-furnished rooms, or about the great formal garden, with its ordered walks and level lawns. And as with knowledge we come to love some old, stern face our childish eyes had thought forbidding, and would not have it changed, there came to her with the years a growing fondness for the old, plain brick-built house. Generations of Allways had lived and died there: men and women somewhat narrow, unsympathetic, a little hard of understanding; but at least earnest, sincere, seeking to do their duty in their solid, unimaginative way. Perhaps there were other ways besides those of speech and pen. Perhaps one did better, keeping to one's own people; the very qualities that separated us from them being intended for their need. What mattered the colours, so that one followed the flag? Somewhere, all roads would meet.

Arthur had to be in London generally once or twice a month, and it came to be accepted that he should always call upon her and "take her out." She had lost the self-sufficiency that had made roaming about London by herself a pleasurable adventure; and a newly-born fear of what people were saying and thinking about her made her shy even of the few friends she still clung to, so that his visits grew to be of the nature of childish treats to which she found herself looking forward—counting the days. Also, she came to be dependent upon him for the keeping alight within her of that little kindly fire of self-conceit at which we warm our hands in wintry days. It is not good that a young woman should remain for long a stranger to her mirror—above her frocks, indifferent to the angle of her hat. She had met the women superior to feminine vanities. Handsome enough, some of them must once have been; now sunk in slovenliness, uncleanliness, in disrespect to womanhood. It would not be fair to him. The worshipper has his rights. The goddess must remember always that she is a goddess—must pull herself together and behave as such, appearing upon her pedestal becomingly attired; seeing to it that in all things she is at her best; not allowing private grief to render her neglectful of this duty.

She had not told him of the Phillips episode. But she felt instinctively that he knew. It was always a little mysterious to her, his perception in matters pertaining to herself.

"I want your love," she said to him one day. "It helps me. I used to think it was selfish of me to take it, knowing I could never return it—not that love. But I no longer feel that now. Your love seems to me a fountain from which I can drink without hurting you."

"I should love to be with you always," he answered, "if you wished it. You won't forget your promise?"

She remembered it then. "No," she answered with a smile. "I shall keep watch. Perhaps I shall be worthy of it by that time."

She had lost her faith in journalism as a drum for the rousing of the people against wrong. Its beat had led too often to the trickster's booth, to the cheap-jack's rostrum. It had lost its rallying power. The popular Press had made the newspaper a byword for falsehood. Even its supporters, while reading it because it pandered to their passions, tickled their vices, and flattered their ignorance, despised and disbelieved it. Here and there, an honest journal advocated a reform, pleaded for the sweeping away of an injustice. The public shrugged its shoulders. Another newspaper stunt! A bid for popularity, for notoriety: with its consequent financial kudos.

She still continued to write for Greyson, but felt she was labouring for the doomed. Lord Sutcliffe had died suddenly and his holding in the *Evening Gazette* had passed to his nephew, a gentleman more interested in big game shooting than in politics. Greyson's support of Phillips had brought him within the net of Carleton's operations, and negotiations for purchase had already been commenced. She knew that, sooner or later, Greyson would be offered the alternative of either changing his opinions or of going. And she knew that he would go. Her work for Mrs. Denton was less likely to be interfered with. It appealed only to the few, and aimed at informing and explaining rather than directly converting. Useful enough work in its way, no doubt; but to put heart into it seemed to require longer views than is given to the eyes of youth.

Besides, her pen was no longer able to absorb her attention, to keep her mind from wandering. The solitude of her desk gave her the feeling of a prison. Her body made perpetual claims upon her, as though it were some restless, fretful child, dragging her out into the streets without knowing where it wanted to go, discontented with everything it did: then hurrying her back to fling itself upon a chair, weary, but still dissatisfied.

If only she could do something. She was sick of thinking.

These physical activities into which women were throwing themselves! Where one used one's body as well as one's brain—hastened to appointments; gathered round noisy tables; met fellow human beings, argued with them, walked with them, laughing and talking; forced one's way through crowds; cheered, shouted; stood up on platforms before a sea of faces; roused applause, filling and emptying one's lungs; met interruptions with swift flash of wit or anger, faced opposition, danger—felt one's blood surging through one's veins, felt one's nerves quivering with excitement; felt the delirious thrill of passion; felt the mad joy of the loosened animal.

She threw herself into the suffrage movement. It satisfied her for a while. She had the rare gift of public speaking, and enjoyed her triumphs. She was temperate, reasonable; persuasive rather than aggressive; feeling her audience as she went, never losing touch with them. She had the magnetism that comes of sympathy. Medical students who came intending to tell her to go home and mind the baby, remained to wonder if man really was the undoubted sovereign of the world, born to look upon woman as his willing subject; to wonder whether under some unwritten whispered law it might not be the other way about. Perhaps she had the right—with or without the baby—to move about the kingdom, express her wishes for its care and management. Possibly his doubts may not have been brought about solely by the force and logic of her arguments. Possibly the voice of Nature is not altogether out of place in discussions upon Humanity's affairs.

She wanted votes for women. But she wanted them clean—won without dishonour. These "monkey tricks"—this apish fury and impatience! Suppose it did hasten by a few months, more or less, the coming of the inevitable. Suppose, by unlawful methods, one could succeed in dragging a reform a little prematurely from the womb of time, did not one endanger the child's health? Of what value was woman's influence on public affairs going to be, if she was to boast that she had won the right to exercise it by unscrupulousness and brutality?

They were to be found at every corner: the reformers who could not reform themselves. The believers in universal brotherhood who hated half the people. The denouncers of tyranny demanding lamp-posts for their opponents. The bloodthirsty preachers of peace. The moralists who had persuaded themselves that every wrong was justified provided one were fighting for the right. The deaf shouters for justice. The excellent intentioned men and women labouring for reforms that could only be hoped for when greed and prejudice had yielded place to reason, and who sought to bring about their ends by appeals to passion and self-interest.

And the insincere, the self-seekers, the self-advertisers! Those who were in the business for even coarser profit! The lime-light lovers who would always say and do the clever, the unexpected thing rather than the useful and the helpful thing: to whom paradox was more than principle.

Ought there not to be a school for reformers, a training college where could be inculcated self-examination, patience, temperance, subordination to duty; with lectures on the fundamental laws, within which all progress must be accomplished, outside which lay confusion and explosions; with lectures on history, showing how improvements had been brought about and how failure had been invited, thus avoiding much waste of reforming zeal; with lectures on the properties and tendencies of human nature, forbidding the attempt to treat it as a sum in rule of three?

There were the others. The men and women not in the lime-light. The lone, scattered men and women who saw no flag but Pity's ragged skirt; who heard no drum but the world's low cry of pain; who fought with feeble hands against the wrong around them; who with aching heart and troubled eyes laboured to make kinder the little space about them. The great army of the nameless reformers uncheered, unparagraphed, unhonoured. The unknown sowers of the seed. Would the reapers of the harvest remember them?

Beyond giving up her visits to the house, she had made no attempt to avoid meeting Phillips; and at public functions and at mutual friends they sometimes found themselves near to one another. It surprised her that she could see him, talk to him, and even be alone with him without its troubling her. He seemed to belong to a part of her that lay dead and buried—something belonging to her that she had thrust away with her own hands: that she knew would never come back to her.

She was still interested in his work and keen to help him. It was going to be a stiff fight. He himself, in spite of Carleton's opposition, had been returned with an increased majority; but the Party as a whole had suffered loss, especially in the counties. The struggle centred round the agricultural labourer. If he could be won over the Government would go ahead with Phillips's scheme. Otherwise there was danger of its being shelved. The difficulty was the old problem of how to get at the men of the scattered villages, the lonely cottages. The only papers that they ever saw were those, chiefly of the Carleton group, that the farmers and the gentry took care should come within their reach; that were handed to them at the end of their day's work as a kindly gift; given to the school children to take home with them; supplied in ample numbers to all the little inns and public-houses. In all these, Phillips was held up as their arch enemy, his proposal explained as a device to lower their wages, decrease their chances of employment, and rob them of the produce of their gardens and allotments. No arguments were used. A daily stream of abuse, misrepresentation and deliberate lies, set forth under flaming headlines, served their simple purpose. The one weekly paper that had got itself established among them, that their fathers had always taken, that dimly they had come to look upon as their one friend, Carleton had at last succeeded in purchasing. When that, too, pictured Phillips's plan as a diabolical intent to take from them even the little that they had, and give it to the loafing socialist and the bloated foreigner, no room for doubt was left to them.

He had organized volunteer cycle companies of speakers from the towns, young working-men and women and students, to go out on summer evenings and hold meetings on the village greens. They were winning their way. But it was slow work. And Carleton was countering their efforts by a hired opposition that followed them from place to place, and whose interruptions were made use of to represent the whole campaign as a fiasco.

"He's clever," laughed Phillips. "I'd enjoy the fight, if I'd only myself to think of, and life wasn't so short."

The laugh died away and a shadow fell upon his face.

"If I could get a few of the big landlords to come in on my side," he continued, "it would make all the difference in the world. They're sensible men, some of them; and the whole thing could be carried out without injury to any legitimate interest. I could make them see that, if I could only get them quietly into a corner."

"But they're frightened of me," he added, with a shrug of his broad shoulders, "and I don't seem to know how to tackle them."

Those drawing-rooms? Might not something of the sort be possible? Not, perhaps, the sumptuous salon of her imagination, thronged with the fair and famous, suitably attired. Something, perhaps, more homely, more immediately attainable. Some of the women dressed, perhaps, a little dowdily; not all of them young and beautiful. The men wise, perhaps, rather than persistently witty; a few of them prosy, maybe a trifle ponderous; but solid and influential. Mrs. Denton's great empty house in Gower Street? A central situation and near to the tube. Lords and ladies had once ruffled there; trod a measure on its spacious floors; filled its echoing stone hall with their greetings and their partings. The gaping sconces, where their link-boys had extinguished their torches, still capped its grim iron railings.

Seated in the great, sombre library, Joan hazarded the suggestion. Mrs. Denton might almost have been waiting for it. It would be quite easy. A little opening of long fastened windows; a lighting of chill grates; a little mending of moth-eaten curtains, a sweeping away of long-gathered dust and cobwebs.

Mrs. Denton knew just the right people. They might be induced to bring their sons and daughters—it might be their grandchildren, youth being there to welcome them. For Joan, of course, would play her part.

The lonely woman touched her lightly on the hand. There shot a pleading look from the old stern eyes.

"You will have to imagine yourself my daughter," she said. "You are taller, but the colouring was the same. You won't mind, will you?"

The right people did come: Mrs. Denton being a personage that a landed gentry, rendered jumpy by the perpetual explosion of new ideas under their very feet, and casting about eagerly for friends, could not afford to snub. A kindly, simple folk, quite intelligent, some of them, as Phillips had surmised. Mrs. Denton made no mystery of why she had invited them. Why should all questions be left to the politicians and the journalists? Why should not the people interested take a hand; meet and talk over these little matters with quiet voices and attentive ears, amid surroundings where the unwritten law would restrain ladies and gentlemen from addressing other ladies and gentlemen as blood-suckers or anarchists, as grinders of the faces of the poor or as oily-tongued rogues; arguments not really conducive to mutual understanding and the bridging over of differences. The latest Russian dancer, the last new musical revue, the marvellous things that can happen at golf, the curious hands that one picks up at bridge, the eternal fox, the sacred bird! Excellent material for nine-tenths of our conversation. But the remaining tenth? Would it be such excruciatingly bad form for us to be intelligent, occasionally; say, on one or two Fridays during the season? Mrs. Denton wrapped it up tactfully; but that was her daring suggestion.

It took them aback at first. There were people who did this sort of thing. People of no class, who called themselves names and took up things. But for people of social standing to talk about serious subjects—except, perhaps, in bed to one's wife! It sounded so un-English.

With the elders it was sense of duty that prevailed. That, at all events, was English. The country must be saved. To their sons and daughters it was the originality, the novelty that gradually appealed. Mrs. Denton's Fridays became a new sensation. It came to be the chic and proper thing to appear at them in shades of mauve or purple. A pushing little woman in Hanover Street designed the "Denton" bodice, with hanging sleeves and square-cut neck. The younger men inclined towards a coat shaped to the waist with a roll collar.

Joan sighed. It looked as if the word had been passed round to treat the whole thing as a joke. Mrs. Denton took a different view.

"Nothing better could have happened," she was of opinion. "It means that their hearts are in it."

The stone hall was still vibrating to the voices of the last departed guests. Joan was seated on a footstool before the fire in front of Mrs. Denton's chair.

"It's the thing that gives me greatest hope," she continued. "The childishness of men and women. It means that the world is still young, still teachable."

"But they're so slow at their lessons," grumbled Joan. "One repeats it and repeats it; and then, when one feels that surely now at least one has drummed it into their heads, one finds they have forgotten all that one has ever said."

"Not always forgotten," answered Mrs. Denton; "mislaid, it may be, for the moment. An Indian student, the son of an old Rajah, called on me a little while ago. He was going back to organize a system of education among his people. 'My father heard you speak when you were over in India,' he told me. 'He has always been thinking about it.' Thirty years ago it must have been, that I undertook that mission to India. I had always looked back upon it as one of my many failures."

"But why leave it to his son," argued Joan. "Why couldn't the old man have set about it himself, instead of wasting thirty precious years?"

"I should have preferred it, myself," agreed Mrs. Denton. "I remember when I was a very little girl my mother longing for a tree upon the lawn underneath which she could sit. I found an acorn and planted it just in the right spot. I thought I would surprise her. I happened to be in the neighbourhood last summer, and I walked over. There was such a nice old lady sitting under it, knitting stockings. So you see it wasn't wasted."

"I wouldn't mind the waiting," answered Joan, "if it were not for the sorrow and the suffering that I see all round me. I want to get rid of it right away, now. I could be patient for myself, but not for others."

The little old lady straightened herself. There came a hardening of the thin, firm mouth.

"And those that have gone before?" she demanded. "Those that have won the ground from where we are fighting. Had they no need of patience? Was the cry never wrung from their lips: 'How long, oh Lord, how long?' Is it for us to lay aside the sword that they bequeath us because we cannot hope any more than they to see the far-off victory? Fifty years I have fought, and what, a few years hence, will my closing eyes still see but the banners of the foe still waving, fresh armies pouring to his standard?"

She flung back her head and the grim mouth broke into a smile.

"But I've won," she said. "I'm dying further forward. I've helped advance the line."

She put out her hands and drew Joan to her.

"Let me think of you," she said, "as taking my place, pushing the outposts a little further on."

Joan did not meet Hilda again till the child had grown into a woman—practically speaking. She had always been years older than her age. It was at a reception given in the Foreign Office. Joan's dress had been trodden on and torn. She had struggled out of the crowd into an empty room, and was examining the damage somewhat ruefully, when she heard a voice behind her, proffering help. It was a hard, cold voice, that yet sounded familiar, and she turned.

There was no forgetting those deep, burning eyes, though the face had changed. The thin red lips still remained its one touch of colour;

but the unhealthy whiteness of the skin had given place to a delicate pallor; and the features that had been indistinct had shaped themselves in fine, firm lines. It was a beautiful, arresting face, marred only by the sullen callousness of the dark, clouded eyes.

Joan was glad of the assistance. Hilda produced pins.

"I always come prepared to these scrimmages," she explained. "I've got some Hazeline in my bag. They haven't kicked you, have they?"

"No," laughed Joan. "At least, I don't think so."

"They do sometimes," answered Hilda, "if you happen to be in the way, near the feeding troughs. If they'd only put all the refreshments into one room, one could avoid it. But they will scatter them about so that one never knows for certain whether one is in the danger zone or not. I hate a mob."

"Why do you come?" asked Joan.

"Oh, I!" answered the girl. "I go everywhere where there's a chance of picking up a swell husband. They've got to come to these shows, they can't help themselves. One never knows what incident may give one one's opportunity."

Joan shot a glance. The girl was evidently serious.

"You think it would prove a useful alliance?" she suggested.

"It would help, undoubtedly," the girl answered. "I don't see any other way of getting hold of them."

Joan seated herself on one of the chairs ranged round the walls, and drew the girl down beside her. Through the closed door, the mingled voices of the Foreign Secretary's guests sounded curiously like the buzzing of flies.

"It's quite easy," said Joan, "with your beauty. Especially if you're not going to be particular. But isn't there danger of your devotion to your father leading you too far? A marriage founded on a lie—no matter for what purpose!—mustn't it degrade a woman—smirch her soul for all time? We have a right to give up the things that belong to ourselves, but not the things that belong to God: our truth, our sincerity, our cleanliness of mind and body; the things that He may one day want of us. It led you into evil once before. Don't think I'm judging you. I was no better than you. I argued just as you must have done. Something stopped me just in time. That was the only difference between us."

The girl turned her dark eyes full upon Joan. "What did stop you?" she demanded.

"Does it matter what we call it?" answered Joan. "It was a voice."

"It told me to do it," answered the girl.

"Did no other voice speak to you?" asked Joan.

"Yes," answered the girl. "The voice of weakness."

There came a fierce anger into the dark eyes. "Why did you listen to it?" she demanded. "All would have been easy if you hadn't."

"You mean," answered Joan quietly, "that if I had let your mother die and had married your father, that he and I would have loved each other to the end; that I should have helped him and encouraged him in all things, so that his success would have been certain. Is that the argument?"

"Didn't you love him?" asked the girl, staring. "Wouldn't you have helped him?"

"I can't tell," answered Joan. "I should have meant to. Many men and women have loved, and have meant to help each other all their lives; and with the years have drifted asunder; coming even to be against one another. We change and our thoughts change; slight differences of temperament grow into barriers between us; unguessed antagonisms widen into gulfs. Accidents come into our lives. A friend was telling me the other day of a woman who practically proposed to and married a musical genius, purely and solely to be of use to him. She earned quite a big income, drawing fashions; and her idea was to relieve him of the necessity of doing pot-boilers for a living, so that he might devote his whole time to his real work. And a few weeks after they were married she ran the point of a lead pencil through her eye and it set up inflammation of her brain. And now all the poor fellow has to think of is how to make enough to pay for her keep at a private lunatic asylum. I don't mean to be flippant. It's the very absurdity of it all that makes the mystery of life—that renders it so hopeless for us to attempt to find our way through it by our own judgment. It is like the ants making all their clever, laborious plans, knowing nothing of chickens and the gardener's spade. That is why we have to cling to the life we can order for ourselves—the life within us. Truth, Justice, Pity. They are the strong things, the eternal things, the things we've got to sacrifice ourselves for—serve with our bodies and our souls.

"Don't think me a prig," she pleaded. "I'm talking as if I knew all about it. I don't really. I grope in the dark; and now and then—at least so it seems to me—I catch a glint of light. We are powerless in ourselves. It is only God working through us that enables us to be of any use. All we can do is to keep ourselves kind and clean and free from self, waiting for Him to come to us."

The girl rose. "I must be getting back," she said. "Dad will be wondering where I've got to."

She paused with the door in her hand, and a faint smile played round the thin red lips.

"Tell me," she said. "What is God?"

"A Labourer, together with man, according to Saint Paul," Joan answered.

The girl turned and went. Joan watched her as she descended the great staircase. She moved with a curious, gliding motion, pausing at times for the people to make way for her.

XVI

It was a summer's evening; Joan had dropped in at the Greysons and had found Mary alone, Francis not having yet returned from a bachelor dinner at his uncle's, who was some big pot in the Navy. They sat in the twilight, facing the open French windows, through which one caught a glimpse of the park. A great stillness seemed to be around them.

The sale and purchase of the *Evening Gazette* had been completed a few days before. Greyson had been offered the alternative of gradually and gracefully changing his opinions, or getting out; and had, of course, chosen dismissal. He was taking a holiday, as Mary explained with a short laugh.

"He had some shares in it himself, hadn't he?" Joan asked.

"Oh, just enough to be of no use," Mary answered. "Carleton was rather decent, so far as that part of it was concerned, and insisted on paying him a fair price. The market value would have been much less; and he wanted to be out of it."

Joan remained silent. It made her mad, that a man could be suddenly robbed of fifteen years' labour: the weapon that his heart and brain had made keen wrested from his hand by a legal process, and turned against the very principles for which all his life he had been fighting.

"I'm almost more sorry for myself than for him," said Mary, making a whimsical grimace. "He will start something else, so soon as he's got over his first soreness; but I'm too old to dream of another child."

He came in a little later and, seating himself between them, filled and lighted his pipe. Looking back, Joan remembered that curiously none of them had spoken. Mary had turned at the sound of his key in the door. She seemed to be watching him intently; but it was too dark to notice her expression. He pulled at his pipe till it was well alight and then removed it.

"It's war," he said.

The words made no immediate impression upon Joan. There had been rumours, threatenings and alarms, newspaper talk. But so there had been before. It would come one day: the world war that one felt was gathering in the air; that would burst like a second deluge on the nations. But it would not be in our time: it was too big. A way out would be found.

"Is there no hope?" asked Mary.

"Yes," he answered. "The hope that a miracle may happen. The Navy's got its orders."

And suddenly—as years before in a Paris music hall—there leapt to life within Joan's brain a little impish creature that took possession of her. She hoped the miracle would not happen. The little impish creature within her brain was marching up and down beating a drum. She wished he would stop a minute. Someone was trying to talk to her, telling her she ought to be tremendously shocked and grieved. He—or she, or whatever it was that was trying to talk to her, appeared concerned about Reason and Pity and Universal Brotherhood and Civilization's clock—things like that. But the little impish drummer was making such a din, she couldn't properly hear. Later on, perhaps, he would get tired; and then she would be able to listen to this humane and sensible person, whoever it might be.

Mary argued that England could and should keep out of it; but Greyson was convinced it would be impossible, not to say dishonourable: a sentiment that won the enthusiastic approval of the little drummer in Joan's brain. He played "Rule Britannia" and "God Save the King," the "Marseillaise" and the Russian National hymn, all at the same time. He would have included "Deutschland uber Alles," if Joan hadn't made a supreme effort and stopped him. Evidently a sporting little devil. He took himself off into a corner after a time, where he played quietly to himself; and Joan was able to join in the conversation.

Greyson spoke with an enthusiasm that was unusual to him. So many of our wars had been mean wars—wars for the wrong; sordid wars for territory, for gold mines; wars against the weak at the bidding of our traders, our financiers. "Shouldering the white man's burden," we called it. Wars for the right of selling opium; wars to perpetuate the vile rule of the Turk because it happened to serve our commercial interests. This time, we were out to play the knight; to save the smaller peoples; to rescue our once "sweet enemy," fair France. Russia was the disturbing thought. It somewhat discounted the knight-errant idea, riding stirrup to stirrup beside that barbarian horseman. But there were possibilities about Russia. Idealism lay hid within that sleeping brain. It would be a holy war for the Kingdom of the Peoples. With Germany freed from the monster of blood and iron that was crushing out her soul, with Russia awakened to life, we would build the United States of Europe. Even his voice was changed. Joan could almost fancy it was some excited schoolboy that was talking.

Mary had been clasping and unclasping her hands, a habit of hers when troubled. Could good ever come out of evil? That was her doubt. Did war ever do anything but sow the seeds of future violence; substitute one injustice for another; change wrong for wrong. Did it ever do anything but add to the world's sum of evil, making God's task the heavier?

Suddenly, while speaking, she fell into a passionate fit of weeping. She went on through her tears:

"It will be terrible," she said. "It will last longer than you say. Every nation will be drawn into it. There will be no voice left to speak for reason. Every day we shall grow more brutalized, more pitiless. It will degrade us, crush the soul out of us. Blood and iron! It will become our God too: the God of all the world. You say we are going into it with clean hands, this time. How long will they keep clean? The people who only live for making money: how long do you think they will remain silent? What has been all the talk of the last ten years but of capturing German trade. We shall be told that we owe it to our dead to make a profit out of them; that otherwise they will have died in vain. Who will care for the people but to use them for killing one another -to hound them on like dogs. In every country nothing but greed and hatred will be preached. Horrible men and women will write to the papers crying out for more blood, more cruelty. Everything that can make for anger and revenge will be screamed from every newspaper. Every plea for humanity will be jeered at as 'sickly sentimentality.' Every man and woman who remembers the ideals with which we started will be shrieked at as a traitor. The people who are doing well out of it, they will get hold of the Press, appeal to the passions of the mob. Nobody else will be allowed to speak. It always has been so in war. It always will be. This will be no exception merely because it's bigger. Every country will be given over to savagery. There will be no appeal against it. The whole world will sink back into the beast."

She ended by rising abruptly and wishing them good-night. Her outburst had silenced Joan's impish drummer, for the time. He appeared to be nervous and depressed, but bucked up again on the way to the bus. Greyson walked with her as usual. They took the long way round by the outer circle.

"Poor Mary!" he said. "I should not have talked before her if I had thought. Her horror of war is almost physical. She will not even read about them. It has the same effect upon her as stories of cruelty."

"But there's truth in a good deal that she says," he added. "War can bring out all that is best in a people; but also it brings out the worst. We shall have to take care that the ideals are not lost sight of."

"I wish this wretched business of the paper hadn't come just at this time," said Joan: "just when your voice is most needed.

"Couldn't you get enough money together to start something quickly," she continued, the idea suddenly coming to her. "I think I could help you. It wouldn't matter its being something small to begin with. So long as it was entirely your own, and couldn't be taken away from you. You'd soon work it up."

"Thanks," he answered. "I may ask you to later on. But just now—" He paused.

Of course. For war you wanted men, to fight. She had been thinking of them in the lump: hurrying masses such as one sees on cinema screens, blurred but picturesque. Of course, when you came to think of it, they would have to be made up of individuals—gallant-hearted, boyish sort of men who would pass through doors, one at a time, into little rooms; give their name and address to a soldier man seated at a big deal table. Later on, one would say good-bye to them on crowded platforms, wave a handkerchief. Not all of them would come back. "You can't make omelettes without breaking eggs," she told herself.

It annoyed her, that silly saying having come into her mind. She could see them lying there, with their white faces to the night. Surely she might have thought of some remark less idiotic to make to herself, at such a time.

He was explaining to her things about the air service. It seemed he had had experience in flying—some relation of his with whom he had spent a holiday last summer.

It would mean his getting out quickly. He seemed quite eager to be gone.

"Isn't it rather dangerous work?" she asked. She felt it was a footling question even as she asked it. Her brain had become stodgy.

"Nothing like as dangerous as being in the Infantry," he answered. "And that would be my only other alternative. Besides I get out of the drilling." He laughed. "I should hate being shouted at and ordered about by a husky old sergeant."

They neither spoke again till they came to the bridge, from the other side of which the busses started.

"I may not see you again before I go," he said. "Look after Mary.

I shall try to persuade her to go down to her aunt in Hampshire. It's rather a bit of luck, as it turns out, the paper being finished with. I shouldn't have quite known what to do."

He had stopped at the corner. They were still beneath the shadow of the trees. Quite unconsciously she put her face up; and as if it had always been the custom at their partings, he drew her to him and kissed her; though it really was for the first time.

She walked home instead of taking the bus. She wanted to think. A day or two would decide the question. She determined that if the miracle did not happen, she would go down to Liverpool. Her father was on the committee of one of the great hospitals; and she knew one or two of the matrons. She would want to be doing something—to get out to the front, if possible. Maybe, her desire to serve was not altogether free from curiosity—from the craving for adventure. There's a spice of the man even in the best of women.

Her conscience plagued her when she thought of Mrs. Denton. For some time now, they had been very close together; and the old lady had come to depend upon her. She waited till all doubt was ended before calling to say good-bye. Mrs. Denton was seated before an old bureau that had long stood locked in a corner of the library. The drawers were open and books and papers were scattered about.

Joan told her plans. "You'll be able to get along without me for a little while?" she asked doubtfully.

Mrs. Denton laughed. "I haven't much more to do," she answered. "Just tidying up, as you see; and two or three half-finished things I shall try to complete. After that, I'll perhaps take a rest."

She took from among the litter a faded photograph and handed it to Joan. "Odd," she said. "I've just turned it out."

It represented a long, thin line of eminently respectable ladies and gentlemen in early Victorian costume. The men in peg-top trousers and silk stocks, the women in crinolines and poke bonnets. Among them, holding the hand of a benevolent-looking, stoutish gentleman, was a mere girl. The terminating frills of a white unmentionable garment showed beneath her skirts. She wore a porkpie hat with a feather in it.

"My first public appearance," explained Mrs. Denton. "I teased my father into taking me with him. We represented Great Britain and Ireland. I suppose I'm the only one left."

"I shouldn't have recognized you," laughed Joan. "What was the occasion?"

"The great International Peace Congress at Paris," explained Mrs. Denton; "just after the Crimean war. It made quite a stir at the time. The Emperor opened our proceedings in person, and the Pope and the Archbishop of Canterbury both sent us their blessing. We had a copy of the speeches presented to us on leaving, in every known language in Europe, bound in vellum. I'm hoping to find it. And the Press was enthusiastic. There were to be Acts of Parliament, Courts of Arbitration, International Laws, Diplomatic Treaties. A Sub-Committee was appointed to prepare a special set of prayers and a Palace of Peace was to be erected. There was only one thing we forgot, and that was the foundation."

"I may not be here," she continued, "when the new plans are submitted. Tell them not to forget the foundation this time. Tell them to teach the children."

Joan dined at a popular restaurant that evening. She fancied it might cheer her up. But the noisy patriotism of the over-fed crowd only irritated her. These elderly, flabby men, these fleshy women, who would form the spectators, who would loll on their cushioned seats protected from the sun, munching contentedly from their well-provided baskets while listening to the dying groans rising upwards from the drenched arena. She glanced from one podgy thumb to another and a feeling of nausea crept over her.

Suddenly the band struck up "God Save the King." Three commonplace enough young men, seated at a table near to her, laid down their napkins and stood up. Yes, there was something to be said for war, she felt, as she looked at their boyish faces, transfigured. Not for them Business as usual, the Capture of German Trade. Other visions those young eyes were seeing. The little imp within her brain had seized his drum again. "Follow me"—so he seemed to beat—"I teach men courage, duty, the laying down of self. I open the gates of honour. I make heroes out of dust. Isn't it worth my price?"

A figure was loitering the other side of the street when she reached home. She thought she somehow recognized it, and crossed over. It was McKean, smoking his everlasting pipe. Success having demanded some such change, he had migrated to "The Albany," and she had not seen him for some time. He had come to have a last look at the house—in case it might happen to be the last. He was off to Scotland the next morning, where he intended to "join up."

"But are you sure it's your particular duty?" suggested Joan. "I'm told you've become a household word both in Germany and France. If we really are out to end war and establish the brotherhood of nations, the work you are doing is of more importance than even the killing of Germans. It isn't as if there wouldn't be enough without you."

"To tell the truth," he answered, "that's exactly what I've been saying to myself. I shan't be any good. I don't see myself sticking a bayonet into even a German. Unless he happened to be abnormally clumsy. I tried to shoot a rabbit once. I might have done it if the little beggar, instead of running away, hadn't turned and looked at me."

"I should keep out of it if I were you," laughed Joan.

"I can't," he answered. "I'm too great a coward."

"An odd reason for enlisting," thought Joan.

"I couldn't face it," he went on; "the way people would be looking at me in trains and omnibuses; the things people would say of me, the things I should imagine they were saying; what my valet would be thinking of me. Oh, I'm ashamed enough of myself. It's the artistic temperament, I suppose. We must always be admired, praised. We're not the stuff that martyrs are made of. We must for ever be kow-towing to the cackling geese around us. We're so terrified lest they should hiss us."

The street was empty. They were pacing it slowly, up and down.

"I've always been a coward," he continued. "I fell in love with you the first day I met you on the stairs. But I dared not tell you."

"You didn't give me that impression," answered Joan.

She had always found it difficult to know when to take him seriously and when not.

"I was so afraid you would find it out," he explained.

"You thought I would take advantage of it," she suggested.

"One can never be sure of a woman," he answered. "And it would have been so difficult. There was a girl down in Scotland, one of the village girls. It wasn't anything really. We had just been children together. But they all thought I had gone away to make my fortune so as to come back and marry her—even my mother. It would have looked so mean if after getting on I had married a fine London lady. I could never have gone home again."

"But you haven't married her—or have you?" asked Joan.

"No," he answered. "She wrote me a beautiful letter that I shall always keep, begging me to forgive her, and hoping I might be happy. She had married a young farmer, and was going out to Canada. My mother will never allow her name to be mentioned in our house."

They had reached the end of the street again. Joan held out her hand with a laugh.

"Thanks for the compliment," she said. "Though I notice you wait till you're going away before telling me."

"But quite seriously," she added, "give it a little more thought—the enlisting, I mean. The world isn't too rich in kind influences. It needs men like you. Come, pull yourself together and show a little pluck." She laughed.

"I'll try," he promised, "but it won't be any use; I shall drift about the streets, seeking to put heart into myself, but all the while my footsteps will be bearing me nearer and nearer to the recruiting office; and outside the door some girl in the crowd will smile approval or some old fool will pat me on the shoulder and I shall sneak in and it will close behind me. It must be fine to have courage."

He wrote her two days later from Ayr, giving her the name of his regiment, and again some six months later from Flanders. But there would have been no sense in her replying to that last.

She lingered in the street by herself, a little time, after he had turned the corner. It had been a house of sorrow and disappointment to her; but so also she had dreamed her dreams there, seen her visions. She had never made much headway with her landlord and her landlady: a worthy couple, who had proved most excellent servants, but who prided themselves, to use their own expression, on knowing their place and keeping themselves to themselves. Joan had given them notice that morning, and had been surprised at the woman's bursting into tears.

"I felt it just the same when young Mr. McKean left us," she explained with apologies. "He had been with us five years. He was like you, miss, so unpracticable. I'd got used to looking after him."

Mary Greyson called on her in the morning, while she was still at breakfast. She had come from seeing Francis off by an early train from Euston. He had sent Joan a ring.

"He is so afraid you may not be able to wear it—that it will not fit you," said Mary, "but I told him I was sure it would."

Joan held our her hand for the letter. "I was afraid he had forgotten it," she answered, with a smile.

She placed the ring on her finger and held out her hand. "I might have been measured for it," she said. "I wonder how he knew."

"You left a glove behind you, the first day you ever came to our house," Mary explained. "And I kept it."

She was following his wishes and going down into the country. They did not meet again until after the war.

Madge dropped in on her during the week and brought Flossie with her. Flossie's husband, Sam, had departed for the Navy; and Niel Singleton, who had offered and been rejected for the Army, had joined a Red Cross unit. Madge herself was taking up canteen work. Joan rather expected Flossie to be in favour of the war, and Madge against it. Instead of which, it turned out the other way round. It seemed difficult to forecast opinion in this matter.

Madge thought that England, in particular, had been too much given up to luxury and pleasure. There had been too much idleness and empty laughter: Hitchicoo dances and women undressing themselves upon the stage. Even the working classes seemed to think of nothing else but cinemas and beer. She dreamed of a United Kingdom purified by suffering, cleansed by tears; its people drawn together by memory of common sacrifice; class antagonism buried in the grave where Duke's son and cook's son would lie side by side: of a new-born Europe rising from the ashes of the old. With Germany beaten, her lust of war burnt out, her hideous doctrine of Force proved to be false, the world would breathe a freer air. Passion and hatred would fall from man's eyes. The people would see one another and join hands.

Flossie was sceptical. "Why hasn't it done it before?" she wanted to know. "Good Lord! There's been enough of it."

"Why didn't we all kiss and be friends after the Napoleonic wars?" she demanded, "instead of getting up Peterloo massacres, and anti-Corn Law riots, and breaking the Duke of Wellington's windows?"

"All this talk of downing Militarism," she continued. "It's like trying to do away with the other sort of disorderly house. You don't stamp out a vice by chivying it round the corner. When men and women have become decent there will be no more disorderly houses. But it won't come before. Suppose we do knock Militarism out of Germany, like we did out of France, not so very long ago? It will only slip round the corner into Russia or Japan. Come and settle over here, as likely as not, especially if we have a few victories and get to fancy ourselves."

Madge was of opinion that the world would have had enough of war. Not armies but whole peoples would be involved this time. The lesson would be driven home.

"Oh, yes, we shall have had enough of it," agreed Flossie, "by the time we've paid up. There's no doubt of that. What about our children?

I've just left young Frank strutting all over the house and flourishing a paper knife. And the servants have had to bar the kitchen door to prevent his bursting in every five minutes and attacking them. What's he going to say when I tell him, later on, that his father and myself have had all the war we want, and have decided there shall be no more? The old folks have had their fun. Why shouldn't I have mine? That will be his argument."

"You can't do it," she concluded, "unless you are prepared to keep half the world's literature away from the children, scrap half your music, edit your museums and your picture galleries; bowdlerize your Old Testament and rewrite your histories. And then you'll have to be careful for twenty-four hours a day that they never see a dog-fight."

Madge still held to her hope. God would make a wind of reason to pass over the earth. He would not smite again his people.

"I wish poor dear Sam could have been kept out of it," said Flossie. She wiped her eyes and finished her tea.

Joan had arranged to leave on the Monday. She ran down to see Mary Stopperton on the Saturday afternoon. Mr. Stopperton had died the year before, and Mary had been a little hurt, divining insincerity in the condolences offered to her by most of her friends.

"You didn't know him, dear," she had said to Joan. "All his faults were on the outside."

She did not want to talk about the war.

"Perhaps it's wrong of me," she said. "But it makes me so sad. And I can do nothing."

She had been busy at her machine when Joan had entered; and a pile of delicate white work lay folded on a chair beside her.

"What are you making?" asked Joan.

The little withered face lighted up. "Guess," she said, as she unfolded and displayed a tiny garment.

"I so love making them," she said. "I say to myself, 'It will all come right. God will send more and more of His Christ babies; till at last there will be thousands and thousands of them everywhere; and their love will change the world!'"

Her bright eyes had caught sight of the ring upon Joan's hand. She touched it with her little fragile fingers.

"You will let me make one for you, dearie, won't you?" she said. "I feel sure it will be a little Christ baby."

Arthur was still away when she arrived home. He had gone to

Norway on business. Her father was afraid he would find it difficult to get back. Telegraphic communication had been stopped, and they had had no news of him. Her father was worried. A big Government contract had come in, while many of his best men had left to enlist.

"I've fixed you up all right at the hospital," he said. "It was good of you to think of coming home. Don't go away, for a bit." It was the first time he had asked anything of her.

Another fortnight passed before they heard from Arthur, and then he wrote them both from Hull. He would be somewhere in the North Sea, mine sweeping, when they read his letters. He had hoped to get a day or two to run across and say good-bye; but the need for men was pressing and he had not liked to plead excuses. The boat by which he had managed to leave Bergen had gone down. He and a few others had been picked up, but the sights that he had seen were haunting him. He felt sure his uncle would agree that he ought to be helping, and this was work for England he could do with all his heart. He hoped he was not leaving his uncle in the lurch; but he did not think the war would last long, and he would soon be back.

"Dear lad," said her father, "he would take the most dangerous work that he could find. But I wish he hadn't been quite so impulsive. He could have been of more use helping me with this War Office contract. I suppose he never got my letter, telling him about it."

In his letter to Joan he went further. He had received his uncle's letter, so he confided to her. Perhaps she would think him a crank, but he couldn't help it. He hated this killing business, this making of machinery for slaughtering men in bulk, like they killed pigs in Chicago. Out on the free, sweet sea, helping to keep it clean from man's abominations, he would be away from it all.

She saw the vision of him that night, as, leaning from her window, she looked out beyond the pines: the little lonely ship amid the waste of waters; his beautiful, almost womanish, face, and the gentle dreamy eyes with their haunting suggestion of a shadow.

Her little drummer played less and less frequently to her as the months passed by. It didn't seem to be the war he had looked forward to. The illustrated papers continued to picture it as a sort of glorified picnic where smiling young men lolled luxuriously in cosy dug-outs, reading their favourite paper. By curious coincidence, it generally happened to be the journal publishing the photograph. Occasionally, it appeared, they came across the enemy, who then put up both hands and shouted

"Kamerad." But the weary, wounded men she talked to told another story.

She grew impatient of the fighters with their mouths; the savage old baldheads heroically prepared to sacrifice the last young man; the sleek, purring women who talked childish nonsense about killing every man, woman and child in Germany, but quite meant it; the shrieking journalists who had decided that their place was the home front; the press-spurred mobs, the spy hunters, chasing terrified old men and sobbing children through the streets. It was a relief to enter the quiet ward and close the door behind her. The camp-followers: the traders and pedlars, the balladmongers, and the mountebanks, the ghoulish sightseers! War brought out all that was worst in them. But the givers of their blood, the lads who suffered, who had made the sacrifice: war had taught them chivalry, manhood. She heard no revilings of hatred and revenge from those drawn lips. Patience, humour, forgiveness, they had learnt from war. They told her kindly stories even of Hans and Fritz.

The little drummer in her brain would creep out of his corner, play to her softly while she moved about among them.

One day she received a letter from Folk. He had come to London at the request of the French Government to consult with English artists on a matter he must not mention. He would not have the time, he told her, to run down to Liverpool. Could she get a couple of days' leave and dine with him in London.

She found him in the uniform of a French Colonel. He had quite a military bearing and seemed pleased with himself. He kissed her hand, and then held her out at arms' length.

"It's wonderful how like you are to your mother," he said, "I wish I were as young as I feel."

She had written him at the beginning of the war, telling him of her wish to get out to the front, and he thought that now he might be able to help her.

"But perhaps you've changed your mind," he said. "It isn't quite as pretty as it's painted."

"I want to," she answered. "It isn't all curiosity. I think it's time for women to insist on seeing war with their own eyes, not trust any longer to the pictures you men paint." She smiled.

"But I've got to give it up," she added. "I can't leave Dad."

They were sitting in the hall of the hotel. It was the dressing hour and the place was almost empty. He shot a swift glance at her.

"Arthur is still away," she explained, "and I feel that he wants me. I should be worrying myself, thinking of him all alone with no one to look after him. It's the mother instinct I suppose. It always has hampered woman." She laughed.

"Dear old boy," he said. He was watching her with a little smile. "I'm glad he's got some luck at last."

They dined in the great restaurant belonging to the hotel. He was still vastly pleased with himself as he marched up the crowded room with Joan upon his arm. He held himself upright and talked and laughed perhaps louder than an elderly gentleman should. "Swaggering old beggar," he must have overheard a young sub. mutter as they passed. But he did not seem to mind it.

They lingered over the meal. Folk was a brilliant talker. Most of the men whose names were filling the newspapers had sat to him at one time or another. He made them seem quite human. Joan was surprised at the time.

"Come up to my rooms, will you?" he asked. "There's something I want to say to you. And then I'll walk back with you." She was staying at a small hotel off Jermyn Street.

He sat her down by the fire and went into the next room. He had a letter in his hand when he returned. Joan noticed that the envelope was written upon across the corner, but she was not near enough to distinguish the handwriting. He placed it on the mantelpiece and sat down opposite her.

"So you have come to love the dear old chap," he said.

"I have always loved him," Joan answered. "It was he didn't love me, for a time, as I thought. But I know now that he does."

He was silent for a few moments, and then he leant across and took her hands in his.

"I am going," he said, "where there is just the possibility of an accident: one never knows. I wanted to be sure that all was well with you."

He was looking at the ring upon her hand.

"A soldier boy?" he asked.

"Yes," she answered. "If he comes back." There was a little catch in her voice.

"I know he'll come back," he said. "I won't tell you why I am so sure. Perhaps you wouldn't believe." He was still holding her hands, looking into her eyes.

"Tell me," he said, "did you see your mother before she died. Did she speak to you?"

"No," Joan answered. "I was too late. She had died the night before. I hardly recognized her when I saw her. She looked so sweet and young."

"She loved you very dearly," he said. "Better than herself. All those years of sorrow: they came to her because of that. I thought it foolish of her at the time, but now I know she was wise. I want you always to love and honour her. I wouldn't ask you if it wasn't right."

She looked at him and smiled. "It's quite easy," she answered. "I always see her as she lay there with all the sorrow gone from her. She looked so beautiful and kind."

He rose and took the letter from where he had placed it on the mantelpiece. He stooped and held it out above the fire and a little flame leaped up and seemed to take it from his hand.

They neither spoke during the short walk between the two hotels. But at the door she turned and held out her hands to him.

"Thank you," she said, "for being so kind—and wise. I shall always love and honour her."

He kissed her, promising to take care of himself.

She ran against Phillips, the next day, at one of the big stores where she was shopping. He had obtained a commission early in the war and was now a captain. He had just come back from the front on leave. The alternative had not appealed to him, of being one of those responsible for sending other men to death while remaining himself in security and comfort.

"It's a matter of temperament," he said. "Somebody's got to stop behind and do the patriotic speechifying. I'm glad I didn't. Especially after what I've seen."

He had lost interest in politics.

"There's something bigger coming," he said. "Here everything seems to be going on much the same, but over there you feel it. Something growing silently out of all this blood and mud. I find myself wondering what the men are staring at, but when I look there's nothing as far as my field-glasses will reach but waste and desolation. And it isn't only on the faces of our own men. It's in the eyes of the prisoners too. As if they saw something. A funny ending to the war, if the people began to think."

Mrs. Phillips was running a Convalescent Home in Folkestone, he told her; and had even made a speech. Hilda was doing relief work among the ruined villages of France.

"It's a new world we shall be called upon to build," he said. "We must pay more heed to the foundation this time."

She seldom discussed the war with her father. At the beginning, he had dreamed with Greyson of a short and glorious campaign that should weld all classes together, and after which we should forgive our enemies and shape with them a better world. But as the months went by, he appeared to grow indifferent; and Joan, who got about twelve hours a day of it outside, welcomed other subjects.

It surprised her when one evening after dinner he introduced it himself.

"What are you going to do when it's over?" he asked her. "You won't give up the fight, will you, whatever happens?" She had not known till then that he had been taking any interest in her work.

"No," she answered with a laugh, "no matter what happens, I shall always want to be in it."

"Good lad," he said, patting her on the shoulder. "It will be an ugly world that will come out of all this hate and anger. The Lord will want all the help that He can get."

"And you don't forget our compact, do you?" he continued, "that I am to be your backer. I want to be in it too."

She shot a glance at him. He was looking at the portrait of that old Ironside Allway who had fought and died to make a nobler England, as he had dreamed. A grim, unprepossessing gentleman, unless the artist had done him much injustice, with high, narrow forehead, and puzzled, staring eyes.

She took the cigarette from her lips and her voice trembled a little.

"I want you to be something more to me than that, sir," she said. "I want to feel that I'm an Allway, fighting for the things we've always had at heart. I'll try and be worthy of the name."

Her hand stole out to him across the table, but she kept her face away from him. Until she felt his grasp grow tight, and then she turned and their eyes met.

"You'll be the last of the name," he said. "Something tells me that. I'm glad you're a fighter. I always prayed my child might be a fighter."

Arthur had not been home since the beginning of the war. Twice he had written them to expect him, but the little fleet of mine sweepers had been hard pressed, and on both occasions his leave had been stopped at the last moment. One afternoon he turned up unexpectedly at the hospital. It was a few weeks after the Conscription Act had been passed.

Joan took him into her room at the end of the ward, from where, through the open door, she could still keep watch. They spoke in low tones.

"It's done you good," said Joan. "You look every inch the jolly Jack Tar." He was hard and tanned, and his eyes were marvellously bright.

"Yes," he said, "I love the sea. It's clean and strong."

A fear was creeping over her. "Why have you come back?" she asked.

He hesitated, keeping his eyes upon the ground.

"I don't suppose you will agree with me," he said. "Somehow I felt I had to."

A Conscientious Objector. She might have guessed it. A "Conchy," as they would call him in the Press: all the spiteful screamers who had never risked a scratch, themselves, denouncing him as a coward. The local Dogberrys of the tribunals would fire off their little stock of gibes and platitudes upon him, propound with owlish solemnity the new Christianity, abuse him and condemn him, without listening to him. Jeering mobs would follow him through the streets. More than once, of late, she had encountered such crowds made up of shrieking girls and foul-mouthed men, surging round some white-faced youngster while the well-dressed passers-by looked on and grinned.

She came to him and stood over him with her hands upon his shoulders.

"Must you, dear?" she said. "Can't you reconcile it to yourself—to go on with your work of mercy, of saving poor folks' lives?"

He raised his eyes to hers. The shadow that, to her fancy, had always rested there seemed to have departed. A light had come to them.

"There are more important things than saving men's bodies. You think that, don't you?" he asked.

"Yes," she answered. "I won't try to hold you back, dear, if you think you can do that."

He caught her hands and held them.

"I wanted to be a coward," he said, "to keep out of the fight. I thought of the shame, of the petty persecutions—that even you might despise me. But I couldn't. I was always seeing His face before me with His beautiful tender eyes, and the blood drops on His brow. It is He alone can save the world. It is perishing for want of love; and by a little suffering I might be able to help Him. And then one night—I suppose it was a piece of driftwood—there rose up out of the sea a little cross that seemed to call to me to stretch out my hand and grasp it, and gird it to my side."

He had risen. "Don't you see," he said. "It is only by suffering that one can help Him. It is the sword that He has chosen—by which one day He will conquer the world. And this is such a splendid opportunity to fight for Him. It would be like deserting Him on the eve of a great battle."

She looked into his eager, hopeful eyes. Yes, it had always been so—it always would be, to the end. Not priests and prophets, but ever that little scattered band of glad sufferers for His sake would be His army. His weapon still the cross, till the victory should be won.

She glanced through the open door to where the poor, broken fellows she always thought of as "her boys" lay so patient, and then held out her hand to him with a smile, though the tears were in her eyes.

"So you're like all the rest of them, lad," she said. "It's for King and country. Good luck to you."

After the war was over and the men, released from their long terms of solitary confinement, came back to life injured in mind and body, she was almost glad he had escaped. But at the time it filled her soul with darkness.

It was one noonday. He had been down to the tribunal and his case had been again adjourned. She was returning from a lecture, and, crossing a street in the neighbourhood of the docks, found herself suddenly faced by an oncoming crowd. It was yelping and snarling, curiously suggestive of a pack of hungry wolves. A couple of young soldiers were standing back against a wall.

"Better not go on, nurse," said one of them. "It's some poor devil of a Conchy, I expect. Must have a damned sight more pluck than I should."

It was the fear that had been haunting her. She did not know how white she had turned.

"I think it is someone I know," she said. "Won't you help me?"

The crowd gave way to them, and they had all but reached him. He was hatless and bespattered, but his tender eyes had neither fear nor anger in them. She reached out her arms and called to him. Another step and she would have been beside him, but at the moment a slim, laughing girl darted in front of him and slipped her foot between his legs and he went down.

She heard the joyous yell and the shrill laughter as she struggled wildly to force her way to him. And then for a moment there was a space and a man with bent body and clenched hands was rushing forward as if upon a football field, and there came a little sickening thud and then the crowd closed in again.

Her strength was gone and she could only wait. More soldiers had come up and were using their fists freely, and gradually the crowd retired, still snarling; and they lifted him up and brought him to her.

"There's a chemist's shop in the next street. We'd better take him there," suggested the one who had first spoken to her. And she thanked them and followed them.

They made a bed for him with their coats upon the floor, and some of them kept guard outside the shop, while one, putting aside the frightened, useless little chemist, waited upon her, bringing things needful, while she cleansed the foulness from his smooth young face, and washed the matted blood from his fair hair, and closed the lids upon his tender eyes, and, stooping, kissed the cold, quiet lips.

There had been whispered talk among the men, and when she rose the one who had first spoken to her came forward. He was nervous and stood stiffly.

"Beg pardon, nurse," he said, "but we've sent for a stretcher, as the police don't seem in any hurry. Would you like us to take him. Or would it upset him, do you think, if he knew?"

"Thank you," she answered. "He would think it kind of you, I know."

She had the feeling that he was being borne by comrades.

XVII

I t was from a small operating hospital in a village of the Argonne that she first saw the war with her own eyes.

Her father had wished her to go. Arthur's death had stirred in him the old Puritan blood with its record of long battle for liberty of conscience. If war claimed to be master of a man's soul, then the new warfare must be against war. He remembered the saying of a Frenchwoman who had been through the Franco-Prussian war. Joan, on her return from Paris some years before, had told him of her, repeating her words: "But, of course, it would not do to tell the truth," the old lady had said, "or we should have our children growing up to hate war."

"I'll be lonely and anxious till you come back," he said. "But that will have to be my part of the fight."

She had written to Folk. No female nurses were supposed to be allowed within the battle zone; but under pressure of shortage the French staff were relaxing the rule, and Folk had pledged himself to her discretion. "I am not doing you any kindness," he had written. "You will have to share the common hardships and privations, and the danger is real. If I didn't feel instinctively that underneath your mask of sweet reasonableness you are one of the most obstinate young women God ever made, and that without me you would probably get yourself into a still worse hole, I'd have refused." And then followed a list of the things she was to be sure to take with her, including a pound or two of Keating's insect powder, and a hint that it might save her trouble, if she had her hair cut short.

There was but one other woman at the hospital. It had been a farmhouse. The man and both sons had been killed during the first year of the war, and the woman had asked to be allowed to stay on. Her name was Madame Lelanne. She was useful by reason of her great physical strength. She could take up a man as he lay and carry him on her outstretched arms. It was an expressionless face, with dull, slow-moving eyes that never changed. She and Joan shared a small *grenier* in one of the barns. Joan had brought with her a camp bedstead; but the woman, wrapping a blanket round her, would creep into a hole she had made for herself among the hay. She never took off her clothes, except the great wooden-soled boots, so far as Joan could discover.

The medical staff consisted of a Dr. Poujoulet and two assistants. The authorities were always promising to send him more help, but it never arrived. One of the assistants, a Monsieur Dubos, a little man with a remarkably big beard, was a chemist, who, at the outbreak of the war, had been on the verge, as he made sure, of an important discovery in connection with colour photography. Almost the first question he asked Joan was could she speak German. Finding that she could, he had hurried her across the yard into a small hut where patients who had borne their operation successfully awaited their turn to be moved down to one of the convalescent hospitals at the base. Among them was a German prisoner, an elderly man, belonging to the Landwehr; in private life a photographer. He also had been making experiments in the direction of colour photography. Chance had revealed to the two men their common interest, and they had been exchanging notes. The German talked a little French, but not sufficient; and on the day of Joan's arrival they had reached an impasse that was maddening to both of them. Joan found herself up against technical terms that rendered her task difficult, but fortunately had brought a dictionary with her, and was able to make them understand one another. But she had to be firm with both of them, allowing them only ten minutes together at a time. The little Frenchman would kneel by the bedside, holding the German at an angle where he could talk with least danger to his wound. It seemed that each was the very man the other had been waiting all his life to meet. They shed tears on one another's neck when they parted, making all arrangements to write to one another.

"And you will come and stay with me," persisted the little Frenchman, "when this affair is finished"—he made an impatient gesture with his hands. "My wife takes much interest. She will be delighted."

And the big German, again embracing the little Frenchman, had promised, and had sent his compliments to Madame.

The other was a young priest. He wore the regulation Red Cross uniform, but kept his cassock hanging on a peg behind his bed. He had pretty frequent occasion to take it down. These small emergency hospitals, within range of the guns, were reserved for only dangerous cases: men whose wounds would not permit of their being carried further; and there never was much more than a sporting chance of saving them. They were always glad to find there was a priest among the staff. Often it was the first question they would ask on being lifted out of the ambulance. Even those who professed to no religion seemed comforted by the idea. He went by the title of "Monsieur le Pretre:" Joan never learned his name. It was he who had laid out the little cemetery on the opposite side of the village street. It had once been an orchard, and some of the trees were still standing. In the centre, rising out of a pile of rockwork, he had placed a crucifix that had been found upon the roadside and had surrounded it with flowers. It formed the one bright spot of colour in the village; and at night time, when all other sounds were hushed, the iron wreaths upon its little crosses, swaying against one another in the wind, would make a low, clear, tinkling music. Joan would sometimes lie awake listening to it. In some way she could not explain it always brought the thought of children to her mind.

The doctor himself was a broad-shouldered, bullet-headed man, clean shaven, with close-cropped, bristly hair. He had curiously square hands, with short, squat fingers. He had been head surgeon in one of the Paris hospitals, and had been assigned his present post because of his marvellous quickness with the knife. The hospital was the nearest to a hill of great strategical importance, and the fighting in the neighbourhood was almost continuous. Often a single ambulance would bring in three or four cases, each one demanding instant attention. Dr. Poujoulet, with his hairy arms bare to the shoulder, would polish them off one after another, with hardly a moment's rest between, not allowing time even for the washing of the table. Joan would have to summon all her nerve to keep herself from collapsing. At times the need for haste was such that it was impossible to wait for the anaesthetic to take effect. The one redeeming feature was the extraordinary heroism of the men, though occasionally there was nothing for it but to call in the orderlies to hold some poor fellow down, and to deafen one's ears.

One day, after a successful operation, she was tending a young sergeant. He was a well-built, handsome man, with skin as white as a woman's. He watched her with curious indifference in his eyes as she busied herself, trying to make him comfortable, and did nothing to help her.

"Has Mam'selle ever seen a bull fight?" he asked her.

"No," she answered. "I've seen all the horror and cruelty I want to for the rest of my life."

"Ah," he said, "you would understand if you had. When one of the horses goes down gored, his entrails lying out upon the sand, you know what they do, don't you? They put a rope round him, and drag him, groaning, into the shambles behind. And once there, kind people like you and Monsieur le Medecin tend him and wash him, and put his entrails back, and sew him up again. He thinks it so kind of them—the first time. But the second! He understands. He will be sent back into the arena to be ripped up again, and again after that. This is the third time I have been wounded, and as soon as you've all patched me up and I've got my breath again, they'll send me back into it. Mam'selle will forgive my not feeling grateful to her." He gave a short laugh that brought the blood into his mouth.

The village consisted of one long straggling street, following the course of a small stream between two lines of hills. It was on one of the great lines of communication: and troops and war material passed through it, going and coming, in almost endless procession. It served also as a camp of rest. Companies from the trenches would arrive there, generally towards the evening, weary, listless, dull-eyed, many of them staggering like over-driven cattle beneath their mass of burdens. They would fling their accoutrements from them and stand in silent groups till the sergeants and corporals returned to lead them to the barns and out-houses that had been assigned to them, the houses still habitable being mostly reserved for the officers. Like those of most French villages, they were drab, plaster-covered buildings without gardens; but some of them were covered with vines, hiding their ugliness; and the village as a whole, with its groups, here and there, of fine sycamore trees and its great stone fountain in the centre, was picturesque enough. It had twice changed hands, and a part of it was in ruins. From one or two of the more solidly built houses merely the front had fallen, leaving the rooms just as they had always been: the furniture in its accustomed place, the pictures on the walls. They suggested doll's houses standing open. One wondered when the giant child would come along and close them up. The iron spire of the little church had been hit twice. It stood above the village, twisted into the form of a note of interrogation. In the churchyard many of the graves had been ripped open. Bones and skulls lay scattered about among the shattered tombstones. But, save for a couple of holes in the roof, the body was still intact, and every afternoon a faint, timid-sounding bell called a few villagers and a sprinkling of soldiers to Mass. Most of the inhabitants had fled, but the farmers and shopkeepers had remained. At intervals, the German batteries, searching round with apparent aimlessness, would drop a score or so of shells about the neighbourhood; but the peasant, with an indifference that was almost animal, would still follow his ox-drawn plough; the old, bent crone, muttering curses, still ply the hoe. The proprietors of the tiny *epiceries* must have been rapidly making their fortunes, considering the prices that they charged the unfortunate *poilu*, dreaming of some small luxury out of his five sous a day. But as one of them, a stout, smiling lady, explained to Joan, with a gesture: "It is not often that one has a war."

Joan had gone out in September, and for a while the weather was pleasant. The men, wrapped up in their great-coats, would sleep for preference under the great sycamore trees. Through open doorways she would catch glimpses of picturesque groups of eager card-players, crowded round a flickering candle. From the darkness there would steal the sound of flute or zither, of voices singing. Occasionally it would be some strident ditty of the Paris music-halls, but more often it was sad and plaintive. But early in October the rains commenced and the stream became a roaring torrent, and a clammy mist lay like a white river between the wooded hills.

Mud! that seemed to be the one word with which to describe modern war. Mud everywhere! Mud ankle-deep upon the roads; mud into which you sank up to your knees the moment you stepped off it; tents and huts to which you waded through the mud, avoiding the slimy gangways on which you slipped and fell; mud-bespattered men, mud-bespattered horses, little donkeys, looking as if they had been sculptured out of mud, struggling up and down the light railways that every now and then would disappear and be lost beneath the mud; guns and wagons groaning through the mud; lorries and ambulances, that in the darkness had swerved from the straight course, overturned and lying abandoned in the mud, motor-cyclists ploughing swift furrows through the mud, rolling it back in liquid streams each side of them; staff cars rushing screaming through the mud, followed by a rushing fountain of mud; serried ranks of muddy men stamping through the mud with steady rhythm, moving through a rain of mud, rising upward from the ground; long lines of motor-buses filled with a mass of muddy humanity packed shoulder to shoulder, rumbling ever through the endless mud.

Men sitting by the roadside in the mud, gnawing at unsavoury food; men squatting by the ditches, examining their sores, washing their bleeding feet in the muddy water, replacing the muddy rags about their wounds.

A world without colour. No other colour to be seen beneath the sky but mud. The very buttons on the men's coats painted to make them look like mud.

Mud and dirt! Dirty faces, dirty hands, dirty clothes, dirty food, dirty beds; dirty interiors, from which there was never time to wash the mud; dirty linen hanging up to dry, beneath which dirty children played, while dirty women scolded. Filth and desolation all around. Shattered farmsteads half buried in the mud; shattered gardens trampled into mud. A weary land of foulness, breeding foulness; tangled wire the only harvest of the fields; mile after mile of gaping holes, filled with muddy water; stinking carcases of dead horses; birds of prey clinging to broken fences, flapping their great wings.

A land where man died, and vermin increased and multiplied. Vermin on your body, vermin in your head, vermin in your food, vermin waiting for you in your bed; vermin the only thing that throve, the only thing that looked at you with bright eyes; vermin the only thing to which the joy of life had still been left.

Joan had found a liking gradually growing up in her for the quick-moving, curt-tongued doctor. She had dismissed him at first as a mere butcher: his brutal haste, his indifference apparently to the suffering he was causing, his great, strong, hairy hands, with their squat fingers, his cold grey eyes. But she learnt as time went by, that his callousness was a thing that he put on at the same time that he tied his white apron round his waist, and rolled up his sleeves.

She was resting, after a morning of grim work, on a bench outside the hospital, struggling with clenched, quivering hands against a craving to fling herself upon the ground and sob. And he had found her there; and had sat down beside her.

"So you wanted to see it with your own eyes," he said. He laid his hand upon her shoulder, and she had some difficulty in not catching hold of him and clinging to him. She was feeling absurdly womanish just at that moment.

"Yes," she answered. "And I'm glad that I did it," she added, defiantly.

"So am I," he said. "Tell your children what you have seen. Tell other women."

"It's you women that make war," he continued. "Oh, I don't mean that you do it on purpose, but it's in your blood. It comes from the days when to live it was needful to kill. When a man who was swift and strong to kill was the only thing that could save a woman and her brood. Every other man that crept towards them through the grass was an enemy, and her only hope was that her man might kill him, while she watched and waited. And later came the tribe; and instead of the one man creeping through the grass, the everlasting warfare was against all other tribes. So you loved only the men ever ready and willing to fight, lest you and your children should be carried into slavery: then it was the only way. You brought up your boys to be fighters. You told them stories of their gallant sires. You sang to them the songs of battle: the glory of killing and of conquering. You have never unlearnt the lesson. Man has learnt comradeship—would have travelled further but for you. But woman is still primitive. She would still have her man the hater and the killer. To the woman the world has never changed."

"Tell the other women," he said. "Open their eyes. Tell them of their sons that you have seen dead and dying in the foolish quarrel for which there was no need. Tell them of the foulness, of the cruelty, of the senselessness of it all. Set the women against War. That is the only way to end it."

It was a morning or two later that, knocking at the door of her loft, he asked her if she would care to come with him to the trenches. He had brought an outfit for her which he handed to her with a grin. She had followed Folk's advice and had cut her hair; and when she appeared before him for inspection in trousers and overcoat, the collar turned up about her neck, and reaching to her helmet, he had laughingly pronounced the experiment safe.

A motor carried them to where the road ended, and from there, a little one-horse ambulance took them on to almost the last trees of the forest. There was no life to be seen anywhere. During the last mile, they had passed through a continuous double line of graves; here and there a group of tiny crosses keeping one another company; others standing singly, looking strangely lonesome amid the torn-up earth and shattered trees. But even these had ceased. Death itself seemed to have been frightened away from this terror-haunted desert.

Looking down, she could see thin wreaths of smoke, rising from the ground. From underneath her feet there came a low, faint, ceaseless murmur.

"Quick," said the doctor. He pushed her in front of him, and she almost fell down a flight of mud-covered steps that led into the earth. She found herself in a long, low gallery, lighted by a dim oil lamp, suspended from the blackened roof. A shelf ran along one side of it, covered with straw. Three men lay there. The straw was soaked with their blood. They had been brought in the night before by the stretcher-bearers. A young surgeon was rearranging their splints and bandages, and redressing their wounds. They would lie there for another hour or so, and then start for their twenty kilometre drive over shell-ridden roads to one or another of the great hospitals at the base. While she was there, two more cases were brought in. The doctor gave but a glance at the first one and then made a sign; and the bearers passed on with him to the further end of the gallery. He seemed to understand, for he gave a low, despairing cry and the tears sprang to his eyes. He was but a boy. The other had a foot torn off. One of the orderlies gave him two round pieces of wood to hold in his hands while the young surgeon cut away the hanging flesh and bound up the stump.

The doctor had been whispering to one of the bearers. He had the face of an old man, but his shoulders were broad and he looked sturdy. He nodded, and beckoned Joan to follow him up the slippery steps.

"It is breakfast time," he explained, as they emerged into the air. "We leave each other alone for half an hour—even the snipers. But we must be careful." She followed in his footsteps, stooping so low that her hands could have touched the ground. They had to be sure that they did not step off the narrow track marked with white stones, lest they should be drowned in the mud. They passed the head of a dead horse. It looked as if it had been cut off and laid there; the body was below it in the mud.

They spoke in whispers, and Joan at first had made an effort to disguise her voice. But her conductor had smiled. "They shall be called the brothers and the sisters of the Lord," he had said. "Mademoiselle is brave for her Brothers' sake." He was a priest. There were many priests among the stretcher-bearers.

Crouching close to the ground, behind the spreading roots of a giant oak, she raised her eyes. Before her lay a sea of smooth, soft mud nearly a mile wide. From the centre rose a solitary tree, from which all had been shot away but two bare branches like outstretched arms above the silence. Beyond, the hills rose again. There was something unearthly in the silence that seemed to brood above that sea of mud. The old priest told her of the living men, French and German, who had stood there day and night sunk in it up to their waists, screaming hour after hour, and waving their arms, sinking into it lower and lower, none able to help them: until at last only their screaming heads were left, and after a time these, too, would disappear: and the silence come again.

She saw the ditches, like long graves dug for the living, where the weary, listless men stood knee-deep in mud, hoping for wounds that would relieve them from the ghastly monotony of their existence; the holes of muddy water where the dead things lay, to which they crept out in the night to wash a little of the filth from their clammy bodies and their stinking clothes; the holes dug out of the mud in which they ate and slept and lived year after year: till brain and heart and soul seemed to have died out of them, and they remembered with an effort that they once were men.

AFTER A TIME, THE CARE of the convalescents passed almost entirely into Joan's hands, Madame Lelanne being told off to assist her. By dint of much persistence she had succeeded in getting the leaky roof repaired, and in place of the smoky stove that had long been her despair she had one night procured a fine calorifere by the simple process of stealing it. Madame Lelanne had heard about it from the gossips. It had been brought to a lonely house at the end of the village by a major of engineers. He had returned to the trenches the day before, and the place for the time being was empty. The thieves were never discovered. The sentry was positive that no one had passed him but two women, one of them carrying a baby. Madame Lelanne had dressed it up in a child's cloak and hood, and had carried it in her arms. As it must have weighed nearly a couple of hundred-weight suspicion had not attached to them.

Space did not allow of any separation; broken Frenchmen and broken Germans would often lie side by side. Joan would wonder, with a grim smile to herself, what the patriotic Press of the different countries would have thought had they been there to have overheard the conversations. Neither France nor Germany appeared to be the enemy, but a thing called "They," a mysterious power that worked its will upon them both from a place they always spoke of as "Back there." One day the talk fell on courage. A young French soldier was holding forth when Joan entered the hut.

"It makes me laugh," he was saying, "all this newspaper talk. Every nation, properly led, fights bravely. It is the male instinct. Women go into hysterics about it, because it has not been given them. I have the Croix de Guerre with all three leaves, and I haven't half the courage of my dog, who weighs twelve kilos, and would face a regiment by himself. Why, a game cock has got more than the best of us. It's the man who doesn't think, who can't think, who has the most courage— who imagines nothing, but just goes forward with his head down, like a bull. There is, of course, a real courage. When you are by yourself, and have to do something in cold blood. But the courage required for rushing forward, shouting and yelling with a lot of other fellows—why, it would take a hundred times more pluck to turn back."

"They know that," chimed in the man lying next to him; "or they would not drug us. Why, when we stormed La Haye I knew nothing until an ugly-looking German spat a pint of blood into my face and woke me up."

A middle-aged sergeant, who had a wound in the stomach and was sitting up in his bed, looked across. "There was a line of Germans came upon us," he said, "at Bras. I thought I must be suffering from a nightmare when I saw them. They had thrown away their rifles and had all joined hands. They came dancing towards us just like a row of ballet girls. They were shrieking and laughing, and they never attempted to do anything. We just waited until they were close up and then shot them down. It was like killing a lot of kids who had come to have a game with us. The one I potted got his arms round me before he coughed himself out, calling me his 'liebe Elsa,' and wanting to kiss me. Lord! You can guess how the Boche ink-slingers spread themselves over that business: 'Sonderbar! Colossal! Unvergessliche Helden.' Poor devils!"

"They'll give us ginger before it is over," said another. He had had both his lips torn away, and appeared to be always laughing. "Stuff it into us as if we were horses at a fair. That will make us run forward, right enough."

"Oh, come," struck in a youngster who was lying perfectly flat, face downwards on his bed: it was the position in which he could breathe easiest. He raised his head a couple of inches and twisted it round so as to get his mouth free. "It isn't as bad as all that. Why, the Thirty-third swarmed into Fort Malmaison of their own accord, though 'twas like jumping into a boiling furnace, and held it for three days against pretty nearly a division. There weren't a dozen of them left when we relieved them. They had no ammunition left. They'd just been filling up the gaps with their bodies. And they wouldn't go back even then. We had to drag them away. 'They shan't pass,' 'They shan't pass!'—that's all they kept saying." His voice had sunk to a thin whisper.

A young officer was lying in a corner behind a screen. He leant forward and pushed it aside.

"Oh, give the devil his due, you fellows," he said. "War isn't a pretty game, but it does make for courage. We all know that. And things even finer than mere fighting pluck. There was a man in my company, a Jacques Decrusy. He was just a stupid peasant lad. We were crowded into one end of the trench, about a score of us. The rest of it had fallen in, and we couldn't move. And a bomb dropped into the middle of us; and the same instant that it touched the ground Decrusy threw himself flat down upon it and took the whole of it into his body. There was nothing left of him but scraps. But the rest of us got off. Nobody had drugged him to do that. There isn't one of us who was in that trench that will not be a better man to the end of his days, remembering how Jacques Decrusy gave his life for ours."

"I'll grant you all that, sir," answered the young soldier who had first spoken. He had long, delicate hands and eager, restless eyes. "War does bring out heroism. So does pestilence and famine. Read Defoe's account of the Plague of London. How men and women left their safe homes, to serve in the pest-houses, knowing that sooner or later they were doomed. Read of the mothers in India who die of slow starvation, never allowing a morsel of food to pass their lips so that they may save up their own small daily portion to add it to their children's. Why don't we pray to God not to withhold from us His precious medicine of pestilence and famine? So is shipwreck a fine school for courage. Look at the chance it gives the captain to set a fine example. And the engineers who stick to their post with the water pouring in upon them. We don't reconcile ourselves to shipwrecks as a necessary school for sailors. We do our best to lessen them. So did persecution bring out heroism. It made saints and martyrs. Why have we done away with it? If this game of killing and being killed is the fine school for virtue it is made out to be, then all our efforts towards law and order have been a mistake. We never ought to have emerged from the jungle."

He took a note-book from under his pillow and commenced to scribble.

An old-looking man spoke. He lay with his arms folded across his breast, addressing apparently the smoky rafters. He was a Russian, a teacher of languages in Paris at the outbreak of the war, and had joined the French Army.

"It is not only courage," he said, "that War brings out. It brings out vile things too. Oh, I'm not thinking merely of the Boches. That's the cant of every nation: that all the heroism is on one side and all the brutality on the other. Take men from anywhere and some of them will be devils. War gives them their opportunity, brings out the beast. Can you wonder at it? You teach a man to plunge a bayonet into the writhing flesh of a fellow human being, and twist it round and round and jamb it further in, while the blood is spurting from him like a fountain. What are you making of him but a beast? A man's got to be a beast before he can bring himself to do it. I have seen things done by our own men in cold blood, the horror of which will haunt my memory until I die. But of course, we hush it up when it happens to be our own people."

He ceased speaking. No one seemed inclined to break the silence.

They remained confused in her memory, these talks among the wounded men in the low, dimly lighted hut that had become her world. At times it was but two men speaking to one another in whispers, at others every creaking bed would be drawn into the argument.

One topic that never lost its interest was: Who made wars? Who hounded the people into them, and kept them there, tearing at one another's throats? They never settled it.

"God knows I didn't want it, speaking personally," said a German prisoner one day, with a laugh. "I had been working at a printing business sixteen hours a day for seven years. It was just beginning to pay me, and now my wife writes me that she has had to shut the place up and sell the machinery to keep them all from starving."

"But couldn't you have done anything to stop it?" demanded a Frenchman, lying next to him. "All your millions of Socialists, what were they up to? What went wrong with the Internationale, the Universal Brotherhood of Labour, and all that Tra-la-la?"

The German laughed again. "Oh, they know their business," he answered. "You have your glass of beer and go to bed, and when you wake up in the morning you find that war has been declared; and you keep your mouth shut—unless you want to be shot for a traitor. Not that it would have made much difference," he added. "I admit that. The ground had been too well prepared. England was envious of our trade. King Edward had been plotting our destruction. Our papers were full of translations from yours, talking about 'La Revanche!' We were told that you had been lending money to Russia to enable her to build railways, and that when they were complete France and Russia would fall upon us suddenly. 'The Fatherland in danger!' It may be lies or it may not; what is one to do? What would you have done—even if you could have done anything?"

"He's right," said a dreamy-eyed looking man, laying down the book he had been reading. "We should have done just the same. 'My country, right or wrong.' After all, it is an ideal."

A dark, black-bearded man raised himself painfully upon his elbow. He was a tailor in the Rue Parnesse, and prided himself on a decided resemblance to Victor Hugo.

"It's a noble ideal," he said. "*La Patrie*! The great Mother. Right or wrong, who shall dare to harm her? Yes, if it was she who rose up in her majesty and called to us." He laughed. "What does it mean in reality: Germania, Italia, La France, Britannia? Half a score of pompous old muddlers with their fat wives egging them on: sons of the fools before them; talkers who have wormed themselves into power by making frothy speeches and fine promises. My Country!" he laughed again. "Look at them. Can't you see their swelling paunches and their flabby faces? Half a score of ambitious politicians, gouty old financiers, bald-headed old toffs, with their waxed moustaches and false teeth. That's what we mean when we talk about 'My Country': a pack of selfish, soulless, muddle-headed old men. And whether they're right or whether they're wrong, our duty is to fight at their bidding—to bleed for them, to die for them, that they may grow more sleek and prosperous." He sank back on his pillow with another laugh.

Sometimes they agreed it was the newspapers that made war—that fanned every trivial difference into a vital question of national honour— that, whenever there was any fear of peace, re-stoked the fires of hatred with their never-failing stories of atrocities. At other times they decided it was the capitalists, the traders, scenting profit for themselves. Some held it was the politicians, dreaming of going down to history as Richelieus or as Bismarcks. A popular theory was that cause for war was always discovered by the ruling classes whenever there seemed danger that the workers were getting out of hand. In war, you put the common people back in their place, revived in them the habits of submission and obedience. Napoleon the Little, it was argued, had started the war of 1870 with that idea. Russia had welcomed the present war as an answer to the Revolution that was threatening Czardom. Others contended it was the great munition industries, aided by the military party, the officers impatient for opportunities of advancement, the strategists eager to put their theories to the test. A few of the more philosophical shrugged their shoulders. It was the thing itself that sooner or later was bound to go off of its own accord. Half every country's energy, half every country's time and money was spent in piling up explosives. In every country envy and hatred of every other country was preached as a religion. They called it patriotism. Sooner or later the spark fell.

A wizened little man had been listening to it all one day. He had a curiously rat-like face, with round, red, twinkling eyes, and a long, pointed nose that twitched as he talked.

"I'll tell you who makes all the wars," he said. "It's you and me, my dears: we make the wars. We love them. That's why we open our mouths and swallow all the twaddle that the papers give us; and cheer the fine, black-coated gentlemen when they tell us it's our sacred duty to kill Germans, or Italians, or Russians, or anybody else. We are just crazy to kill something: it doesn't matter what. If it's to be Germans, we shout 'A Berlin!'; and if it's to be Russians we cheer for Liberty. I was in Paris at the time of the Fashoda trouble. How we hissed the English in the cafes! And how they glared back at us! They were just as eager to kill us. Who makes a dog fight? Why, the dog. Anybody can do it. Who could make us fight each other, if we didn't want to? Not all the king's horses and all the King's men. No, my dears, it's we make the wars. You and me, my dears."

There came a day in early spring. All night long the guns had never ceased. It sounded like the tireless barking of ten thousand giant dogs. Behind the hills, the whole horizon, like a fiery circle, was ringed with flashing light. Shapeless forms, bent beneath burdens, passed in endless procession through the village. Masses of rushing men swept like shadowy phantoms through the fitfully-illumined darkness. Beneath that everlasting barking, Joan would hear, now the piercing wail of a child; now a clap of thunder that for the moment would drown all other sounds, followed by a faint, low, rumbling crash, like the shooting of coals into a cellar. The wounded on their beds lay with wide-open, terrified eyes, moving feverishly from side to side.

At dawn the order came that the hospital was to be evacuated. The ambulances were already waiting in the street. Joan flew up the ladder to her loft, the other side of the yard. Madame Lelanne was already there. She had thrown a few things into a bundle, and her foot was again upon the ladder, when it seemed to her that someone struck her, hurling her back upon the floor, and the house the other side of the yard rose up into the air, and then fell quite slowly, and a cloud of dust hid it from her sight.

Madame Lelanne must have carried her down the ladder. She was standing in the yard, and the dust was choking her. Across the street, beyond the ruins of the hospital, swarms of men were running about like ants when their nest has been disturbed. Some were running this way, and some that. And then they would turn and run back again, making dancing movements round one another and jostling one another. The guns had ceased; and instead, it sounded as if all the babies in the world were playing with their rattles. Suddenly Madame Lelanne reappeared out of the dust, and seizing Joan, dragged her through a dark opening and down a flight of steps, and then left her. She was in a great vaulted cellar. A faint light crept in through a grated window at the other end. There was a long table against the wall, and in front of it a bench. She staggered to it and sat down, leaning against the damp wall. The place was very silent. Suddenly she began to laugh. She tried to stop herself, but couldn't. And then she heard footsteps descending, and her memory came back to her with a rush. They were German footsteps, she felt sure by the sound: they were so slow and heavy. They should not find her in hysterics, anyhow. She fixed her teeth into the wooden table in front of her and held on to it with clenched hands. She had recovered herself before the footsteps had finished their descent. With a relief that made it difficult for her not to begin laughing again, she found it was Madame Lelanne and Monsieur Dubos. They were carrying something between them. She hardly recognized Dubos at first. His beard was gone, and a line of flaming scars had taken its place. They laid their burden on the table. It was one of the wounded men from the hut. They told her they were bringing down two more. The hut itself had not been hit, but the roof had been torn off by the force of the explosion, and the others had been killed by the falling beams. Joan wanted to return with them, but Madame Lelanne had assumed an air of authority, and told her she would be more useful where she was. From the top of the steps they threw down bundles of straw, on which they laid the wounded men, and Joan tended them, while Madame Lelanne and the little chemist went up and down continuously. Before evening the place, considering all things, was fairly habitable. Madame Lelanne brought down the great stove from the hut; and breaking a pane of glass in the barred window, they fixed it up with its chimney and lighted it. From time to time the turmoil above them would break out again: the rattling, and sometimes a dull rumbling as of rushing water. But only a faint murmur of it penetrated into the cellar. Towards night it became quiet again.

How long Joan remained there she was never quite sure. There was little difference between day and night. After it had been quiet for an hour or so, Madame Lelanne would go out, to return a little later with a wounded man upon her back; and when one died, she would throw him across her shoulder and disappear again up the steps. Sometimes it was a Frenchman and sometimes a German she brought in. One gathered that the fight for the village still continued. There was but little they could do for them beyond dressing their wounds and easing their pain. Joan and the little chemist took it in turns to relieve one another. If Madame Lelanne ever slept, it was when she would sit in the shadow behind the stove, her hands upon her knees. Dubos had been in the house when it had fallen. Madame Lelanne had discovered him pinned against a wall underneath a great oak beam that had withstood the falling debris. His beard had been burnt off, but otherwise he had been unharmed.

She seemed to be living in a dream. She could not shake from her the feeling that it was not bodies but souls that she was tending. The men themselves gave colour to this fancy of hers. Stripped of their poor, stained, tattered uniforms, they were neither French nor Germans. Friend or foe! it was already but a memory. Often, awakening out of a sleep, they would look across at one another and smile as to a comrade. A great peace seemed to have entered there. Faint murmurs as from some distant troubled world would steal at times into the silence. It brought a pang of pity, but it did not drive away the quiet that dwelt there.

Once, someone who must have known the place and had descended the steps softly, sat there among them and talked with them. Joan could not remember seeing him enter. Perhaps unknowing, she had fallen to sleep for a few minutes. Madame Lelanne was seated by the stove, her great coarse hands upon her knees, her patient, dull, slow-moving eyes fixed upon the speaker's face. Dubos was half standing, half resting against the table, his arms folded upon his breast. The wounded men had raised themselves upon the straw and were listening. Some leant upon their elbows, some sat with their hands clasped round their knees, and one, with head bent down, remained with his face hidden in his hands.

The speaker sat a little way apart. The light from the oil lamp, suspended from the ceiling, fell upon his face. He wore a peasant's blouse. It seemed to her a face she knew. Possibly she had passed him in the village street and had looked at him without remembering. It was his eyes that for long years afterwards still haunted her. She did not notice at the time what language he was speaking. But there were none who did not understand him.

"You think of God as of a great King," he said, "a Ruler who orders all things: who could change all things in the twinkling of an eye. You see the cruelty and the wrong around you. And you say to yourselves: 'He has ordered it. If He would, He could have willed it differently.' So that in your hearts you are angry with Him. How could it be otherwise? What father, loving his children, would see them suffer wrong, when by stretching out a hand he could protect them: turn their tears to gladness? What father would see his children doing evil to one another and not check them: would see them following ways leading to their destruction, and not pluck them back? If God has ordered all things, why has He created evil, making His creatures weak and sinful? Does a father lay snares for his children: leading them into temptation: delivering them unto evil?"

"There is no God, apart from Man."

"God is a spirit. His dwelling-place is in man's heart. We are His fellow-labourers. It is through man that He shall one day rule the world."

"God is knocking at your heart, but you will not open to Him. You have filled your hearts with love of self. There is no room for Him to enter in."

"God whispers to you: 'Be pitiful. Be merciful. Be just.' But you answer Him: 'If I am pitiful, I lose my time and money. If I am merciful, I forego advantage to myself. If I am just, I lessen my own profit, and another passes me in the race.'"

"And yet in your inmost thoughts you know that you are wrong: that love of self brings you no peace. Who is happier than the lover, thinking only how to serve? Who is the more joyous: he who sits alone at the table, or he who shares his meal with a friend? It is more blessed to give than to receive. How can you doubt it? For what do you toil and strive but that you may give to your children, to your loved ones, reaping the harvest of their good?"

"Who among you is the more honoured? The miser or the giver: he who heaps up riches for himself or he who labours for others?"

"Who is the true soldier? He who has put away self. His own ease and comfort, even his own needs, his own safety: they are but as a feather in the balance when weighed against his love for his comrades, for his country. The true soldier is not afraid to love. He gives his life for his friend. Do you jeer at him? Do you say he is a fool for his pains? No, it is his honour, his glory."

"God is love. Why are you afraid to let Him in? Hate knocks also at your door and to him you open wide. Why are you afraid of love? All things are created by love. Hate can but destroy. Why choose you death instead of life? God pleads to you. He is waiting for your help."

And one answered him.

"We are but poor men," he said. "What can we do? Of what use are such as we?"

The young man looked at him and smiled.

"You can ask that," he said: "you, a soldier? Does the soldier say: 'I am of no use. I am but a poor man of no account. Who has need of such as I?' God has need of all. There is none that shall not help to win the victory. It is with his life the soldier serves. Who were they whose teaching moved the world more than it has ever yet been moved by the teaching of the wisest? They were men of little knowledge, of but little learning, poor and lowly. It was with their lives they taught."

"Cast out self, and God shall enter in, and you shall be One with God. For there is none so lowly that he may not become the Temple of God: there is none so great that he shall be greater than this."

The speaker ceased. There came a faint sound at which she turned her head; and when she looked again he was gone.

The wounded men had heard it also. Dubos had moved forward. Madame Lelanne had risen. It came again, the thin, faint shrill of a distant bugle. Footsteps were descending the stairs. French soldiers, laughing, shouting, were crowding round them.

XVIII

Her father met her at Waterloo. He had business in London, and they stayed on for a few days. Reading between the lines of his later letters, she had felt that all was not well with him. His old heart trouble had come back; and she noticed that he walked to meet her very slowly. It would be all right, now that she had returned, he explained: he had been worrying himself about her.

Mrs. Denton had died. She had left Joan her library, together with her wonderful collection of note books. She had brought them all up-to-date and indexed them. They would be invaluable to Francis when he started the new paper upon which they had determined. He was still in the hospital at Breganze, near to where his machine had been shot down. She had tried to get to him; but it would have meant endless delays; and she had been anxious about her father. The Italian surgeons were very proud of him, he wrote. They had had him X-rayed before and after; and beyond a slight lameness which gave him, he thought, a touch of distinction, there was no flaw that the most careful scrutiny would be likely to detect. Any day, now, he expected to be discharged. Mary had married an old sweetheart. She had grown restless in the country with nothing to do, and, at the suggestion of some friends, had gone to Bristol to help in a children's hospital; and there they had met once more.

Neil Singleton, after serving two years in a cholera hospital at Baghdad, had died of the flu in Dover twenty-fours hours after landing. Madge was in Palestine. She had been appointed secretary to a committee for the establishment of native schools. She expected to be there for some years, she wrote. The work was interesting, and appealed to her.

Flossie 'phoned her from Paddington Station, the second day, and by luck she happened to be in. Flossie had just come up from Devonshire. Sam had "got through," and she was on her way to meet him at Hull. She had heard of Joan's arrival in London from one of Carleton's illustrated dailies. She brought the paper with her. They had used the old photograph that once had adorned each week the *Sunday Post*. Joan hardly recognized herself in the serene, self-confident young woman who seemed to be looking down upon a world at her feet. The world was strong and cruel, she had discovered; and Joans but small and weak. One had to pretend that one was not afraid of it.

Flossie had joined every society she could hear of that was working for the League of Nations. Her hope was that it would get itself established before young Frank grew up.

"Not that I really believe it will," she confessed. "A draw might have disgusted us all with fighting. As it is, half the world is dancing at Victory balls, exhibiting captured guns on every village green, and hanging father's helmet above the mantelpiece; while the other half is nursing its revenge. Young Frank only cares for life because he is looking forward to one day driving a tank. I've made up my mind to burn Sam's uniform; but I expect it will end in my wrapping it up in lavender and hiding it away in a drawer. And then there will be all the books and plays. No self-respecting heroine, for the next ten years will dream of marrying anyone but a soldier."

Joan laughed. "Difficult to get anything else, just at present," she said. "It's the soldiers I'm looking to for help. I don't think the men who have been there will want their sons to go. It's the women I'm afraid of."

Flossie caught sight of the clock and jumped up. "Who was it said that woman would be the last thing man would civilize?" she asked.

"It sounds like Meredith," suggested Joan. "I am not quite sure."

"Well, he's wrong, anyhow," retorted Flossie. "It's no good our waiting for man. He is too much afraid of us to be of any real help to us. We shall have to do it ourselves." She gave Joan a hug and was gone.

Phillips was still abroad with the Army of Occupation. He had tried to get out of it, but had not succeeded. He held it to be gaoler's work; and the sight of the starving populace was stirring in him a fierce anger.

He would not put up again for Parliament. He was thinking of going back to his old work upon the Union. "Parliament is played out," he had written her. "Kings and Aristocracies have served their purpose and have gone, and now the Ruling Classes, as they call themselves, must be content to hear the bell toll for them also. Parliament was never anything more than an instrument in their hands, and never can be. What happens? Once in every five years you wake the people up: tell them the time has come for them to exercise their Heaven-ordained privilege of putting a cross against the names of some seven hundred gentlemen who have kindly expressed their willingness to rule over them. After that, you send the people back to sleep; and for the next five years these seven hundred gentlemen, consulting no one but themselves, rule over the country as absolutely as ever a Caesar ruled over Rome. What sort of Democracy is that? Even a Labour Government—supposing that in spite of the Press it did win through—what would be its fate? Separated from its base, imprisoned within those tradition-haunted walls, it would lose touch with the people, would become in its turn a mere oligarchy. If the people are ever to govern they must keep their hand firmly upon the machine; not remain content with pulling a lever and then being shown the door."

She had sent a note by messenger to Mary Stopperton to say she was coming. Mary had looked very fragile the last time she had seen her, just before leaving for France; and she had felt a fear. Mary had answered in her neat, thin, quavering writing, asking her to come early in the morning. Sometimes she was a little tired and had to lie down again. She had been waiting for Joan. She had a present for her.

The morning promised to be fair, and she decided to walk by way of the Embankment. The great river with its deep, strong patience had always been a friend to her. It was Sunday and the city was still sleeping. The pale December sun rose above the mist as she reached the corner of Westminster Bridge, turning the river into silver and flooding the silent streets with a soft, white, tender light.

The tower of Chelsea Church brought back to her remembrance of the wheezy old clergyman who had preached there that Sunday evening, that now seemed so long ago, when her footsteps had first taken her that way by chance. Always she had intended making inquiries and discovering his name. Why had she never done so? It would surely have been easy. He was someone she had known as a child. She had become quite convinced of that. She could see his face close to hers as if he had lifted her up in his arms and was smiling at her. But pride and power had looked out of his eyes then.

It was earlier than the time she had fixed in her own mind and, pausing with her elbows resting on the granite parapet, she watched the ceaseless waters returning to the sea, bearing their burden of impurities.

"All roads lead to Calvary." It was curious how the words had dwelt with her, till gradually they had become a part of her creed. She remembered how at first they had seemed to her a threat chilling her with fear. They had grown to be a promise, a hope held out to all. The road to Calvary! It was the road to life. By the giving up of self we gained God.

And suddenly a great peace came to her. One was not alone in the fight, God was with us: the great Comrade. The evil and the cruelty all round her: she was no longer afraid of it. God was coming. Beyond the menace of the passing day, black with the war's foul aftermath of evil dreams and hatreds, she saw the breaking of the distant dawn. The devil should not always triumph. God was gathering His labourers.

God was conquering. Unceasing through the ages, God's voice had crept round man, seeking entry. Through the long darkness of that dim beginning, when man knew no law but self, unceasing God had striven: until at last one here and there, emerging from the brute, had heard—had listened to the voice of love and pity, and in that hour, unknowing, had built to God a temple in the wilderness.

Labourers together with God. The mighty host of those who through the ages had heard the voice of God and had made answer. The men and women in all lands who had made room in their hearts for God. Still nameless, scattered, unknown to one another: still powerless as yet against the world's foul law of hate, they should continue to increase and multiply, until one day they should speak with God's voice and should be heard. And a new world should be created.

God. The tireless Spirit of eternal creation, the Spirit of Love. What else was it that out of formlessness had shaped the spheres, had planned the orbits of the suns. The law of gravity we named it. What was it but another name for Love, the yearning of like for like, the calling to one another of the stars. What else but Love had made the worlds, had gathered together the waters, had fashioned the dry land. The cohesion of elements, so we explained it. The clinging of like to like. The brotherhood of the atoms.

God. The Eternal Creator. Out of matter, lifeless void, he had moulded His worlds, had ordered His endless firmament. It was finished. The greater task remained: the Universe of mind, of soul. Out of man it should be created. God in man and man in God: made in like image: fellow labourers together with one another: together they should build it. Out of the senseless strife and discord, above the chaos and the tumult should be heard the new command: "Let there be Love."

The striking of the old church clock recalled her to herself. But she had only a few minutes' walk before her. Mary had given up her Church work. It included the cleaning, and she had found it beyond her failing strength. But she still lived in the tiny cottage behind its long strip of garden. The door yielded to Joan's touch: it was seldom fast closed. And knowing Mary's ways, she entered without knocking and pushed it to behind her, leaving it still ajar.

And as she did so, it seemed to her that someone passing breathed upon her lips a little kiss: and for a while she did not move. Then, treading softly, she looked into the room.

It welcomed her, as always, with its smile of cosy neatness. The spotless curtains that were Mary's pride: the gay flowers in the window, to which she had given children's names: the few poor pieces of furniture, polished with much loving labour: the shining grate: the foolish china dogs and the little china house between them on the mantelpiece. The fire was burning brightly, and the kettle was singing on the hob.

Mary's work was finished. She sat upright in her straight-backed chair before the table, her eyes half closed. It seemed so odd to see those little work-worn hands idle upon her lap.

Joan's present lay on the table near to her, as if she had just folded it and placed it there: the little cap and the fine robe of lawn: as if for a king's child.

Joan had never thought that Death could be so beautiful. It was as if some friend had looked in at the door, and, seeing her so tired, had taken the work gently from her hands, and had folded them upon her lap. And she had yielded with a smile.

Joan heard a faint rustle and looked up. A woman had entered. It was the girl she had met there on a Christmas Day, a Miss Ensor. Joan had met her once or twice since then. She was still in the chorus. Neither of them spoke for a few minutes.

"I have been expecting every morning to find her gone," said the girl. "I think she only waited to finish this." She gently unfolded the fine lawn robe, and they saw the delicate insertion and the wonderful, embroidery.

"I asked her once," said the girl, "why she wasted so much work on them. They were mostly only for poor people. 'One never knows, dearie,' she answered, with that childish smile of hers. 'It may be for a little Christ.'"

They would not let less loving hands come near her.

HER FATHER HAD COMPLETED HIS business, and both were glad to leave London. She had a sense of something sinister, foreboding, casting its shadow on the sordid, unclean streets, the neglected buildings falling into disrepair. A lurking savagery, a half-veiled enmity seemed to be stealing among the people. The town's mad lust for pleasure: its fierce, unjoyous laughter: its desire ever to be in crowds as if afraid of itself: its orgies of eating and drinking: its animal-like indifference to the misery and death that lay but a little way beyond its own horizon! She dared not remember history. Perhaps it would pass.

The long, slow journey tried her father's strength, and assuming an authority to which he yielded obedience tempered by grumbling, Joan sent him to bed, and would not let him come down till Christmas Day. The big, square house was on the outskirts of the town where it was quiet, and in the afternoon they walked in the garden sheltered behind its high brick wall.

He told her of what had been done at the works. Arthur's plan had succeeded. It might not be the last word, but at least it was on the road to the right end. The men had been brought into it and shared the management. And the disasters predicted had proved groundless.

"You won't be able to indulge in all your mad schemes," he laughed, "but there'll be enough to help on a few. And you will be among friends. Arthur told me he had explained it to you and that you had agreed."

"Yes," she answered. "It was the last time he came to see me in London. And I could not help feeling a bit jealous. He was doing things while I was writing and talking. But I was glad he was an Allway. It will be known as the Allway scheme. New ways will date from it."

She had thought it time for him to return indoors, but he pleaded for a visit to his beloved roses. He prided himself on being always able to pick roses on Christmas Day.

"This young man of yours," he asked, "what is he like?"

"Oh, just a Christian gentleman," she answered. "You will love him when you know him."

He laughed. "And this new journal of his?" he asked. "It's got to be published in London, hasn't it?"

She gave a slight start, for in their letters to one another they had been discussing this very point.

"No," she answered, "it could be circulated just as well from, say, Birmingham or Manchester."

He was choosing his roses. They held their petals wrapped tight round them, trying to keep the cold from their brave hearts. In the warmth they would open out and be gay, until the end.

"Not Liverpool?" he suggested.

"Or even Liverpool," she laughed.

They looked at one another, and then beyond the sheltering evergreens and the wide lawns to where the great square house seemed to be listening.

"It's an ugly old thing," he said.

"No, it isn't," she contradicted. "It's simple and big and kind. I always used to feel it disapproved of me. I believe it has come to love me, in its solemn old brick way."

"It was built by Kent in seventeen-forty for your great-great grandfather," he explained. He was regarding it more affectionately. "Solid respectability was the dream, then."

"I think that's why I love it," she said: "for it's dear, old-fashioned ways. We will teach it the new dreams, too. It will be so shocked, at first."

They dined in state in the great dining-room.

"I was going to buy you a present," he grumbled. "But you wouldn't let me get up."

"I want to give you something quite expensive, Dad," she said. "I've had my eye on it for years."

She slipped her hand in his. "I want you to give me that Dream of yours; that you built for my mother, and that all went wrong. They call it Allway's Folly; and it makes me so mad. I want to make it all come true. May I try?"

It was there that he came to her.

She stood beneath the withered trees, beside the shattered fountain. The sad-faced ghosts peeped out at her from the broken windows of the little silent houses.

She wondered later why she had not been surprised to see him. But at the time it seemed to be in the order of things that she should look up and find him there.

She went to him with outstretched arms.

"I'm so glad you've come," she said. "I was just wanting you."

They sat on the stone step of the fountain, where they were sheltered from the wind; and she buttoned his long coat about him.

"Do you think you will go on doing it?" he asked, with a laugh.

"I'm so afraid," she answered gravely. "That I shall come to love you too much: the home, the children and you. I shall have none left over."

"There is an old Hindoo proverb," he said: "That when a man and woman love they dig a fountain down to God."

"This poor, little choked-up thing," he said, "against which we are sitting; it's for want of men and women drawing water, of children dabbling their hands in it and making themselves all wet, that it has run dry."

She took his hands in hers to keep them warm. The nursing habit seemed to have taken root in her.

"I see your argument," she said. "The more I love you, the deeper will be the fountain. So that the more Love I want to come to me, the more I must love you."

"Don't you see it for yourself?" he demanded.

She broke into a little laugh.

"Perhaps you are right," she admitted. "Perhaps that is why He made us male and female: to teach us to love."

A robin broke into a song of triumph. He had seen the sad-faced ghosts steal silently away.

A Note about the Author

Jerome K. Jerome (1859–1927) was an English writer who grew up in a poverty-stricken family. After multiple bad investments and the untimely deaths of both parents, the clan struggled to make ends meet. The young Jerome was forced to drop out of school and work to support himself. During his downtime, he enjoyed the theatre and joined a local repertory troupe. He branched out and began writing essays, satires and many short stories. One of his earliest successes was *Idle Thoughts of an Idle Fellow* (1886) but his most famous work is *Three Men in a Boat* (1889).

A Note from the Publisher

Spanning many genres, from non-fiction essays to literature classics to children's books and lyric poetry, Mint Edition books showcase the master works of our time in a modern new package. The text is freshly typeset, is clean and easy to read, and features a new note about the author in each volume. Many books also include exclusive new introductory material. Every book boasts a striking new cover, which makes it as appropriate for collecting as it is for gift giving. Mint Edition books are only printed when a reader orders them, so natural resources are not wasted. We're proud that our books are never manufactured in excess and exist only in the exact quantity they need to be read and enjoyed.

Discover more of your favorite classics with Bookfinity™.

- Track your reading with custom book lists.
- Get great book recommendations for your personalized Reader Type.
- Add reviews for your favorite books.
- AND MUCH MORE!

Visit **bookfinity.com** and take the fun Reader Type quiz to get started.

Enjoy our classic and modern companion pairings!